States

of

Passion

Translated
from the Arabic
by Max Weiss

States

of

Passion

Nihad

Sirees

PUSHKIN PRESS

Pushkin Press
71–75 Shelton Street
London wc2h 9jq

Original text © Nihad Sirees 1998
English translation © Max Weiss 2018

States of Passion was first published as حالة شغف in Lebanon, 1998
First published by Pushkin Press in 2018

 Supported using public funding by
ARTS COUNCIL ENGLAND

This book has been selected to receive financial assistance from English PEN's PEN Translates programme, supported by Arts Council England. English PEN exists to promote literature and our understanding of it, to uphold writers' freedoms around the world, to campaign against the persecution and imprisonment of writers for stating their views, and to promote the friendly co-operation of writers and the free exchange of ideas. www.englishpen.org

3 5 7 9 8 6 4 2

ISBN 13: 978-1-78227-347-9

Designed and typeset by Tetragon, London
Printed and bound by CPI Group (UK) Ltd, Croydon cro 4yy

www.pushkinpress.com

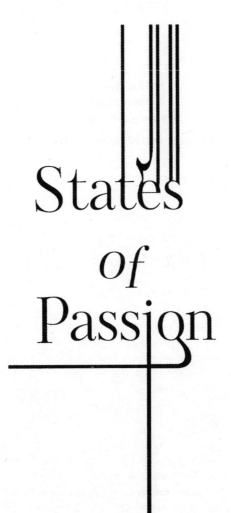

States

of

Passion

The Tale of the Tale, or the Prologue,
or the Preface, or Whatever Heading Novelists
Typically Use to Introduce Their Novels

T HE WORLD IS SO STRANGE. The strangest things are the stories you overhear here and there. I had never once thought of myself as a storyteller, mind you, gathering people around me in order to tell them about something I happened to hear or see with my own two eyes. That would be a waste of breath because I'm no good at the art of narrative anyway, of telling stories at all. But sometimes life, this strange life we all cling to, gives us a job we never thought we were cut out for, and this strange life gave me an incredible job. To tell stories… to tell all of you a curious tale I once heard in a moment that was even more unusual than the story itself.

I work at the Agricultural Bank, where I head up a division, which is to say I'm not the director or a worker or a mighty accountant whose task it is to balance the annual budget and then breathe a sigh of relief once the ledger is clean. The peasants got used to calling us experts, my colleagues and me. Our job was to trek out into the fields in Land Rovers, to ensure the state agricultural plan was being implemented properly, to survey the cultivated lands, and to dole out loans to the peasants, which might come in the form of seeds or empty sacks or other things I'm quite good at talking about; so much so, in fact, that I wish they could have been the subject matter I ended up writing about, because I would have been able to present you with a scientific treasure, replete with precise statistics. However, and there's nothing shameful about this, really, I've undertaken something else altogether, namely, to write a story... That's right, a story. Please don't laugh... I'm already embarrassed enough to have embarked upon this kind of work in the first place. I'm definitely not cut out for it. It never occurred to me that I might pick up a pen and write literary prose one day instead of agricultural reports and explanations of the rural development projects, which I can slash and joust my way through like a knight in shining armour. On second thought, who knows? You might just wind up loving what I have to say here, because this isn't something I made up, or, as writers like to say, this isn't a product of my own thoughts or imagination, which is more often than not crammed with dry facts and figures. No, all there is to it is that I happened to hear what I'm about to relate to you, and I simply had to write it down. I'll fill you in on the details later, as we used to say at the Agricultural Bank, my good people.

It all started last winter while we were out on one of those exhausting expeditions, travelling by Land Rover between villages. There were three of us: the driver, my assistant Mr Tameem and myself. We had wrapped up our work in one village just before sunset and were about to take off for another called Abu al-Fida. In order to get there we would have to drive back to the narrow asphalt road, which we would then follow for a few kilometres before turning off once again in order to head east on a godforsaken dirt path. Even though we should have stayed the night in that first village, my idea, a burning desire really, was to be done with our last village before the following afternoon so we could get back to Aleppo as quickly as possible, which led me to insist that we go out in wet and stormy weather. By the time night had fallen, it was cold, pouring rain, and the sky was dark. The windscreen was coated in condensation from the humidity outside and the breath from the three of us trapped inside.

We struggled not to let our fear show whenever the harsh wind and frightening downpour got so bad that we had to scrape the water off the glass with our bare hands so the driver could see the road. Although the two of them were trying to keep quiet, I could tell that my colleague and the driver wanted to scream in my face and accuse me of stupidity and recklessness.

Things got worse still when the car broke down all of a sudden. I felt cold sweat dripping down my forehead, under my arms. The driver tried to restart the car several times, but to no avail. This workhorse of a Land Rover, which had got us out of sticky situations on more than a few occasions in the past, in much worse weather conditions, became immovable, a stubborn hunk of metal. The driver switched on his flashlight and hopped out of the car, lifted the hood and fiddled with the engine, spewing curses all the while.

"Bitch, son of a bitch. Fuck this job."

I smiled and turned around, encouraging my assistant Tameem to smile as well, but he glared back at me with hatred in his eyes, then looked away and muttered repeatedly, "God help us." He wiped the window clean with his coat sleeve and

9

tried to get a look outside. Tearing that smile off my face, I followed his lead and peered outside myself, but my vision ran smack into a dark wall obscured by ropes of torrential rain. Flashlight beams leaking out from under the hood managed to provide some light.

I jumped when the driver slammed the engine hood shut, shooting a derisive and vengeful message my way as he climbed back in the car, sopping wet from head to toe. Falling back into his seat, his face illuminated in the flashlight glow, he said through gritted teeth:

"It's no use, sir. The car's dead."

For a while I remained silent, wishing he would switch off the flashlight so I could hide my embarrassment. They were staring at me as if I were a circus monkey, as if I could come up with a magical solution to our predicament. I asked him to switch it off, making up the excuse that we needed to conserve energy. I took a deep breath and mumbled a few scattered words that were meant to indicate to the others just how hard I was thinking about a fix, even though I was fully aware of how empty my head actually was, how utterly incapable I was of offering even the feeblest suggestion. One of the drawbacks to being a team leader is having to put up with the insults and sarcasm of employees without being able to tell them to stop; doing so would immediately cause them to erupt in laughter, and lead to losing their respect once and for all. I subsequently dreamt about that happening more than a few times, imagining Mr Tameem and the driver laughing at me as I drowned in embarrassment, tossing and turning in bed so violently that my wife had to wake me up and calm me down.

"What do we do now?" they asked. Because I had ordered them to leave the first village, to leave the warm shack, the guest house redolent with the aroma of bitter coffee, the seductive glances Merhej's daughter threw towards Mr Tameem suggesting, to him alone, of course, so many many things… Since this was all my fault, it was now up to me to find an acceptable solution to the predicament I had got them, and myself, into.

Before going any further with the story, I think it's necessary for me to tell you something about Merhej's daughter. I hope the reader will forgive me for making these detours, but I warned you at the outset that I don't know the first thing about how to write stories in a properly literary fashion. Besides, I have to say what's on my mind as soon as it occurs to me, or else the reader might miss out on some important details that I deem necessary, especially since I could then forget about them altogether.

Now, this Merhej is an elderly man, fast approaching the age of seventy, and he's married to three women. He does nothing all day but sit in Abu Jasim's guesthouse—Abu Jasim, whom the government had appointed *mukhtar* after its previous village headman, Shaykh Aswad, passed away, and because they forbade his son from inheriting the position, as was generally the custom; this because for some reason Shaykh Aswad's son was not well liked by the sub-district director of the Office of Peasant Affairs. Despite his marriage to a second, and then a third wife, Merhej had not been blessed with the birth of a son. And so his three wives seemed to be pregnant constantly, giving birth over and over until he came to have more than twenty children. Since there were no male children

11

to work in the fields, he ordered his daughters to take care of the animals and planting and harvesting as well as to wait on us hand and foot whenever we came to visit. As a matter of courtesy he would order his daughters to see after our every request, fetching water from the well or picking up food from the main house or cleaning the guesthouse where we stayed and other chores like that.

Mr Tameem would insist upon going to visit the village of Abu Jasim and his daughter whenever we had a job in that area. It didn't take long for me to figure out what was going on. Merhej's daughter was sending lascivious glances his way, smiling at him suggestively. Then she'd walk out of the guesthouse, and my colleague would follow after her a few minutes later, not coming back until after midnight. When he did finally return, he'd jump under the covers without saying a word out of fear that he and this girl would cause a scandal.

But I was onto everything that was taking place. Although I was somewhat envious, I kept my mouth shut. My insistence that we persevere through stormy and wet weather that day might have had something to do with envy, with my extreme frustration at approaching fifty years old, nearly twice Mr Tameem's age.

I'd rather not cop to this, but those of you who are still reading right now deserve to know the real reason we stayed out there. I wouldn't want anyone to imagine for a second that I was the head of a failed division.

Let's get back to our story, though. I've already explained how I was in an unenviable position. I could feel the pressure of their stares despite the fact that our eyes never met in the dark car, as I took shelter in the silence. What silence, though?

The rain was pounding the car like chickpeas, making a sound that reminded me of popcorn kernels when they cook and split open and bang the pan they're frying in.

I opened the car door and went outside. That was all I had the strength to do. Suddenly I noticed that the darkness wasn't so dark, that the sky was illuminated with dim light, the source of which I couldn't make out. It was a light in the darkness, a light scattered in a single pattern, preventing the darkness from being pitch-black. I moved away from the car, in the direction we would have kept going if the Land Rover hadn't broken down. My colleague and the driver weren't concerned with what I was doing. Maybe they both thought acting crazy like this was the right thing for me to do.

As I started to walk, I didn't feel wet, much the way a swimmer feels while in the water, not noticing at all the fact that he's wet, thinking instead about how to traverse the coming distance. My feet were searching for the dirt road created by the residents and the livestock of the village of Abu al-Fida. Whenever the topography beneath my feet shifted, I would adjust my course to the left or to the right. I walked without thinking about anything at all, discovering something else in the process: my rational mind. In order not to think about anything, no matter what it might be, but especially my physical safety, I started counting my steps. I continued to talk out loud and keep track of my steps until I heard the howling of wild dogs approaching. At that point I froze. Discerning the difference between the sound of my racing heartbeat and the sound of the storm coming down from the sky, I swivelled around and tried to figure out the direction the barking was coming from. But my God was that difficult, which is why

I decided to just keep walking. The howling was getting closer, and for the rest of my life nobody will ever believe me when I say that I didn't care. Why should I care about some stupid dogs after successfully getting away from the driver and Mr Tameem, who hated me so much all because of Merhej's daughter? In that moment I also hated myself for coveting her.

Just then the wall of water stretching between earth and sky was peeled away to reveal hundreds of animal eyes shining in the gloom: fixed, motionless, round, shimmering with phosphorescent colours, surrounding me on all sides. Muffled growls revolved around me as these creatures watched. *What am I going to do?* I thought, or rather, I blurted out loud, as if I could ask those eyes for advice. I didn't know what to do other than to keep walking, with slow and sure-footed movements, without breaking into a run. People had always warned me not to run away from wild dogs. The dogs followed me, circling around me. Apparently they were searching for my most vulnerable point. But that's a load of bullshit—my entire being was one big, walking weak spot.

The dogs were tracking me from all sides, alternating between barking and growling. They sparred with each other as well, nipping at each other's heels. I blubbered at them that not all of the guests had arrived for the feast yet. Then I noticed another pair of eyes in the distance out in front of me, most likely belonging to another wolf that had decided to wait and let me come to him, or maybe belonging to their alpha, to whom they had been leading me all along. Whoever it was, I was headed right for him. But would anyone believe me if I said that I stopped right there, stupefied, and the dogs stopped along with me? I felt warmth rising to my head and a violent shiver. It was the kind of shiver experienced by a man about to be hanged, the noose already wrapped around his neck, when they abruptly tell him he has been pardoned, that the law has just been changed. But that pair of eyes turned out to be two electric lamps beaming out through the window of a house.

By the time I was a few metres away from that house, the dogs had started to retreat, as if their mission of delivering me there safely was complete.

The house was unlike any of those we used to see during our visits to villages in the area. It had been built out of white stone, cut and engraved in the Aleppo style. There were designs carved into the stones above the front door and over the windows. I found the existence of the house strange, as if I were in some kind of a dream just before death, but there I was, standing there, while the dogs began to sniff each others' butts, prancing around in the rain, entirely unaffected by it. What was the story of this house? How could it have sprung up so precisely at the moment when I most needed it?

The windows were curiously large. I approached the one that was illuminated and looked inside. There was a large mirror reflecting the light outside, which is what had allowed me to see the lamp and its reflection from so far away. The room was cavernous, furnished in the style of wealthy urbanites: oil paintings hanging from the walls, elegant, comfortable furniture. Sitting beside a giant fireplace there was an old man dressed in black evening wear, staring motionless at the floor, his back hunched. Believe me, if the fireplace hadn't been in use, blowing warmth and life all around, I would have thought the old man was dead. I drew away from the window, climbed the two steps up to the large, decorative front door, and rang the bell.

A dignified man who was clearly from the city opened the door. He stood there for a moment scrutinising my appearance. He clearly found my presence there strange and wanted to ask what could possibly have brought me there. For what it's worth, I also found his presence there quite strange. But instead, after informing me that he was the butler, he politely asked me, in a smooth accent quite similar to—but not quite—an Egyptian one, what I wanted. I told him how I'd got lost in the wilderness, how I would like to speak to the man of the house in order to ask for his help. To allay the butler's concerns, I told him who I was, about my job and my assignment. He hesitated for a moment, and I thought he might not let me in. He shut the door and walked away. A few minutes later he returned to open the door once again and invited me inside.

This house and its owners were strange. Everything about it left you confused. In the same way I had stood outside beforehand, marvelling at its very existence in these distant parts, I also stood inside, amazed by its elegance and neatness, marvelling at the owner; from the look of the antiques hanging on the walls, he had travelled the world without leaving a single foreign city unexplored, returning with valuable *objets* to hang on the wall or place on the shelves full of treasures. I'd ask him how it came to be that a man could leave the world behind, come here and build a fancy house that he lived in all by his lonesome.

The butler showed me to the small room off the corridor that was used as a storeroom for old junk, where he invited me to dry off and change out of my wet clothes into others he had grabbed off the shelf for me. There was an electric heater with hot metal coils that the butler had switched on so I could warm up. I drew closer to it and stood there, fighting off the cold that had settled deep into my bones, the damp causing steam to start rising from my clothes. I quickly got changed, as the butler instructed me to do, because I was excited to meet the owner of the house.

Then the butler showed me to the room I had looked into through the window when I was still outside. The old man had a hard time getting up to greet me. Although he didn't smile, the man was very kind, and the warmth in his eyes comforted me, made me feel like less of a stranger in his beautiful treasure-filled house. To be sure, I'd say I felt much more at ease with the old man than with his butler; there was something unfriendly about him that made you feel he despised you.

The old man was seventy years old, or thereabouts. He respectfully asked me what my name was and where I was from; this, despite the fact that I was certain the butler had already told him. He searched his memory and remembered other people with the same last name as mine, explaining to me how he had known them back in the day. Then he proceeded to tell me about his life, how he was alone in this world, that he didn't have anyone other than his butler. He had run away from the city after having lived there for a while but then got bored, the same way he had got bored of hundreds of other cities he had passed through during his travels. Finally, he said:

"After all the amazing things I've seen, life has taught me not to trust anyone, no matter who they might be. But, my brother, you're different from the others. I can tell from what your eyes are saying to me. You're my guest. Come and sit with me until this rain lets up."

I thanked him and then told him what had happened to me and my colleague Mr Tameem, how the car broke down and I'd had to abandon them for personal reasons. Then I asked him to send someone to look for the car and the people stranded inside. He immediately ordered the butler to do exactly what I had requested. After pouring us some tea, the butler took off right away. I could sense that the butler wasn't too pleased about this, so I felt the need to beg his forgiveness. The old man and I were left to sit there near the fireplace, listening to old songs by Umm Kulthum as they played on the stereo in the corner nearest him. I watched how he would drift off into these songs from the Thirties or perhaps from the Forties. He drifted far, far away with the songs, "May God Increase Your Beauty", "May Night Go On and On and Never Let Me Go" and "O, Neighbourhood Doctor". I respected his silence and tranquillity, his desire to keep listening. Umm Kulthum's songs came to an end and the broadcaster, or perhaps the one who had made the recording, announced that the next songs would be by Mounira al-Mahdiya. The band started to play, "He Can Forget Anyone But Me" followed by "Your Love Covers Everything, Sidi" and "The Best Time for Fooling Around Is After Dinner".

The atmosphere was electric. The warmth and the classic songs and the silence only added to the magic. Those melodies blended in with the sound of the old man's breathing. Why did he enjoy listening to the oldies? He seemed taciturn by nature, but I wanted to get him to explain to me why he had decided to go off the grid like this and live in the middle of nowhere. When the recording finished, I asked him:

"Tell me, respected sir, what made you come and live here? It may be impolite to ask but the question keeps nagging at me."

He raised his head, gazed at me with a gentle and resigned expression, and said:

"You have every right to ask, my new friend, but mine is a long story. It would take a very long time to hear the whole thing. To tell you the truth, I enjoy telling it, and would love to have someone around who wanted to hear my stories, but my butler keeps me from talking too much because he says it's better for my health not to."

"Please, old man, tell me the story. Ever since I was a little boy, I've loved stories. I've craved hearing them."

Handing me his cup, he asked with his customary gentleness:

"Would you mind pouring me another cup of tea?"

"At your service."

After pouring the tea, I dropped in two sugar cubes for him. After all, he was a diabetic. He sipped his tea with two shaking hands, which must have been the result of Parkinson's, or something like that, I thought, and then he began to tell me his tale, which was the strangest thing I had ever heard in my entire life.

On the Margin of the Story

I WANT TO JUMP AHEAD for a moment and inform you, dear reader, what happened both while and after these stories were being told. I stayed in the old man's house for five days and five nights, because that's how long it took the septuagenarian to get through all the events and details. He was quite generous and hospitable, without any skin off of his nose. That's an expression I stole from some literary work. We stayed up very late into the night, catching some sleep during the daytime and not waking up until mid-afternoon. There were particular aspects of the story that kept me there that whole time, until the story was finished. I don't want to get too far ahead of myself and give everything away before its time, but there's no harm in saying that the butler tried to stop the old man from talking.

By the time I finally made it home, my family had given up hope of ever finding me. The office had been searching for me with the assistance of the police as well as the efforts of dozens of village leaders whom I know and who know me as well. After heading off in search of the Land Rover and the driver and Mr Tameem, the butler came back two hours later to inform us that he couldn't find any trace of the car. I concluded that the two of them had managed to fix it somehow and continue on their way to the village of Abu al-Fida. Later they would tell me how they had waited there for me until morning, but when I didn't come back they went to get help towing the car. Unfortunately, the old man's house didn't even have a telephone from which I could call the office or my house during the entire time I spent there. Because what the old man was telling me remained so captivating, I forgot all about calling the city, and it never once occurred to me that they might believe I'd got lost in the wilderness on that stormy and rainy night, and had been eaten by wolves, which led to my colleague being hauled in for questioning. He remained under suspicion even after I finally made it home in one piece.

The stories affected me so deeply that I felt as though they had become a part of my own life. My family felt the same way, especially my wife, who believed that something terrible must have happened to my mind because I decided to get out of the car in such frightening weather. But it was really nothing more than the fact that I was taken by those stories I'm about to narrate for you starting in the next chapter.

All that's left for me to explain to you is the form of writing that you'll find here. As I mentioned at the outset, I'm not accustomed to writing literary texts or such modes of expression. All I've ever been good at is writing accounting reports that are only of interest to my bosses at the Agricultural Bank. Am I even capable of writing as long a story as this one?

I was convinced that this story needed to live for ever in a book. As you know, the old man had reached a ripe old age and he had only a short time left. If it had ever occurred to him to write it down, he would have done so a long time ago and not allowed it to fester in his chest. That's why I found myself facing this great and challenging task. How should this story, or these stories, be preserved? And who would have written them down, if I hadn't done so?

One day I heard about this well-known poet who was very good at writing prose, and so I went to see him, to ask him to listen to me tell the story so that he could then write it down in his own words. After I had convinced him to hear part of the story, he told me to stop, begged off writing, and wished me well. Truth be told, he did the right thing, because there is something in this story that offends common decency, as they say, despite my own belief that nothing can offend common decency anymore, not these days. Once I made it home, my preoccupations and fears about dying and the story dying with me became more and more pronounced. That's why I decided to write it down myself. And yet, dear reader, I found that I am not very good at writing stories, so please forgive me. Just yesterday I opened up a literary book and discovered that the author had introduced his book with a caveat for his reader that the book wasn't complete, as perfection is a characteristic of the Creator. If professional writers offer their own excuses, then certainly I can write now and apologise later.

It remains for me to say that I tried going back to the old man's house another time, but couldn't find it again. I also tried once more in the summertime, relying on a compass and asking all the peasants and the shepherds where the house might be, but none of them could tell me anything. That was strange, of course, but I assure you that I actually showed up there on that stormy, rainswept night.

So here you have these stories. You'll find me emerging from the frame of the story in order to speak with the old man, to discuss what I heard with him from time to time, or you may find me describing the old man and his butler and the house where I stayed for five days, or you may hear me talking about the shocking events that happened to me there. So, I beg your forgiveness… and God is behind every good intention.

CHAPTER ONE

How Innocent Widad Appeared in a Photograph with the French High Commissioner

T HE OLD MAN SAID...

"It all started on 27th September 1936...

"The train was slowly pulling into al-Sham Station, its whistle blowing nonstop.

"Widad didn't stand up to look out the window the way most of the other passengers did. She was glued to her seat, trying hard not to make eye contact with the man sitting across from her, beside the compartment door, who was staring at her intently. She wished he would get up and stick his head out the window the way everyone else did as the Orient Express passed through the narrow tunnel. Her eyelashes fluttering, she stole a quick glance. She wished he would turn his eyes away from her, towards the sky, towards the first city buildings that had come into view, towards the trees that were slowly receding behind them, or even towards the picture of the Eiffel Tower hanging above her head in the wooden compartment. But he just kept on staring at her, which was particularly unnerving given how her mother had always warned her to be modest around men. He might have smiled at her if she hadn't retreated further inward, pushing herself against the window, looking down at her hands, which were folded in her lap.

"She abandoned her sense of sight, and was aware of what was going on by way of her ears alone. The train was coming to a halt, even as it continued to sound its whistle. She could hear the conversations of other passengers in the corridor, then some enthusiastic cheering, because the train was carrying several notable people, and it was expected that they would receive an ebullient reception. She wished she could get up to see the celebrations, but that man continued to gawk at her, threatening to ogle her behind if she stood. She had to remain where she sat until the train stopped, at which point she would be able to get away. But what if everyone except for the two of them disembarked from the train? She shuddered. Her forehead felt warm. She experienced a few seconds of panic, the kind of terror she used to feel on nights that were filled with thunder and lightning, when her mother would tell her what men were capable of doing to a little girl. But now her fear was due to something real, because there was a man sitting across from her, staring right at her, oblivious to all the other passengers who were amusing themselves by looking outside and shouting patriotic chants against France, cheering the returning delegation. Which delegation? What was the delegation? And why were they cheering for it? Where was it coming from?

"She had waited on the platform at Maydan Ekbas Station for more than three hours before the train coming from Istanbul on its way to Aleppo finally arrived. They had sent Bayonet Abduh to see her off, a feeble-minded crazy boy whom they had given the name Bayonet because one day when he crossed over the border—Maydan Ekbas is located near the Turkish-Syrian border—a Turkish soldier stabbed him with his bayonet. From then on he walked with a limp, which led people to make fun of him even more. There was a third infirmity that made him seem even funnier to people: there was a gaping hole in his upper row of teeth that made him whistle unintentionally whenever he spoke. Before her mother died, Widad always had a good time with Bayonet Abduh when he came over to their house. He would come round often in order to do odd jobs for them, but also to amuse Widad, that sweet girl who would laugh and laugh whenever he moved or ran or spoke. He would joyfully lie down on his back and start giggling, his hands and legs flailing in the air. Sometimes, when she wasn't paying attention or while she was laughing with her eyes closed, he would touch her and experience a strange sensation that left him feeling happy all day long, sapping some of his strength, which might send him to sit under a tree in the shade. She never understood what those caresses meant to him, what they did to him. One day when the village imam Shaykh Abd al-Sabbour saw what he was doing he scolded him and then chased after him with a pomegranate switch threateningly held high in the air. At the time Widad couldn't understand the anger of the shaykh and his muezzin. She hated the shaykh. When he sat at her ill mother's bedside whispering to her and staring at Widad, she became convinced that he was badmouthing her because of how much she hated him. That's what she thought, anyway. When they were alone together at night, her mother would repeat warnings about men, but Widad never thought of Bayonet Abduh as being one of them. She never felt afraid of him.

"On the verge of losing Widad for ever, Bayonet Abduh spent those three hours waiting for the Orient Express in tears. Despite his impaired mind, he knew that Widad's mother had decided to send her to Aleppo after her death. He saw Shaykh Abd al-Sabbour hand her an addressed envelope that contained a letter and some money, so she wouldn't be left waiting all alone any longer than an eighteen-year-old girl could handle. The carriage that was supposed to pick her up was often delayed. In an attempt to beat back her sadness and make her forget her fears, he made her laugh the way he had always done. She was nervous of what lay in store for her. This was her first time travelling alone by train. Widad distracted him, too, chatting away the whole time, lying to him by saying that she would be back soon, knowing full well that she wasn't coming back. And as the train rolled into the station, preceded by a long, drawn-out whistle, Abduh's mood changed. Bayonet Abduh scampered around with glee at the sight of those carriages adorned with flags and banners, which caused him so much joy that the other half of his rational mind flew away altogether. At this point she started to cry even as he laughed harder, oblivious to her. It was difficult for her to get a grip on him, to calm him down, until she squeezed his hand firmly and dragged him over towards one of the undecorated cars. By the door she took his hand in both of hers, mustering up the courage to board the train and leave the village in which she had been born, and which she had never left before.

"She hopped up onto the train and searched for an empty seat in one of the compartments. After stowing her suitcase on the overhead shelf, she sat down. Abduh stood there beneath the window. Rubbing the hand Widad had held just a moment before, he gazed up at her sitting there on the other side of the glass. Tears cut paths down her cheeks. Just before the train departed Abduh felt like he was the happiest person in the world and started hooting, giggling in order to make his little girl laugh in turn, but she kept on crying until the train left the platform. Once Bayonet Abduh and the train station were far behind her, she wiped away her tears and looked away from the window, immediately meeting the stare of the man who would spend the entire trip fixated on her without raising the slightest notice from any of the other travellers in the compartment.

"She heard other voices that gradually blended in with the sounds of the train whistle and the passengers' chanting and the screeching of iron against iron. The sound of music was approaching, getting louder, and she felt a sudden affection towards the station where the train was about to stop. Without even looking at the man, she quickly turned her face towards the window. A huge crowd of people had gathered to welcome the delegation arriving by train. They were chanting raucously, holding up banners and flags, waving towards the first few cars. A state music troupe started to play military marches. She smiled in spite of herself. This jam-packed reception had cheered her up.

"'They're here to greet the delegation…'

"She spun around instinctively, irritation written all over her face. The man was talking to her, having moved closer to the window as well. Just then the other passengers came in to get their bags, chattering and making a lot of noise. She thought about getting up, too, but she might bump into this man if she did, so she remained in her seat. It was the first time she had looked at his face up close like this. His eyes were red, staring into hers as if he wanted to penetrate them, as if he were marvelling at something that only she possessed. In that instant she felt that she had to get out of there. The situation was getting dangerous. She mumbled something from her seat, looking at him solicitously as if to ask whether she could get up and leave. Taking advantage of the fact that they were the only ones left in the compartment, though, he thrust out his hand and touched her face. She recoiled and started shivering as the music grew louder, feeling as though nobody would be able to hear her even if she shouted.

"'I beg of you,' she found herself pleading.

"His hand continued to roam around her cheeks, her chin, and her nose. She couldn't calm down. Heat was spreading across her face. She saw no other option than to shove him away and run out of there. As he fell back into his seat, she grabbed her suitcase and rushed out. Looking back to check whether he was coming after her, she saw that he was just sitting there, smiling, elated. Fearing that he was about to pounce, she raced off, in search of somewhere she could jump down onto the platform. This was pretty near impossible, though, because the crowd was mobbing the train, blocking the exits on both sides. She had to zip from one car to another several times before she managed to find a way out.

"The musical troupe continued to perform military marches. Crowds of people undulated through the station, rolling back and forth, until the platforms were jammed. Some people were forced to climb up onto the train, to leap up onto the roof and scamper over to the car where the delegation was about to disembark, just to catch a glimpse of them. When the head of the delegation peeked his head out—that was Hashim al-Atassi, by the way—he heard a powerful roar. Welcomers tried to slip past the French policemen to get closer to the train. But orders are orders. The policemen had been instructed to keep the people away from the car as the delegation descended so that High Commissioner Monsieur Damien de Martel would be able to approach and shake hands with the Nationalists returning from Paris.

"The High Commissioner approached, in his gleaming white suit, his chest festooned with various medals and commendations. After Hashim al-Atassi drew in so close that the High Commissioner was able to detect the scent of Paris in autumn, he went on to shake hands with all the remaining members of the delegation; they disembarked from the train one by one, waiting on the steps until it was their turn to shake hands or embrace. Every time one of them appeared on the train steps, they would receive raucous applause and renewed chanting from the assembled audience. Although they had spent six days on the train, none of them looked worn out or overwhelmed from all the sitting and boredom. They had prepared themselves before arriving at Aleppo Station by trimming their beards, washing their faces, and changing their clothes. The sight of them was so affecting that a number of the greeters broke down in tears. Then His Excellency the High Commissioner invited them to pose next to him for a souvenir photograph. The photograph was composed to memorialise the fact that the delegation had just returned from splendid Paris to occupied Aleppo, arranged so that the train would appear in the background behind them. At the moment the flashbulb popped to illuminate the shot, Widad appeared on the train steps with her suitcase, which is why she can be seen in the photograph that was later circulated to all the local periodicals as well as newspapers in the capital. Her face looked so innocent there just above de Martel's head. There are some who say they even saw her on the front page of French newspapers in Paris. The photograph was enlarged and hung on the walls inside the offices of the High Commissioner and the National Bloc as well as in some of the delegation members' homes.

"When the crowd noticed her standing there on the train steps, innocent and afraid, their voices started to die down and then fell silent, until nothing could be heard but the sound of the marching band, still being conducted by the swinging hands of Sergeant Samuel, who now turned in the direction of Widad. The members of the band were no more disciplined than he was, though, and although still playing, they, too, craned their necks to look at that peasant woman who had popped out of the delegation's train clutching her ancient suitcase, a scarf tied around her head to keep her hair concealed from the eyes of men in the city. Even the ministers and urban notables who had shown up to greet the delegation were flabbergasted to see such a beautiful peasant woman. The *mufti* was the only one who tried to look away, but even he didn't manage to do so, concluding that perhaps she was a *djinn* or an angel come down from heaven in order to safeguard the delegation on their journey, which was why there could be no harm in gazing upon her. The High Commissioner found that silence strange, and he wheeled around backwards. It took some time for him to comprehend what was happening, to understand what that young lady was doing there. Because of his stare, and the looks from members of the delegation,

Widad's confusion grew even greater. It seemed necessary for her to explain herself, so she hesitantly said, in a muffled voice:

"'I couldn't find anywhere else to get out...'

"At first the High Commissioner didn't understand what the young lady had said, and continued to stare back at her like an idiot, but then everyone else burst out laughing at such an unexpected sight. The people of Aleppo have a good sense of humour despite everything that's said about them. De Martel became convinced the whole thing was just an accident, so he thought nothing more of the peasant woman whose beauty had stolen the hearts of all the welcomers. The delegation was invited to get moving, the chants started back up, and the marches rang out once more. The French police forged a path for the delegation through the crowds that had started to surge forward because every person wanted to catch a glimpse of the head of the National Bloc, Hashim al-Atassi, who was also heading up the delegation, or at Saadallah al-Jabiri, the Aleppan native son and elegant politician. There were others who didn't know where to look because it was quite rare for so many Syrian nationalists and politicians to be gathered together alongside the officers of colonial rule.

"They left the station, led by the High Commissioner, whose white suit fitted tightly around his corpulent body, and followed by the people and the musical troupe playing a stirring military composition. It wasn't long before Widad was standing on the platform by herself, her suitcase by her side and her anxiety subsiding. She stood there next to the train even as the engine continued to spew out its soft white steam. But she was unsure about what was going to happen to her, seeing as how she had never dreamt there would be this kind of reception in the vast city called Aleppo, whose men her deceased mother had always warned her about. *If she were to find out down in her grave in the Maydan Ekbas cemetery how the men had welcomed her at the station, would she change her mind about them?* she wondered. Widad shrugged her shoulders, silently answering her own question, and then took out the envelope with the address where she was supposed to go. She picked up her suitcase and walked out of the station. She stood outside, as the Maydan Ekbas imam Shaykh Abd al-Sabbour had instructed her to do, waiting for the carriage that would take her to her destination. But what cabs would be running at this hour? The square and the streets had all been deserted by the people she could now see far off in the distance, forming a huge crowd that accompanied the carriages and the cars transporting the delegation and the official welcoming committee, their chanting becoming indistinguishable from the tune played by the military band."

The butler walked in carrying a pot of hot tea. The old man suddenly fell silent, as if ceding the space for him to do his job of pouring the tea. But it occurred to me that the old man might have become silent because he was trying to keep something from his servant. Or maybe he just wanted to rest for a moment. Whatever the case, the butler poured the tea without making a sound, gracefully serving each of us a cup. If the old man had kept talking I wouldn't even have noticed the presence of a third person in the room. Instead I sensed that the old man's silence indicated that I should pay close attention to what the butler was doing. I was reminded of the uneasy feeling I'd had from the first moment he had greeted me at the front door. I kindly thanked him all the same before starting to sip the hot tea I couldn't seem to get enough of; the cold had seeped into my bones during my long trek in the wilderness after I'd inexplicably walked away from the Land Rover. As soon as he left and closed the door behind him, the old man's calm and mellifluous voice continued...

"Widad stood outside the station for a whole hour, until the carriage being pulled along by a single horse arrived to pick her up. She handed the driver the address and settled into the back seat, placing her trust in this driver, a man who inspired confidence, and watched the city roll past.

"She privately wondered how this city had looked to her mother eighteen years before.

"Her mother had told Widad about that fateful day when she ran away from the city. She had hopped onto a train bound for the north, which she had caught at that very station one day in the midst of the Great War in which everyone and every country had fought. The war had been nearing an end, thousands of Turks were massing at the station, every one of them searching for a place on trains bound for Turkish territory. Veteran politicians, decommissioned officers, former governors, high-ranking bureaucrats in the Ottoman administration, men whom the Sultan had stripped of their *pasha* titles, one-time administrators from provinces and sub-districts that had been lost during the devastating military hostilities. The station was also filled with affluent women and well-fed children as well as the mistresses of military personnel anxious about their future.

"All those people, unconcerned with their appearances, which they had once paid such close attention to, filled the platforms at the station. Under their arms they were clutching bags and suitcases, in which they had packed everything they could save or plunder from the provinces they once ruled. The convoys were arriving nonstop, and when there was no more space to set foot on the station floor, they unloaded their cargo from the carriages and the pack animals, which they later voluntarily set free, because the spirit is more valuable than any material possession. They filled the square outside the station as well. When the train arrived, they all surged towards it as one, shouting as they tried to find a way towards the doors in order to stake out a spot inside. Every person tried to identify himself, but who cared about ranks or titles anymore? Anyone who was able to get on one of the cars would then start wailing when he realised he had left behind a friend or a wife or a child...

"It was only with great difficulty that her mother managed to find herself a place in one of the livestock cars. She was five months pregnant at the time, though her pregnancy wasn't yet obvious, so in order to secure a space for herself she had to exaggerate the size of her belly. People took pity on her and helped her to get on board. From where she sat on the train she witnessed the painful conclusion of Ottoman rule in Syria.

"The train didn't start moving until night-time. Those on the run were trying to convince the conductors to get the train moving as quickly as possible. Rumours were flying at the speed of light about the worst possible consequences for anyone who got left behind. Enemy forces were encroaching on Aleppo. At first they said they had got as close as Khan al-Sabeel, then in the evening, news broke confirming that the English had taken control of Shaykh Saeed, on the outskirts of Aleppo, which distressed everyone and made many women weep. But her mother wasn't concerned. She was an Arab who wanted to flee to Turkey before the borders were closed so that she could find Captain Cevdet, the Turkish officer who had helped make a baby in her belly just before getting called up unexpectedly to join his division, somewhere along the southern front.

"Inside the train compartment, once everyone was able to relax, convinced that luck was on their side now that the train had started inching its way towards safer shores, the men discovered how beautiful her mother was. The train was moving very slowly because of its heavy load of humanity. All eyes started to burrow into her, tracking her every move, the eyes of men and women alike, hungry eyes, brimming with vengeance and jealousy. This denied her the freedom to think about her handsome officer, whom she loved so desperately, the one for whom she had given up everything. She had to keep her shame concealed the whole time. The compartment was so crowded that she had to continuously shove away all the men who wanted to rub up against her in the darkness, exhaling their warm breath in her face. In the morning the army rescued her from the hell of those men. When the train rolled into Maydan Ekbas Station to stock up on water and fuel, something pushed them past the point of no return, something so shocking and harsh and merciless that everyone raised their voices in disapproval, weeping and crying on each other's shoulders before falling silent and being forced to go along with it: all civilians would have to disembark and continue their journey on foot so the army could transport its wounded and its supplies across the border as quickly as possible. As everyone else continued their journey into Turkish territory however they could, Widad's mother decided to stay put in Maydan Ekbas.

"The village station was the nerve centre, where the retreating forces would have to pass through on their way to the Turkish interior. That's why she stayed there on the platform, waiting for the train carrying her beloved Captain Cevdet to arrive. Whenever another train rolled in from the south, she would jump to her feet, straining to see him, in case he stepped off. She spent days like this, but there was no sign of him. Finally the English soldiers started to arrive, chasing away and fighting the retreating Turks, which was when she realised that she had lost the Captain for good. So instead of going back to Aleppo, which was impossible anyway, she decided to rent a house in the village and stay there until she gave birth to her child.

"In order to convince the people of the village to accept her living among them, her mother made up a story... a second life that was entirely imaginary. She would never tell them the truth, secretly burying it away for ever, and instead she led them to believe that she was Captain Cevdet's wife, that her entire family had died in the war, and that she had been travelling to Turkey in order to search for her officer husband and his family but the arrival of the English and the ongoing hostilities between them and the Turks along the border had prevented her from doing so. Her mother was beautiful, graceful. The people of the village had never seen such a beautiful woman before, not even the wealthy Turkish women who would pass through town as they fled back to Istanbul. Her innocent face, her delightful way with words, and her tears that could make stones speak—what chance did those simple-minded villagers stand? What convinced them of her sincerity even more was the way she lived her life after giving birth to a beautiful little girl she named Widad. She quietly and humbly took on whatever work there was in order to feed and take care of her daughter. By the time Widad had matured into an attractive young woman who resembled her mother in her gracefulness and innocence and charms, the village seemed to have hardly noticed her. Some young men attempted to approach her mother in order to ask for Widad's hand but she refused to marry her off; she wouldn't let any of those boys get near the house except for that nutty kid, Bayonet Abduh, and that was only after she got to know him a little bit first. For reasons that weren't clear, she constantly sowed the fear of men in her strikingly beautiful daughter, which led Widad to be nervous around them. When her mother was diagnosed with a horrible case of tuberculosis and learnt that she would die soon, she started talking to Widad about Aleppo and some of the people she knew there. She tried to express her affection for the city, wanted her daughter to go there after her death. She told Widad about a dear friend of hers named Khojah Bahira, and gave her a letter of introduction, but asked her to say nothing of that name for the moment, until she passed away, insisting that she avoid letting anyone in the village hear her mention Khojah Bahira's name, and that she ask her nothing about her.

"The carriage driver turned around and stole a quick glance at the young girl's face, muttering *mashallah* under his breath. Widad stared out at the city streets with a mixture of sadness and awe. Every street, every intersection, every building reminded her of her mother. She imagined her walking down the street, arm in arm with the Turkish officer, or crossing the street alone in front of the carriage as she hunted for her man, lost in the Great War. But why had her mother refused to go to Aleppo? Why had she never brought her here, instead limiting herself to describing it and instilling in Widad's heart a fondness for it? Nothing made any sense. Her mother was dead, leaving behind a thousand questions that confused Widad. Who was this Khojah Bahira? Why had their friendship remained such a mysterious secret? And why had she wanted Widad to go and see her after she died? As I just said, nothing made any sense in the mind of our beautiful young woman. It was as confusing as the layout of the ancient city."

The old man said…

"Her mother Badia was beautiful and bold. She wasn't shy like her daughter Widad. Maybe everything that happened to her led her to raise her daughter differently, in such a way that might prevent her from making the same mistakes. All mothers want a life for their daughters that will be different from the lives they lived, especially Badia, who had run away from home when the war broke out. Men started disappearing from the streets and from their houses. During wartime men were condemned either to go off to war or to disappear. This was their fate. Turkish gendarmes were on every street corner waiting to ambush them. They would seize them and then take them God knows where. This was what had happened to her recently married brother Muhammad Ali. But her father ran away. Every so often he would send them supplies and some cash, but he'd run away all the same. The house became a home for women only. Its law was women's law. Her own mother was stern and irascible. Most of the women in the house were beautiful, which was why her mother imposed such strict rules upon them. This was also the reason Badia fled to Aleppo in the first place. She had often entertained her sisters and her brother's wife by tying a scarf around her waist and dancing for them. She decided to take advantage of her talent and to try making a living out of it.

"Life in their village wasn't unbearable. The society of women took care of itself and things went on as normal. Badia's arrival in Aleppo, though, happened to coincide with the first signs of famine. The streets were full of sick people. She once came across the body of an old man who had died of hunger lying in an alley. Badia was horrified. She had heard so much about the city before her arrival and had dreamt about it, but now she was frightened of what lay in store for her there. She knew this was not normal. As she arrived, fleeing her mother's strict rules, people were dying of hunger. Had it not been for a man who passed by as she was leaning against a door and who mercifully gave her some change, she might have turned around and gone right back to the village, back to her mother's regime. When he asked her if she was good at anything besides begging, she told him she knew how to do the washing and the cleaning, how to cook and how to dance. That's right, she had the audacity to mention dancing. And she really did know how to shake her hips and her breasts. It's a good thing she did, too, because sweeping and cleaning and cooking had no value in those days, especially since there was nothing to cook or eat anyway. Get up and come with me, the man told her. While she followed him, she munched

41

on a cracker he had bought in order to tide her over until he could sort something better out.

"But where was this samaritan, who materialised at just the right moment, taking her?" I asked the old man, desperate to find out Badia's fate. The captivating story had had such an effect on me that my cup of tea had gone cold; I had forgotten all about it as soon as the kindly old man began again to tell his story. He said I had to be patient if I wanted to hear the story all the way to the end. I begged his pardon and picked up my cup of tea, which is when I discovered that it was cold, despite the warmth that was radiating from the heater. There's something I want the reader to be aware of, which is that I was keen to hear the story of the mother so that we could get back to the story of the daughter. What was most enjoyable about the way the old man told the story was how he bounced back and forth from one to the other without a clear rhyme or reason, without necessarily finishing the first story before moving on to the second. I don't know why, exactly, but it was satisfying... Now, let's get back to the story of Badia, and I apologise to the reader for this intervention on my part but I find it necessary to appear in the text every now and then because my time there with the old man, my listening to his story... that is also a story in its own right.

The old man said that the one I called a samaritan took her to see one of the most famous singers in the city at that time—Khojah Bahira—handing her over in exchange for nine gold liras, and Badia would never see him again.

"That son of a bitch sold her?" I asked, trembling with rage.

"Yes, he sold her. But don't take the word 'sold' to mean that he actually sold her. He could tell from her beautiful face and what she had told him about knowing how to dance that if he presented her to Khojah Bahira she would compensate him for it. That was something normal. Bahira was a singer well known throughout the city. She loved to be surrounded by beautiful young ladies. Besides, she needed a dancer to accompany her at her concerts. That's why he got his compensation.

"When Khojah Bahira laid eyes on Badia she nearly collapsed under her own weight." (This literary turn of phrase was the old man's, and he used it several times while telling the story.) "Badia was beautiful, extremely beautiful. She was a rare specimen who had fallen into Khojah Bahira's hands because Khojah would undoubtedly be able to appreciate her value. We know that women who make their living in this line of work tend not to be so pretty. Some are even thought of as repulsive: overweight, swarthy, flabby and old. Except for the Jews, that is, who were famous for their beauty. Music groups in the theatres used to compete with one another over them, as with this one Jewish woman in particular who would elicit audible gasps from people in the audience, not only because of her stirring voice but also because of her beautiful face, supple body, and her creamy-white skin.

"Khojah Bahira took Badia in, cared for her, and then helped to coach her movement, teaching her essential skills of dance such as the ability to hold her legs and her torso still while rapidly shaking her hips and swinging her hands. This was a kind of movement Badia had never been very good at; she moved constantly instead, in a way that gave her a more masculine appearance, which is not what women like Bahira wanted to see. Dominant femininity was necessary for a dancer. Bahira continued to give her lessons, teaching Badia all of her moves and her skills until she had perfected Oriental dance and Bahira was satisfied.

"Bahira, the veteran singer who was well known all over town, was funny looking. Her face, her body, and the way she moved were mannish. She also looked like a man. She wore men's clothing, strutted around in public like that, sometimes even wearing a red fez on her head. She loved it when people mistook her for a man. She had always dreamt of being up on a wooden stage wearing trousers and a man's shirt, with a watch in her waistcoat pocket that would allow her to show off her chain for all to see. At weddings, inside the atmosphere of the harem, her appearance caused huge excitement among the female audience. She wasn't bothered by the comments and harsh words some women spread about her; in fact she liked to hear what they said and would respond in kind, or even up the ante. She was a manly woman with a foul mouth.

"Bahira wasn't her real name. Nobody knew what it was, even if some people let their imaginations run wild, claiming she was actually called Husayn or Abed… or Abu Steve or some other man's name because of how much she looked like one. Bahira was originally from Aleppo, from the Qastal al-Mosht neighbourhood, her parents' only child, and in order to protect her from other children, they told everyone she was a boy, cutting her hair short and dressing her like all the other boys until she began to go out with girls even though she was one herself. Nobody ever seemed to notice. This story is one hundred per cent true. In those days, she went by the name Subhi. It was even said that she had assembled a gang of young men under her command without any of them knowing she was a girl. The gang would maraud houses and farms, robbing and plundering. One day the gang tried to rob a prostitute's house. That woman started to cry, pleading with them because she didn't have anything for them to steal in the first place. Instead, she offered them the opportunity to have sex with her for free. The idea appealed to them. Subhi, that is, Bahira, nearly lost his status as leader of the gang. He was afraid she might reveal his secret sex in front of all of them. He tried to talk them out of it but the gang nearly came to blows over it because they were all desperate to try that thing they had heard so much about but had never done. Now the opportunity was being presented to them by chance, and for free, so why was Subhi trying to prevent them, that filthy animal? In the end he agreed and the guys went in one after the other to see the prostitute. They came out giggling. The whole thing was a lot of fun. Finally it was Subhi's turn, leader of the pack. Because of his fear of having his sexual identity exposed, he decided to go in last. He found the woman lying spread eagled, exhausted and in surrender. Bahira was overwhelmed with a powerful desire to caress the whore's body. She moved in closer and started gently stroking her body. The prostitute found what the head of the gang was doing a bit strange. Instead of doing what he was supposed to, this gangster was caressing her gently, kissing her, and exploring her body and its curves until she started to feel pleasure. Bahira also felt that way, discovering her own attraction to girls.

"From that moment forward, Bahira became much closer to the members of her gang. The truth that she had been so afraid her pals might discover was relegated to secondary importance. She could have sex with female whores just like the other guys, and she experienced tremendous pleasure in

NIHAD SIREES

doing so. She even suggested to the guys in the gang several times that they should go to the woman's house. Because she was poor she recommended that they pay her. And so the gang became regular customers of that woman. Each and every time Bahira rediscovered her lust for women's bodies, and her distaste for men. One day the whore whispered in one of the gang member's ears that their boss wasn't a real man because he made do with just touching her, even though they were sexual caresses. When he relayed what the woman had told him to the other guys in the gang, they started to monitor Subhi, discovering after a while that he didn't piss standing up the way they did, or that he hardly ever pissed at all. Subhi would say that he didn't have to go whenever the guys lined up and whipped out their cocks to piss. He would back away from them when they were doing that. As far as the guys in the gang were concerned, this was a real disaster, an earth-shaking scandal. What kind of a gang was led by a hermaphrodite, someone who was neither female nor male? The shame of it… They hoped things weren't as they seemed, that the whore was mistaken. Besides, how could they take the word of some prostitute seriously and doubt the leader of their gang? They had to find out for themselves. But how? Could they just ask Subhi directly? That was impossible. Questions like that weren't asked. They were insulting. What if the whole thing was a misunderstanding and that lowlife was just trying to break them up so she could be rid of them?

"They were crossing the Queiq River over the al-Qarri Bridge. They had stolen a chicken from a nearby farm, slaughtered it, and then started a fire so they could roast it. They swam in the river and dared each other to dive under the

46

water wheel that had swallowed a number of boys and men in the past. When they lay down on the ground to dry off they saw Subhi, who usually didn't join them in the water, lying there as well. He was fast asleep. At that moment they made their decision to pin him down by his hands and feet while one of them tore off his pants and shirt. They had to get an answer to the question right then and there, while they had the chance. If Subhi was a boy like them they would all have a good laugh and make the whole thing look like a joke. So that Subhi wouldn't be offended by what they were doing all the boys stripped naked. They took off their clothes, including the last scrap of clothing that covered their genitals. Then they drew closer to him while he was sleeping, and with a signal from the one who'd had the idea in the first place, they grabbed hold of Subhi and started to tear his clothes off. He woke up and tried to defend himself but they had already got a good hold on him. They were all laughing. They ripped off his pants and then the rest of his clothes. When his genitals appeared they all stopped laughing. They discovered what they had feared most: Subhi was a girl.

"In the midst of such shock they hardly noticed the shame. How had it never occurred to them that their leader might be a girl? Bahira ran off in tears, back home to the city all by herself. They were tongue-tied. Bahira had been able to deceive them that whole time because she looked like a young man in so many ways—her face, her legs, her hands. She had muscles and would roughhouse the way boys do. She resembled them in almost every respect, except for the one thing that distinguished them below the waist. Bahira had managed to fool them by never peeing in front of them. What about her breasts, though? They were fifteen years old. Bahira had a chest like the other girls her age. Did she wrap her chest? After she was kicked out of the gang, they chose another boy to be their boss, and the first decision he made was to rape Bahira. But she was onto what was happening and steered well clear of them. She made a weighty decision of her own, resolving never to get married, if for no other reason than the fact that the bodies of men and boys repulsed her.

"She began to detest the society of men, which was one reason why she became a wedding singer. When she was eighteen years old her mother discovered that she had a beautiful voice. She may have reached puberty, but what kind of maturity could that be if she fantasised about being with women? She had a slender body without any flab. Her chest had blossomed so much that it was impossible to squeeze it flat with wraps. She no longer felt repressed because she had no desire to be with men at all. She preferred to be with the gentler sex instead; to be with women, that is. Her own gender prepared her well for that kind of relationship. In this country it's impossible for anyone who isn't a woman to penetrate women's society, even if the woman is like Bahira and looks like a man. When her mother first discovered that she had such a melodious voice, she started encouraging her to sing in the presence of friends and neighbours without it ever occurring to her that Bahira might wind up becoming a wedding singer someday. Bahira's fame spread throughout the city, into every household. She sang at weddings, women's gatherings and baby showers, especially when a baby boy was born. She used to show up at those parties with her band, which everyone knew would consist entirely of women as well.

She became accustomed to being on stage dressed in men's clothes, sometimes wearing a fez on her head or painting on a curlicued moustache, a white rose always stuck in her coat pocket. She became well known for her male stage persona, which is what made the women of the city into such dedicated fans, they even worshipped her. The mere mention of her name evoked a kind of Bahira fever.

"The fact that she liked women added to her reputation. Her love for girls, really. Stories of her passion and her female lovers ricocheted around the salons and the bathhouse gatherings. She wasn't ashamed. On the contrary, she was proud, boasting of her latest adventure as well as her frantic struggle to hold on to her lovers, to keep them away from jealous women and rivals who were also known to like women. Those women also vied to win the heart of a beautiful woman who had only recently come into their circle. Khojah Bahira moved in on one of the musicians, a blonde zither player, winning her away from her ex-lover, Khojah Samah, and enticing her to join her band instead. The doorbell rang and Badia walked in with the man who had brought her round to earn nine gold liras during a time of war and poverty, when people were dying of starvation.

With a cunning smile curling up on his face, the kindly old man asked me, "So, now do you understand why Khojah Bahira was so happy about Badia that she would pay the man in gold for bringing her over?"

"Yes, I do, my good sir. I imagine she must have been phenomenally beautiful, an attractive young lady hand delivered to an older woman who liked women. But tell me, please, didn't that make the other female musicians in Khojah Bahira's band jealous, especially the one you mentioned, the blonde zither player Bahira had stolen from her ex-lover, Khojah Samah?"

"The blonde was absolutely dying of jealousy. You've never seen a woman like that, or maybe you have. I have no right to question the encounters and experiences you've had in life, but just imagine a woman that two established women had been competing over. Suddenly she becomes uninteresting to her current lover, who starts to pour all of her energy into teaching Badia about the fundamentals of dance, as both an art and a science, taking a keen interest in her beauty and her elegance."

"So what happened to the blonde?"

"She left Khojah Bahira, went back to Khojah Samah."

I laughed to hear the old man say that. The story was just getting better and better. Apparently I had a thing for stories about female lovers. In order to seem as though I knew something about such matters, I explained to the old man, "I think they call them *banat al-ishreh*."

"That's right, *banat al-ishreh*."

"I don't know the origin of that expression. Do you, my good man?"

"I think *banat al-ishreh* refers to women who are with other women the same way men are with women. That's how they got the name anyway. Throughout the city's history there are tales of women who live together like any other family. As if they were man and wife. There's always one who takes on the role of the man while the other takes on the woman's role."

"Is the former necessarily more important than the latter?"

"In general, yes, which is why the more important one, that is to say, the man of the house, is called *ablaya*, which means older sister in Turkish. The other one belongs to the *ablaya*, which is why she's called her 'little girl'."

"Then what happened to Badia? I've started to grow fond of her. She's the mother of our hero Widad, the one who arrived in Aleppo by train with a pre-addressed envelope in her hand and who was unwittingly captured in a photo with the French High Commissioner."

"Hold on. First I need to tell you something about Khojah Samah. But it's getting late. I see that the butler has already gone to bed. What do you say we both go upstairs so we can get some rest and then pick up the story in the morning?"

I agreed. It had been a particularly exhausting day for me. If I wanted to pay close attention to his stories and fix them in my memory, I would need all of my strength. I stood up and guided the old man to his room. He was very frail, trembling as he climbed the stairs. Just getting to his room required extraordinary effort. I opened the door for him and switched on the light before helping him into bed. I didn't leave his side until I was sure he was comfortable and tucked in under the thick blankets. He thanked me and wished me good night. I made to leave but a quick glance around the room stopped me in my tracks. The walls were covered with framed photographs. There wasn't enough room for another picture even if he had wanted to add another to his collection. Photographs were also strewn all over the small writing desk, on the nightstands on either side of the bed, and on the vanity. There were pictures of men and women, children and old people, all from the same class, and they all had some kind of relationship to him. The old man was watching me. I could sense that he didn't want me to paw through his pictures and his past. My intuition wasn't correct that time, though, as he would tell me later how much he appreciated my curiosity. I said goodnight, switched off the light, and left the room.

I was exhausted. And despite my fascination with the old man—his house and his bedroom, his photographs and his servant—I fell asleep as soon as my head hit the pillow. I made certain that the door was securely closed. I'm very careful about things like that, which I chalk up to an old fear that lives in my heart.

When I woke up the next day my head was heavy. I opened my eyes but stayed in bed. I wanted to hold on to that uncanny feeling of waking up in an unrecognisable place, or at least in an unfamiliar bedroom.

It was nearly eleven o'clock but the grey light of day and the sound of the pouring rain made it seem much earlier. Meanwhile the room seemed much cosier than it had the night before when I first arrived. It was a simple but elegant bedroom. The walls had no photographs like those in the old man's room. There was a single landscape painting hanging on the wall. All the furniture was made out of carved oak, which they must have brought from Aleppo. Since I come from there, I'm well aware that my city is known for that kind of craftsmanship. I didn't hear a sound, not even the typical sounds of the countryside. It was a kind of tranquillity a citydweller like me would never dream of. I enjoyed lying there in the quiet. Then it dawned on me that I might have heard something moving around inside the room while I was sleeping, but because of how worn out I was from the cold and the damp that had seeped into my bones, I slept through it without having the strength to get up, turn on the light, and seek out the source of the noise.

This is when I got a little bit scared. I got up and examined the door to make sure it was locked. Then I checked the window that looks out on the backyard garden and found the lock secure. Most likely it had only been a dream. The idea calmed me down. I went into the bathroom, washed and shaved, with all the new supplies the butler had provided just for me, and started to get dressed. Just then I heard a light tapping on the door, followed by the voice of the butler inviting me to come downstairs for breakfast.

When I got downstairs, I found the old man sitting at the table waiting for me. I wished him good morning and sat down in a place that had been set for me. Despite the numerous treasures and wooden boxes and paintings and decorative ivory tusks and pieces of fancy china and other things the old man had acquired during his travels all over the world, the dining room was more sparsely decorated than I remembered it being the night before. Those trinkets made the dining room and the living room look classy, and demonstrated that the old man had good taste. As we ate breakfast in silence, the servant would come around to pour us some milk or offer us a fresh plate of fried eggs.

Amid the silence that descended upon the three of us while we ate, I was able to get a good look at the old man's face. Now he looked less old than he had seemed to me the night before: he had a warm, familiar face, a shiny head with thinning hair, faint wrinkles spreading along both sides of his face. His eyes were honey-coloured and hadn't completely faded yet. The old man was easy on the eyes, gentle, whereas I found the servant more mysterious and even hostile. Listening to the sounds he made as he greeted me, I realised that they were the same sounds I had heard while I was in bed the night before. I shivered slightly.

We had coffee in the living room beside the wood-burning fireplace. After the servant served us and then left us alone, the old man continued telling his story. In his soft, deep voice, he said:

"I mentioned I'd tell you something more about Khojah Samah. The story wouldn't be complete without her."

"That's great. I'm all ears. And I'm honoured that you would take so much time to talk to me."

And he said…

"Khojah Samah was a real threat to Khojah Bahira. They competed for singing gigs at the fanciest and best-known houses in town. They were friends with women belonging to the most influential families in Aleppo so that they wouldn't miss the chance to perform at engagement parties and weddings. They would conspire against each other, each trying to prevent the other from getting to some event so that she could take her place. They would also compete with one another to be the first woman to perform the most beautiful and hottest songs. They angled for the newest records from the Egyptian 'Gramophone Limited' label. On one occasion, Khojah Samah was even able to get her hands on the latest record by 'Maestro' Shaykh Sayed El Safti before the agent in Damascus, which enabled her to sing his hit song, 'My Heart, Who Told You to Love Me?' at a party attended by the governor himself before anyone had even heard it, which impressed everyone so that they were raving about her for days. This, of course, elicited the resentment and envy of Khojah Bahira.

"Samah was more beautiful than Bahira, who looked like a man. She was feminine, white-skinned and curvy, with a round face, unlike Bahira, whose face was more rectangular. She always wore a white rose in her hair, which made her look even more lovely and womanly. She had also been blessed with a wide mouth and full lips, which gave the impression that she was constantly in a lustful mood. Although their appearances were quite different, they were strikingly similar in other ways. Samah also had a thing for women. She had refused to get married because of these feelings, and she would also steal young women and sweethearts from Bahira, her singers and dancers as well. Bahira would do the same thing, and her latest conquest was to steal the blonde zither player from Samah and turn her into her girlfriend. When Badia showed up, she took her place in Bahira's life and heart. The zither player was so intensely jealous that she left and went back to Samah, her first *ablaya*.

"So Badia's arrival was a stroke of good fortune for Khojah Bahira. She showed up at just the right time because Samah had recently scored a few victories against Bahira. Samah surrounded herself with a number of talented women in high demand among elite circles. Her band boasted talented and beautiful female musicians, and despite the fact that she had lost the blonde zither player for a time, it was hardly a catastrophe since there were other women who had similar skills or were even more talented. Things were going in the opposite direction for Bahira. She wasn't in a good spot, and the blonde zither player didn't much improve her standing with the public despite Bahira's valiant attempts to perform fashionable songs that were coming from Egypt, especially

those written by Muhammad Effendi Othman and Dawud
Husni…"

Interrupting the flow of the story, I asked:

"But why were things better for Khojah Samah than for
Khojah Bahira? Why were all those beautiful women in her
band and why did Bahira's group have so few?"

"It might have had something to do with how bossy Bahira
was. She treated her girls very harshly. She was prickly, and
loved to be in charge. In charge of what? Other human beings,
which made girls run away from her. She used to monitor
their every move."

"She's really more like a man. Then again, I'd say that
kind of spirit is pretty common among women, too, so why
didn't…"

"There's something else, though, that set Khojah Samah
apart, like I said. She was beautiful and blonde and looked like
a real woman, even though she was one of the *banat al-ishreh*.
Apparently the women who were with her wanted their *ablaya*s
to be women in every sense of the term."

"Was Badia comfortable working alongside a singer who
had homosexual tendencies?"

Returning to the story, the old man said:

"Bahira continued to take an interest in Badia until she
had turned her into a dancer who met her standards, someone
she could show off at gatherings held in private homes or at
weddings. She transformed her from a young woman who
had run away from her mother's rules in some backwater
town into a beautiful woman and a professional dancer. If
that man had run into Badia again after Bahira was finished
with her, he would never have believed that she was the same

woman. She took care over her clothes, her hair and her skin. She had been taught how to walk properly after Bahira noticed the way she would throw her feet in front of her like a peasant, a gait that was looked down upon in the city. Badia's dancing became more balanced and she was taught how to create movement out of rhythm, to constantly change things up. Bahira always advised Badia to show off her slim figure and not to be ashamed of doing so. She wanted her to become a real dancer who would be cheered by both men and women alike, just as she wanted her to become an exceptionally beautiful woman who stole hearts and drew gasps of wonder from anyone who saw her. The more Bahira realised how valuable Badia was, the better she became at planning, including how to get her out into public and introduce her to the scene. Before Bahira allowed another woman to meet her she would invite Badia into her bed, caress her and feed her the taste of love for the first time. That country girl had no idea what a woman like that could do to her.

"Badia was happy about everything that was happening to her. Bahira had rescued her from an unpredictable fate in the starving city streets. The best she thought she could hope for once those conditions of war and hunger had abated would be to get sent back to her mother. But Bahira had saved her from that dark future, giving her the opportunity to enjoy creature comforts most people couldn't dream of, not least the innocent rural girl she once was. She promised her love and silk clothing and gold. She promised her fame and her name in lights. She promised her all that and more, but only as long as she remained faithful to her *ablaya*, only as long as she didn't cheat on her with anyone at all, but especially not

57

with Samah the woman stealer. She warned her that as soon as she stepped into the limelight she would hear gentle whispers and tempting promises and endless expressions of wonder. She also told her that a lot of women were going to fall in love with her, but those feelings were worthless because there was no one on earth who loved her the way Bahira did. Bahira had moulded her and brought her back to life. Therefore she had to listen and forget about all the horrible things she had been through. There was nothing truer than Bahira and her promises, her love and her touch. Then there were the men. They were fearsome savages. She had to be careful around them, stay away from them. They stirred up women's worries, put fetuses in their wombs, which was precisely why she had to stay away from them. Men were Bahira's mortal enemies. A *bint al-ishreh* girl could steal a young lady right out from under Bahira's nose and she'd quickly win her back. But if a man snatched away Bahira's lover, there'd be no hope of getting her back once she got married and lost her virginity, once her belly had swollen and she became busy taking care of children. Bahira never tired of telling her about men, how vile they were, about their disgusting penises. Badia started to despise them. Bahira described them as fearsome savages who had giant snouts they used to tear out women's insides. The angelic antidote was Bahira's touch in bed late at night. She would hold Badia in her arms and kiss her, then take off her clothes and pleasure her until she started to gasp. Badia loved what happened to her in Bahira's bed. One time Khojah Bahira left her there without touching her, just left her there to sleep, as if she were punishing her for some kind of sin she had committed. But Badia had become used to her touch and

58

wouldn't go to sleep without being touched. Bahira could hear her moan and toss and turn in bed. Bahira knew that Badia was ready. She wasn't worried at all about presenting her to mixed company. And that's what happened.

"Khojah Bahira wanted her to be a bombshell in the Aleppo scene. She didn't just want to bring her out at some run-of-the-mill wedding where a surprise like this wouldn't be noticed. She presented her at a party hosted by the Turkish governor's wife, which was attended by the Turkish and Arab and Circassian wives of the most important men in high society. Khojah Bahira was expected to sing for them at the governor's house, and it was customary for her dancer to go with her. It never occurred to any of those people in attendance that an angel in a dance costume would come out to see them. While Khojah Bahira sang, she watched more than a hundred eyes suddenly widen as they became fixated on the extremely beautiful Badia, who danced so gracefully that it melted their hearts. All at once the ladies, young and old, felt as if they had been taken prisoner by that white beauty moving so smoothly and rhythmically. Some of them moaned silently and some of them moaned out loud. The next day the whole city was talking about Badia, the dancer, and requests for her to perform at parties in the salons of the most important houses in town started pouring in to Bahira, to the extent that the Khojah's house lost its tranquillity because of the sheer number of visitors arriving to meet bodacious Badia and see her up close. Many of them tried to impress her, having fallen in love the moment they'd seen her dance. But Khojah Bahira greeted all visitors and female admirers and made sure that Badia sat next to her, close enough to touch.

Most of the time she would hold her palm between her hands to make clear that she was Bahira's girlfriend and that their chances of winning Badia's affections were nil. Bahira even asked Badia to kiss her in front of those visitors whenever she felt like it. She would announce to the public that she was her *ablaya*, even asking her servant to tell all the visitors and female admirers that Bahira and Badia were still asleep in bed, and make them wait in the salon. A little while later, the two of them would show up in their house clothes and welcome the guests, looking as if they had just made love, and had been interrupted in the middle of a steamy moment.

"When they heard from their wives what a revelation she was, men would also come over to Khojah Bahira's house in order to meet Badia: Turkish officers, associates of the governor, high-profile businessmen, civil servants, even a German marshal, a Turkish *pasha* and Arab notables. Bahira would willingly show her off in front of women and female dignitaries, but in front of men she did so only because she had no other choice. She was afraid of men. Khojah Samah, Bahira's main competitor in singing and women's affection, would fume as she kept track of what was going on. She dispatched a few spies to bring her back a precise description of this well-known courtesan.

Samah tried to seduce Badia. She made her promises through her emissaries but Bahira kept a close eye on them. They confronted her with stern, mannish faces and an iron will, ready to go to war for Badia's sake. Over the course of more than two years, Bahira dominated women's entertainment in the city, and was the happy lover of its most beautiful and graceful dancer. Badia had no real equal, and Bahira was able to protect her, leaving all the other courtesans no other choice but to sigh from a distance.

"No matter how careful we are, though, we all eventually forget about the misfortune we're so afraid might befall us. Bahira was afraid that other women like her were going to steal Badia away. She was also afraid of men with malicious intent. She assiduously worked to make Badia hate them. They were the root of all women's misfortune, in her opinion. On one occasion, when some respectable men were visiting, Badia fell in love with one of them. The man was Captain Cevdet, the handsome Turkish officer who stole Badia's heart, and broke Khojah Bahira's as well. He was a strapping young man with irresistible charm. He came to Bahira's house in the company of a high-ranking Ottoman officer, and sat there silently waiting for the chance to steal a glance at Badia's beauty without anyone else noticing. He might have seemed bashful, but deep down inside he was a courageous adventurer. He fell in love with Badia at once. His eyes were sharp and deep-set, like those of an eagle; Badia felt a pleasant ripple wash over her whenever she looked into them. She fell in love with him, too, but she didn't dare tell anyone about it or let her *ablaya* know. He would come to Bahira's street and stand on the corner for hours. As soon as Badia noticed he was there, she would stand by the window and gaze down at him, allowing him a clear view of herself. He confessed his love for her through gestures, and invited her outside to meet him. She began thinking about him whenever she was awake and dreaming about him whenever she was asleep, until her resistance grew weak, and she started to invent excuses to go outside to see him. She would take a servant with her, one

she could easily bribe to say nothing. So Cevdet was able to
meet her and become her lover. Badia learnt that not all men
are bad, and that some parts of their bodies even taste good.

"One day she started to feel nauseous. It had been a while
since she'd last had her period. She was pregnant with Widad.
What was she going to do? Cevdet took her to see a *shaykh*
who married them right away. She had to tell her *ablaya*,
Bahira, but she was too scared to do so until the day the war
grew so fierce that they claimed Damascus was about to fall
into the hands of the Arab and British armies. At that point
Captain Cevdet had to accompany his senior officer to the
south in order to defend against the advance of those armies.
It was a tearful goodbye, and Badia cried out of fear for her
beloved Turkish officer, fear for her unknown future. Cevdet
left her alone and worried about her growing belly, worried
that Bahira might find out. Thankfully the celebrations came
to an end now that the Ottomans had been defeated—who
would celebrate with singing and dancing under such circumstances? When Badia heard that Damascus had fallen
and Ottoman soldiers were retreating to Turkey by train, she
ran away from her *ablaya* Khojah Bahirah. She also went by
train, hiding out in Maydan Ekbas Station as she watched
the trains coming from the south, so that her beloved Turkish
officer would be able to find her and the two of them could
then live together as they had planned. But the war came to
an end, and the entire Turkish army left Syria. The English
army arrived and Captain Cevdet never showed up. Khojah
Bahira had to endure that devastating loss, the loss of Badia,
as well as the *schadenfreude* of Khojah Samah."

CHAPTER TWO

How Khojah Bahira Introduced Widad to Her First Kiss

T HE OLD MAN STOPPED TALKING and asked if he could take a break. I got up to toss some more wood onto the fire. I had really taken a shine to him, waiting for any reason to rush to his aid. I'd tuck in the blanket that he kept on his lap to help with his arthritis. Whenever he fell silent in order to rest, I kept quiet, too, so that I wouldn't encourage him to keep talking and become even more worn out. When he was quiet, his hands would tap, and he'd watch his fingers tremble even as he tried to keep them still. I prayed to God he didn't have Parkinson's, which my father suffered from. I know how bad the physical and psychological pain is for those unlucky enough to have this terrible disease. I learnt from the doctor who treated my father that Parkinson's afflicts men who have lived a very active life. He told me that the boxer Muhammad Ali had it, which really hammered home for me what he meant by an active life.

So had the old man also lived a full life? And how did he know so much about the women in this story? Did he have some kind of relationship with them? Had he known them or even lived with them? Was the old man actually telling me the story of his own life, I wonder? Questions swirled around inside my head as I added more wood to rekindle the fire and help keep the old man warm. Glancing over at him, I noticed that he was still tapping, staring down at his trembling hands. Instead of sitting back down, I drew closer to the window and gazed out at the barren fields that stretched into the distance and had been washed vigorously with rain. Just then I heard something, a movement, or possibly some breathing behind the door next to the window. I started to have all kinds of doubts about the servant, particularly because of his inscrutable and stern face, his dusky eyes which were darker than those of the old man. I repeatedly thought about the noise I thought I had heard in my room which had been locked from the inside. If I hadn't been so soundly asleep that my mind refused the possibility of anything bad happening, I would have got up to switch on the light and seek out the source of the sound. At this point, dear reader, I'd like to confess that, in that moment, standing by the window, I felt a little bit afraid, especially since the house was shrouded in mystery, its furnishings and lighting as well as the way the servant behaved and the way he looked at you. The most mysterious thing about the house was its very existence there. I calmly moved closer to the door, still looking outside, and then suddenly turned back to the old man and found him still fixated on his hands. Then I looked back at the door and opened it confidently, instinctively, without a plan. My suspicion was correct. The hallway was dimly lit and the servant was quickly turning from me, trying to get away, though he continued to stare right at me. We stood there for a couple of seconds before the servant fully wheeled around and scurried away without any obvious confusion or a smile. Once he had rounded the corner and disappeared, I shut the door and walked back to the window.

I would have liked a moment to think about the whole thing but the old man interrupted my train of thought. He called out for me, so I returned to my place opposite him and adjusted the blanket on his lap. I decided to return to the matter of the servant later on, once I was back in the bedroom for my afternoon nap.

"Where were we?" the old man asked me.

"Before we get back to the story, I'd like to ask you something. Why did Badia send her daughter to Khojah Bahira? I don't understand it, especially seeing as how Badia had herself run away from her long before. Khojah Bahira was a domineering woman, a ladykiller. Badia must have been okay with whatever might happen to her daughter."

"Definitely. I agree it's confusing, but apparently she regretted what she had done after she left her *ablaya* Bahira. Badia seems to have been thinking that she should have trusted Bahira and steered well clear of men. During the time she lived with Bahira she had been treated like a princess, so on her deathbed she thought the best way to protect her daughter would be to send her to Bahira instead of marrying her to some country bumpkin with whom she would live out the rest of her days in Maydan Ekbas, turning into an ordinary country woman."

"Didn't it ever occur to her to take Widad to her *ablaya* before she died?"

"Women aren't miracle workers, son. You've got to keep the matter of reputation in mind."

"But wouldn't you agree with me, old man, that she escaped the restrictions of her mother in the context of the First World War because she longed for freedom, and that she did the exact same thing again when she ran away from Bahira's rules?"

"Badia spent her entire life bouncing from the authority of one woman to another. She had bad luck. She believed that if she ran away from her mother's house she'd be able to live any way she pleased, beyond the control of another woman, including her mother. But as soon as she arrived in the city, she fell under the sway of another woman."

"So when she met Captain Cevdet, she thought she could throw off the control of women once and for all."

"That's right, but the Captain let her down. Maybe the man couldn't take on his responsibility because he was killed in one of the battles that took place outside of Damascus. Whatever the case, he let her down. In order to finish what she had started, she moved to that village with a train station and decided to live there and raise her daughter. Still, it does seem that she suffered a lot. She turned into an unremarkable woman, but pride prevented her from behaving as if she had been defeated. The important thing is that she wasn't going to deprive her daughter of what she herself had been able to enjoy, and so decided to send her to Khojah Bahira's house, but not until after she had passed away."

"Which means that she believed life with a woman could be better than living with a man; I mean, she arrived at the same conclusion about men that her *ablaya* had tried to convince her of before."

"Eighteen years in the village made her regret following after men, which is why she tried to instil the fear of men in her daughter, not to let her be friends with anyone except Bayonet Abduh."

I didn't know very much about the *banat al-ishreh*, just a few rumours we used to spread. Men used to love talking about them, embellishing their own stories or those told by famous *banat al-ishreh* in the city, however they wished.

"As far as I know," I said to the old man, "the *banat al-ishreh* have nothing against marriage. Even some of the most famous ones in Aleppo are married and have families and children."

"That's right. A woman wants to be taken care of, no matter her sexual preference, longs to be under someone's supervision, whether that's her father or her husband. Most women get married while they're young, or you might say they get married at an early age, before they have developed their own will. Most of the time their friendships develop in women's spaces, which city women attend all the time."

"You're talking about the *qabool* reception, as they call it in Aleppo."

"Yes. A woman at one of those *qabools* becomes familiar with this kind of relationship. She'll see women sitting together in pairs, talking to one another, laughing and having a good time, even embracing and caressing and kissing. After a while some other lady will approach her, pissing off her girlfriend and stirring up feelings of jealousy. That's the way this companionship blossoms, far from the prying eyes of men. I'm sure you know that men aren't allowed to attend these women's gatherings."

"Of course I do. Eastern men guard their honour in front of other men. Women do nothing of the sort."

"Ordinarily a man will go home and inquire about his wife. He might be told that she has a visitor, one of her friends,

67

naturally, and after a while he'll be able to confirm that she's been with a woman when he finds her coming out of the living room as his wife says goodbye to her. But as for what went on between the two of them, he has no idea whatsoever."

"I've heard of some men who knew about their wives' relationships with their girlfriends."

"A relationship between a woman and her *ablaya* can get more serious and dramatic things do happen. For example, many women talk about relationships with arguments and breakups and getting back together, stories that might find their way to men who then pass it on to the husband."

"And what usually comes of this?"

"Many men simply remain silent. But if a relationship is discovered and turns into a public scandal they'll lean on their wives to end it. Most of the time, though, they can't put a stop to it, and some will divorce their wives as a result."

"The situation can lead to divorce?"

"It only leads to divorce when the woman is really serious about her *ablaya*. If the *ablaya* happens to be wealthy, for example, she might encourage her girlfriend to get divorced, she might offer to buy her a house so they can live together as if they were married. Another thing that might drive the husband towards divorce is if his wife starts to shirk her marital obligations, turns frigid because of her relationship with her *ablaya*."

"But that sounds a lot like what we'd call lesbianism today."

"Right, lesbianism."

"So what about Khojah Bahira? Where does she fit in to all this?"

"Bahira was an *ablaya*. She was the dominant one in relationships. She'd just find a new girlfriend if she got bored or if something happened or if she met a more beautiful girl. When Badia first showed up with that man, Bahira was involved in a very serious relationship with the blonde zither player whom she had previously won away from Khojah Samah. But Bahira dropped her with icy coldness when she first set eyes on Badia's loveliness and beauty and sweetness; she fell in love with her at first sight. That was why the blonde had to go."

The subject of *banat al-ishreh* diverted me for a bit because of the tantalising details he had shared with me. I decided to look deeper into the matter as soon as I got back to Aleppo, to meet some of the women known to be a part of that society, or at least send my wife Nadia to meet them and then ask her to report back on whatever they had to say. Most of those women are too embarrassed to talk about such things with men, unfortunately, which is why I warn you, dear reader, that my information might only wind up being imperfect. You'll have to follow up yourself, or by way of your own wife, if you want to get into it as deeply as I have.

Anyway, I wanted the old man to get back to our story. He was the only one who could tell it, and he was rapidly growing weary of talking about it. My time was running short. There was also the matter of the mysterious servant who might wind up kicking me out of there before I had the chance to hear the end of the story, which is why I said to the old man:

"We left Widad in that horse-drawn carriage with the driver stealing a glimpse of her beautiful face. She was holding an envelope on which Khojah Bahira had written an address. What happened next?"

He glanced up at me, with gratitude in his eyes for my having reminded him of Widad. What was his relationship to her?! He nodded a few times as he squeezed his hands together in order to keep them from shaking. Then he started speaking in his calm, soft voice, finding the proper tone for the story, moving away from the everyday conversation we had been engaged in a moment before.

"The carriage driver stopped outside a house with high walls that had a small blackened wooden oriel window with five panes of glass, three in the front and two along the sides. The wooden door of the house was clad in metal embossed with an elegant pattern. Widad paid the driver his fare, took up her suitcase and got out. The driver continued to watch her as he had during the entire trip. He repeatedly blessed the Prophet for her beauty. He had never come across such a beautiful young woman before. Then he asked God to protect her from evil men and drove away. She stood there in front of the house, in that quiet part of the chichi Farafrah neighbourhood.

"She fidgeted outside the house. She shimmied up a tree to climb onto the wall. Then she glanced over the street before climbing back down, holding on tight to the rough stone wall. Had her mother Badia once stood in the exact same place she was standing now, Widad thought. How had she felt then? Widad suddenly became scared of the unknown, which was going to open up and swallow her whole as soon as she knocked on the shiny black door. Had her mother also been afraid? She gathered her courage and drew closer, climbing the low steps to reach the knocker. Her hand froze once she had got hold of it. From inside the house she could hear the sound of a *kamancheh*. She concluded that the house was quite spacious because the sound of the *kamancheh* was obviously coming from far away. Someone was practising the new Umm Kulthum song, 'To the Country of My Beloved'. She was familiar with the instrument because a street vendor used to park his cart loaded with all sorts of colourful little items in the village square, pull out his *kamancheh* and start playing sad Kurdish songs. She would go to the square with Bayonet Abduh to look at the colourful women's headscarves. She used to thrill at the arrival of the street vendor just because of the opportunity to listen to him play his sad songs. She was actually uninterested in the colourful headscarves she knew so well since she browsed through them so often.

"She rapped on the door with the metal knocker, took a step backwards, and waited. The *kamancheh* stopped. A few seconds later she heard footsteps and then the door opened, producing a loud screech because it was so heavy. A woman in her twenties stood there, and when she saw that the visitor was also a woman, she opened the door wider, a quizzical expression on her face. This was the woman who had been practising *kamancheh*. Her name was Suad. She was homely, with hair suspended in hot curlers reaching down to her shoulders, and dressed in a diaphanous robe that extended to just below the knee and showed off her forearms and her legs. Smiling at the peasant who stood there with an old suitcase in one hand and an envelope in the other, looking so friendly and harmless, she asked:

"'Can I help you, sweetie?'

"'I'm looking for Khojah Bahira.'

"'What do you want with her?'

"Widad was flummoxed. What should she tell this inquisitive woman?

71

NIHAD SIREES

"'I need to give her this letter,' she said, nodding towards the envelope in her hand.

"'A letter?' It seemed as though Suad was having a bit of fun with her. Apparently she was enjoying messing with this peasant girl who became increasingly embarrassed with every question. 'Who's it from?'

"'From my mother. Is Khojah Bahira here?'

"Just then the *kamancheh* player opened the door all the way and invited her to come inside. She watched Widad breathe a sigh of relief after she'd started sweating on account of all these questions from the woman. She walked up the two remaining steps that separated the house from the street, walked past the woman with all the questions, and stopped. The woman closed the door and patted Widad on the shoulder to comfort her, asking her to follow her down the long corridor into the courtyard.

"Windows on the western and eastern sides looked over the square open-air courtyard. On the other two sides were staircases leading to the sleeping quarters and the rooftops. There was a large *iwan* furnished with chairs and pillows on the facing side, as though a concert was held there every night. The *kamancheh* leant against one of those chairs. In the middle of the courtyard was a pool with a fountain that was switched off for the time. Floating in the stagnant water was a piece of muslin, some roses, and leaves from the surrounding trees.

"Suad guided Widad towards the *iwan* and invited her to sit down and wait. She smiled again, gently patting her in a reassuring manner, before saying:

"'Khojah Bahira is at the *hammam*.'

72

"Widad nodded and then watched Suad as she left through one of the doors. As soon as she was alone she began to inspect the courtyard, the windows and the trees. Sitting there with her mother's letter to Khojah Bahira in her lap, she unconsciously played with the envelope. She was nervous. What if the Khojah read the letter and kicked her out? Where would she go? She didn't know anyone in this city. She looked up towards the upstairs bedroom windows and jumped suddenly, letting out a soft squeal that nobody but she could hear. There were two women in their underwear standing by the window, staring down at her and smiling. Why did everyone in this house smile at her so much? They were clinging to one another, each holding on to the other's waist, standing cheek to cheek. Widad looked away, primarily out of fear and also out of embarrassment, until burning curiosity drove her to look again. Now there was just one woman looking down at her, still smiling seductively, her arms folded across her chest, but she disappeared when the other woman dragged her away from the window.

"Widad glanced over at the *kamancheh* leaning against the chair and thought of the Kurdish street vendor, remembering his melancholy songs. Whereas all the Kurds in Maydan Ekbas play the horn, this man preferred to play the *kamancheh*. Isn't that strange? She also thought of Bayonet Abduh, about saying goodbye to him that morning. He stood on the railway station platform, in tears over their separation. She missed him. Apart from her fear and bewilderment in that house full of women, she was simply sad.

"Just then, the clacking of wooden shoes on the floor jolted her out of her reverie. Two women swaddled in bath towels were standing in the doorway Suad the *kamancheh* player had gone through. Suad had returned with these two women. All three of them were staring at her. The first woman looked just like a man, although Widad was sure she was a woman because an opening in her towel revealed her small breasts.

"Widad knew this was Khojah Bahira. The woman drew closer to her, inspecting the beautiful face of this peasant girl who looked like an angel come down from heaven. As she joined her in the *iwan*, she continued to examine her without looking away. Her companion from the *hammam* started to feel jealous about her *ablaya*'s behaviour, the jealousy of a girlfriend who had once been confident that she'd be taken care of for the rest of her life even if she couldn't always keep a close watch on her Khojah. Now Bahira was standing across from this peasant girl as if hypnotised. Then she pulled herself together and hurried back to her room. Suad said, as though she were trying to rouse Bahira:

"'She says she's brought a letter for you from her mother.'

"Widad handed the envelope to Bahira, who took it from her without looking at it. In fact, she already knew what the letter said and who had sent it. Still staring at Widad, she asked:

"'You're Badia's daughter, aren't you?'

"'Yes.'

"'Please, have a seat.'

"Widad sat back down with Bahira seated in front of her. She had recognised Widad because of her striking resemblance to her mother. She had never forgotten Badia. Bahira had never loved anyone the way she had loved her, and after Badia ran away, she spent years dreaming of the day she would return to her. She was haunted by Badia's image. Badia was her great love, the one who got away. Suad now understood why this beautiful peasant girl had cast such a spell over Khojah Bahira. She asked:

"'Badia's her mother?'

"Widad wheeled around and nodded.

"'Where is she now?' Bahira asked.

"'Dead. You meant the world to her.'

"She said this as if imploring Khojah Bahira not to kick her out. Bahira choked up, sorrowfully shaking her head over her lost lover. She bowed her head in sadness and held the letter in her hands. She unfolded it and started to read. She forgot where she was, the towel slipping from her body as Widad looked away, locking eyes with Suad, who smiled at her tenderly.

"'Are you hungry?'

"'I ate on the way.'

"'I'll heat something up for you.'

She went to the kitchen, leaving the two of them alone. Widad watched her go, to avoid the embarrassment of looking at Bahira's body. She had felt great affection for that woman from the moment she opened the door. Widad needed someone to take care of her and it seemed they weren't going to kick her out into the street. She had to turn back around and look at the Khojah.

"'God rest her soul,' Bahira said, folding the letter back up and wrapping the towel around her naked body again. 'Do you know what the dearly departed wrote to me?'

Widad nodded her head. She had always known.

"'I know, ma'am.'

"'She asked me to welcome you, to let you live here and work with me, for me, to take care of you. Is that what you want?'

"'Yes, it is. There's nowhere else for me to go.'

"'You can stay here.'

"Widad looked away and saw the Khojah's companion from the *hammam* standing by the bedroom door, wearing a red slip and brushing her wet hair. She wasn't happy about what she was hearing. Just then Bahira got up and moved closer to Widad.

"'Your mother tells me your name's Widad.'

"'That's right.'

"'It's a beautiful name…'

"Bahira repeated Widad's name several times and then reached for the headscarf Widad had wrapped around her head, untied it and took it off, marvelling at her beauty. She stroked her hair, smiling. Widad looked towards the woman in the red slip to find her enviously watching what was going on. Bahira bent down and kissed Widad on the cheek in a way that was anything but motherly.

"'Come on, I'll show you where you're going to sleep.'

"Widad stood, picked up her suitcase and followed Khojah Bahira. The eyes of the three women met, but Bahira was unaffected by the clear jealousy of the one in the red slip."

The rain was becoming more intense. Raindrops started to crash against the windowpane in an unsettling way. The old man stopped to take a breath. Seeing that he was going to relax for a bit, I looked out at the pouring rain. It was coming down so hard that I couldn't see the desolate fields beyond the front fence. I thought about my colleague Mr Tameem and the Land Rover driver, hoping that they had managed to find help. Just then the old man picked up the story. He wanted to tell it to me as much as I wanted to hear it.

"Bahira loved to be constantly surrounded by the members of her band, which was why she had bought that spacious house in the Farafrah neighbourhood, so that the greatest possible number of women could live with her. In addition to Suad the *kamancheh* player there was Aisha the percussionist as well as the zither player Farida, whom Widad had seen looking down through the window of the upstairs bedroom they shared. They were so close that they slept in the same bed. They were lovers, of course; everybody knew it, and nobody would interfere in their private lives or try to keep them apart. In short, they were happy together. The one in red lingerie was the group's dancer. Her name was Raheel and she was a red-headed Jew. She had been part of Bahira's group for three years, from the time that Bahira wooed her away from one of the city theatres. It was said that Bahira fell in love with her the first time she saw her face, proposing immediately that she become the lead dancer for her group and her girlfriend. Raheel agreed and ever since had lived in Bahira's room and slept in her bed. Like all Bahira's lovers, she also used the same bathroom and was never too far away. She obeyed her *ablaya*'s strict rules. The other members of the troupe were Bahiya the overweight *oud* player who was married and lived with her husband. He used to be her family's servant, and she'd married him and they'd moved to the city together. Some people say that he pimped her out when they were forced to sell her body to make enough money to eat.

77

"This was the environment Widad had arrived in. Her beauty floored Bahira, made her head spin. The Khojah was a connoisseur of beauty and passion and she was quick to fall in love. She took care of Widad from the moment they met, preventing her from being alone with anyone else. She always wanted Widad to be alone in her room, and lo and behold it turned out to be the one right next to Bahira's room, which meant that Suad had had to move to a room in the other wing so that Widad could take hers.

"Raheel was annoyed when Widad showed up. It made her feel defeated and jealous to see how interested Bahira was in this new arrival, how she would never stop looking at her, attending to her every need. She knew her *ablaya* well. When Bahira had brought her back from the theatre, she had taken care of her in exactly the same way. At that time Bahira had been with a woman who wasn't good at anything other than making love. She wasn't a musician or a singer or a dancer. She was beautiful and attractive, which was all that mattered. She was curvy, with darkish skin, but she was also spoilt and flirtatious, and if it weren't for those two qualities then people might have found Khojah Bahira's feelings for her strange. The way she flirted and behaved like a baby endeared her to many people. She had other attributes, of course: she was good at modulating her voice in a way that would make everyone around her vibrate whenever she spoke. She bickered with Bahira a lot, which she believed would make her *ablaya* more enamoured of her, but Bahira eventually grew bored of her and ended up hiring Raheel. One of the most important clauses of their agreement was that Raheel would become her girlfriend. That's right, it was part of the deal. Nobody should find this strange, the old man said. Bahira made agreements like that a few times in her life. When Raheel moved to the house in Farafrah, the flirty brat hadn't moved out yet. It wasn't like the Khojah to kick out her ex-girlfriends as soon as she had decided to drop them in favour of someone else. Instead, she'd flit from one to the other in a way that everyone else could hear and see. Simply put, she got used to shifting her attention from the old one to the new one, even though the old one still shared a room, a bathroom and a bed with her. So she installed Raheel in a room the two of them would later share while the brat was moved into the room where Widad wound up staying. When the time was right, Bahira left that room for another one, leaving the brat to sleep all by herself, as if nothing had ever happened between them. In order to make that happen, she'd gradually shift her attention from this one to the other, maintaining the old affection, as she called it. Most of the time the ex-lover felt that she was about to leave, and so she would push back and cry out of jealousy and fear of being abandoned. If the old girlfriend argued with the new one, Bahira would promise the new one that she would break up with the old one.

"Raheel knew all of this, chapter and verse, when Widad showed up. The same thing had happened to her when she took the place of another woman. She had once been new and beloved. Now she would be the ex. Sleep eluded her. She became anxious all the time, extremely sensitive, and she picked up the habit of spying on the two of them whenever Bahira was with Widad. Bahira began to stay up all night in Widad's room. She would sit at her bedside and tell her about her mother, Badia, the only person these two women knew in

79

common. Raheel started to loathe the night, especially when the women had to stay home because the band wasn't playing a show. She would find herself coming out of her room to spy on her *ablaya* through the window that looked down on the courtyard. She might find Bahira talking to Widad or listening as she described her life with her mother in Maydan Ekbas. Every few minutes Bahira would reach out to touch innocent Widad or wipe a tear from her cheek. When Bahira was feeling bold, she would cradle Widad in her arms and kiss her, trying to assuage her sadness over her dead mother. As Bahira headed back to her room, Raheel would come to her, and would feel less jealous and jilted. Raheel was clever, and through her intelligence and patience she managed to put off Bahira's moving out of her room and into Widad's for a pretty long time. She even started taking care of Widad right in front of Bahira.

"The goal at that point was to transform Widad from a beautiful peasant into a woman who would be acceptable in high-class Aleppo society. She had inherited quite a few of her mother's traits, which meant that this was not an impossible task. The ladies would have to give Widad a makeover: cutting and curling her hair, plucking her eyebrows and redrawing them, removing the hair from her arms and her legs in the traditional manner, using sugar paste, and then selecting the fabrics and styles of dress that would suit Widad's slender frame and her beautiful and well-proportioned body. Bahira attended to all of this with assistance from Suad, who had offered Widad her friendship from the moment she'd entered the house. Suad wasn't afraid of Bahira. She was a trust-worthy and friendly woman who had interests beyond the world of women. She was waiting for her Prince Charming rather than a female saviour like Bahira. This was why the Khojah could ask for Suad's help with Widad's body without fear that she would pose a challenge to her in the future. But Raheel would insinuate herself as soon as they were finished attending to Widad. She would break through every barrier and open up every door in order to join them in plucking her hair or choosing her underwear. She gave her opinion honestly, without any disrespect, in a way that satisfied Bahira and her womanly sensibility. Raheel's *ablaya* would remain silent in the face of her interference, her barging in through closed doors, without ever kicking her out.

"There was one thing that Raheel took advantage of in order to postpone Bahira moving from her bed to Widad's. Badia had never taught her daughter anything about their profession, which meant she didn't know how to dance or play an instrument. Her voice wasn't refined enough to sing. Widad was little more than a beautiful ornament, a doll anyone would long to possess. The ladies couldn't make her into anything other than a stunningly beautiful woman: graceful, reserved, a person with a kind heart and a pleasant disposition. She was delightful to look at when she sat there, even more so when she walked or moved or turned around. When she laughed, her face would become slightly red in an adorable fashion. But Khojah Bahira needed a dancer, and Raheel was the one who drew oohs and aahs from the mouths of men and women alike whenever she danced. She was considered to be among the best dancers of any group in the city. So Bahira had to wait until she could find a suitable replacement, because Raheel refused to remain in the group if Bahira abandoned her bed.

81

"On nights when there wasn't any work at a wedding or a party at someone's house, the women would congregate in the *iwan* in order to play music and sing their favourite songs, including 'Love Ain't Easy' and 'Love Has Made Me Squeal'. They might spice up their evenings with little ditties such as 'I'm the Reason for What Happened' or 'Oh Sweetie, How You Make Me Laugh'. Suad would crack jokes, making them all laugh. Watching Widad laugh was a pleasure for everyone. Suad was so good at mimicking both men and women that she made people crack up. Whenever they got together she would act out Aisha and Faridah's hilarious infatuation with one another. They were never apart, caressing one another even in front of Widad; she had begun to see this as something completely natural, which was just what Bahira wanted with all her heart. Widad would laugh heartily as she watched Suad impersonate Faridah slobbering all over Aisha's cheek or mimic the two of them in an argument. She would do an impression of everyone: Bahira singing or Raheel dancing, Aisha beating the hand drum, or the heavy-set *oud* player and the way she would fall asleep in the arms of her pimp of a husband. Suad's impressions would have them all in hysterics.

Whenever they insisted on it, Raheel would get up and dance. Widad loved the way she moved and never took her eyes off her. She thought Raheel was amazing. She had never seen a woman dance with such skill and such flair, and she started asking her to dance for her. If she wasn't in the mood and demurred, Widad would be disappointed. This pleased Raheel, and she began performing special routines just for her, leaning towards her and bending over in front of her and inviting her to join her in the dance. She did this because she was fond of her. What had ultimately brought about this change in Raheel was her refusal to succumb to Bahira's neglect. If her *ablaya* were to leave her one day for Widad, she wouldn't resent Widad for that. She'd blame the Khojah who could never be fully satiated.

"On one occasion Bahira was sitting beside Widad. She was hanging on to her the way Aisha and Faridah would sit together, as if it were totally natural. Raheel calmly watched her *ablaya* out of the corner of her eye but she was furious inside. No matter how annoyed she might get, she had learnt well how to hide her displeasure and her jealousy. She stood up and asked Aisha and Faridah and Suad to play for her so she could dance. She wanted her *ablaya* to realise that she wasn't going to be able to get rid of her so easily. She wanted Bahira to see that any other love she experienced would pale in comparison to theirs.

"The women played a dance number by Dawud Husni and Widad began clapping along to the beat. Raheel got up and stood in front of them with her legs spread wide open, her eyes locked on Bahira, and started dancing the bee for her."

"The bee?" I asked the old man in confusion, as I had never heard of that dance before.

"That's right, the bee," the old man said. "It's a really inappropriate, lewd dance."

"Did Raheel always dance that way for her *ablaya* Bahira?"

"Hardly. This was the first time Raheel had ever danced that way in Bahira's house. The Khojah was quite surprised to see her do so. The important thing is that she was looking straight at Bahira, who was mesmerised by what her old girl-friend was up to."

"That's sexy."

"It's true. Now let me tell you exactly what happened, and what the consequences were."

"By all means."

"Raheel was performing as if a bee had got under her clothes, as if she were hunting for it and trying to kill it. She writhed in pain from all the bee stings, arching her hips towards Bahira, who was silent and stunned, hanging on Raheel's every move. All of a sudden Raheel started taking off her clothes, one piece at a time, in order to look for the imaginary bee. She was groaning, as if in pain from the bee stings, mouthing the word 'bee' while she searched for it in the folds of every piece of clothing and then finding herself forced to remove it to capture the insect. All eyes were enjoyably following her the whole time, not least Bahira's, Aisha's and Faridah's. Widad was amazed by Raheel's ability to bend and act. She believed that what was happening was an ordinary occurrence, just another day at Khojah Bahira's house. A few moments later Raheel was totally naked except for her lacy underwear. But the bee seemed to be hiding in there as well. She started feeling around for it, writhing on the ground. When Raheel finally decided to strip off the last piece of clothing that covered her, Bahira got up, grabbed her and pulled her towards her bedroom.

"This all happened to the wonder of the other women. When the music stopped, the ensuing silence allowed them to hear Raheel weeping as Bahira cursed her harshly. Suad noticed Widad's concern over what was happening in the other room, so she started to play the *kamancheh* once again and Aisha followed suit. Then Faridah did the same. Suad stood up and took Widad by the hand, inviting her to dance. Widad got up, but she wouldn't dance. She was no good at dancing and didn't want to embarrass herself in front of the more experienced women. She just swayed with the beat, reached out her hand and shuffled a few baby steps along with the rhythm of the *darbuka*. Then she started to wave one hand and extend the other, taking one step forward then one step back, shyly stomping the ground, rosy-cheeked, smiling bravely. This wasn't quite dancing in Suad's opinion, but still it was sweeter than cane sugar. Mind-blowing. She learnt a new move, touching her temple with her fingertips as she held the back of her hand with the other one, shaking from side to side. They giddily cheered her on. She was moving without a plan, on pure feminine instinct. Just then something caught her attention over by the doorway to Bahira's room. Bahira and Raheel were standing there watching her. Raheel had wrapped herself in a white sheet and was clinging to Bahira, who had wrapped her arm around her. Raheel seemed to have been crying. Widad was embarrassed and sat down, hiding her face in her hands.

"Raheel's dance had been a farewell number. She had decided to leave. With her bee dance she had wanted to leave Bahira in a state of extreme excitement. They held one another the whole night, never closed their eyes. Raheel cried as Bahira cradled her. Bahira had rediscovered her passionate affection for the girlfriend she had lost with Widad's arrival. They spoke to one another in a whisper, their mouths and ears close together.

"'Stay with me, Raheel. I need you. You're my dancer and my sweetheart.'

"'I have to go. I know what's going to happen to me. That's why I'm leaving in the morning.'

"'Nothing's going to happen. You're imagining things… I love you.'

"'And you'll love Widad next. I've got to make room for her on my own terms. I don't want to leave after I've already become an ex-girlfriend past her prime. I love you, too, Bahira, but I know what's going to happen, so just let me go.'

"'Tonight I discovered just how much I love you, Raheel. I don't even love Widad yet.'

"'You *discovered* that? It's because I danced the bee for you. Do you know why I did that? Because I watched you sitting there next to Widad. You were all over her. You started falling for her. Your feelings are unpredictable and I can't dance the bee for you every day.'

"'You were amazing, Raheel. But it isn't right for you to dance like that in front of Widad. She doesn't understand yet.'

"'I know. And Widad was amazing in that little number we saw her do. Wasn't she great?'

"'No comment.'

"'Did you even know she danced? Her moves are heart-stopping, *ablaya*. Just keep her dancing like that. You'll see, everyone's going to fall in love with her.'

"'People aren't going to like this. It isn't even dance. She was just flailing around. The women *love* you.'

"'You're wrong. You're just saying that to make me feel better. What is dance anyway, *ablaya*? It's bodily flexibility, natural movement. It's *la danse pour la danse*. Good dance is instinctive. Bahira, the dancer forgets everyone else and dances only for herself. That's what Widad was doing just now. You know what they say—the gazelle is graceful by nature. A good dancer is one who doesn't even realise she's dancing.'

"Bahira remained silent, aware that everything Raheel was saying was true. Raheel had rekindled a fire that had been extinguished in Bahira's loins; she had been on the brink of falling in love with Widad. But Raheel had her charms, making it hard for her to know what to do. She wished she could have both women, despite knowing full well this was out of the question. As she burrowed her face into her ear, Bahira heard Raheel repeat, 'I'm leaving in the morning.'

"In the morning Raheel went to say goodbye to Widad. She stood in front of that innocent woman, who didn't fully understand how things worked. Widad was confused, and twiddled her thumbs like a little girl.

"'Why are you leaving?' Widad asked. 'I'm starting to like you, all of you.'

"'I have to go. I've also started to like you.'

"'So why do you have to go, then? Please don't go. We'll stay up late together. I loved to see you dancing yesterday.'

"Raheel smiled at her. She didn't understand what was going on. She got closer and kissed her.

"'Forget about what happened yesterday,' she whispered.

"'I wish you'd teach me how to dance... not necessarily *that* one...'

"'Dance however you feel. I was watching you and thought it was good. Just keep doing what you're doing. People are going to love you. Goodbye.'

"Raheel left the house. All the woman stood there and saw her off except for Bahira. She stayed in her room—at peace, though, because she was free, and ready for a new adventure in which Widad would play a starring role."

We sat down to lunch at 3:30. The old man had the same habits as the elderly in Aleppo: sleep in late, which meant that he didn't have breakfast until 11:15, eat lunch late, have little more than a glass of warm milk at 10 p.m., and totter off to bed well after midnight. Because I had stayed up late the night before listening to him tell the beginning of the story, I had to adhere to his sleeping and eating schedule. I didn't find it difficult. I was already accustomed to waking up early for work at the Agricultural Bank. I was constantly exhausted and had to nap every afternoon in order to regain the strength I lost during the awful night before last. I found myself thanking God I didn't get sick after being caught out in the rain. Ordinarily I catch cold if I don't dry my hair after showering. Isn't that odd? I think the reason was how intrigued I was by the story.

I snap back to the house where the old man and I are sitting at the dining-room table, waiting for the servant to serve us lunch. The old man was taciturn, which was his custom whenever he stopped telling the story. In those moments I respected his silence and remained silent myself. The rain was coming down hard outside. The dining room adjoining the salon was well heated, and the warmth radiating from the wood-burning fireplace in the living room reached us. I'd learnt just a little while before that the servant's name was Ismail. He had set the table with two decorative china plates and three sets of spoons and forks and knives, European style, so we could enjoy several courses: soup, main dishes and dessert. That day I discovered that Ismail preferred the old man and his guests to sit at a table bare except for cutlery and napkins so he could serve the food in the proper order, which required his going back and forth to the kitchen.

When he first walked in with the soup—vegetable soup, by the way—he cast me a discomfiting look and loomed over me before filling my bowl. He then stepped behind the old man's chair and filled his, glaring at me until he left the room once again. I sipped my soup, comfortable, unafraid, unaffected by Ismail's unpleasant glances in my direction. We also had some seasonal salad. But when it was time to serve the main course I got a little nervous when he presented me with a skewer of spiced meat doused in lemon and garlic but served the old man a plate of steamed vegetables.

I started to fear the servant, and carefully inspected the food and drink he served me. There was no cause for alarm if he served me from the same pot from which he served his master, but when he prepared food especially for me, it was worth stopping to think about it. I didn't trust him. Let me repeat this for the umpteenth time: I could tell he didn't like me and wanted to harm me in some way, or at least get me out of there before I could figure out why. I stared at the skewer of meat without touching it as the old man vigorously tucked into his steamed vegetables, despite the pain caused by eating with his dentures in. When Ismail returned carrying a dessert tray with crème caramel—which his boss seemed to like because of his gum pain—I noticed his surprise and visible disappointment at finding I hadn't eaten any of the meat. This meant there was a strong possibility he had spiked the food with something that would make my stay at the house as short as possible. He took away the food and replaced it with the plate of caramel without asking any questions. After finishing my dessert, I peeled an orange. When I had finished eating that, I praised God, thanked the old man, and got up to wash my hands.

I let the water run over my hands longer than usual, then dried them and studied my face in the mirror. As I backed away I suddenly bumped into Ismail. He wasn't carrying plates from the table and wasn't coming out of the kitchen, because the washroom was on the other side of the house. He was spying on me, pure and simple. We stood toe to toe for a few seconds. I exhaled in his face and he exhaled in mine. I was trying to conceal how unnerved I was, how frightened, even as he looked down on me in that fancy, highfalutin outfit so commonly worn by servants in palatial homes. I sensed that he was having a bit of fun with me, demonstrating how easy it was for him to to scare me. I had to take a step backwards and to the right in order to head towards the living room, where I wanted to sit and calm myself down. But he came at me with a terrifying look on his face, harsh and sadistic.

"Excuse me?" I found myself asking.

"You didn't touch your meat," he said with his mouth clenched.

I told him I wasn't feeling well, then pulled back and walked away even as I could feel him standing there watching me.

I collapsed into my chair by the fireplace, heart racing. I was afraid he would follow me there before the old man arrived, but I spent five minutes alone, confused and frightened, without his appearing. Then the old man entered and I sprang up to help him sit down.

He thanked me and said, "Let's have some tea and then go up for a nap. We can continue the story later."

I told him I also needed a nap. He nodded and fell silent. A few moments later the servant came in carrying a tea tray laden with fine china. I asked for mine without sugar. He poured the tea, handed each of us our cup, and then left without making eye contact with either of us. We sipped our tea in silence as the rain kept pouring outside.

I went up to my room and sat beside the window, looking down on the desolate landscape being washed by the rain. I couldn't see farther than sixty metres beyond the back-garden fence. Despite the appeal of a warm bed in a world soaked with rain, I refused to lie down. I needed to think about the servant's behaviour. I had already planned to spend some time thinking about it. What did Ismail want from me? Did he want me to leave? If he hadn't wanted me there, he would have tried to keep me out from the first moment I showed up on their doorstep, after the wild dogs had led me there. The first hour I'd spent there, I'd felt he was a kind person. He even got my room ready, changing the sheets and warming them up, leaving a new razor out for me. What could have transformed him into a person who hated me so much that he would spy on me and even try to bring me harm, or worse?

"What does this prick want?" I heard myself whisper. Then, in an audible voice, I asked myself, "Did he come into my room last night while I was sleeping? If he did, how did he manage to do so if I had locked the door and made sure the window was shut? What was he doing in my room while I was sleeping anyway? Did he have a knife? Or a gun?"

So many questions, and I couldn't come up with an answer to any of them.

All of a sudden it dawned on me that the whole thing had to do with the story the old man was telling me. The way he treated me had changed ever since the kindly old man had started to open up and tell me his story. The whole thing began to take shape in my cloudy mind. Ismail had something to do with the story the old man was telling. At that point I still didn't know how he was related to the story or what his relationship with Widad or Khojah Bahira might have been. I had to hear more of the story before I could understand the relationship between the old man and his story, let alone how Ismail was related to it all. But why would Ismail want to prevent me from listening to the story? After all, what was I going to tell anyone? I decided I would fight to stick around and hear it to the end. It wasn't only a story. It was more than that. It was the revelation of something unknown. Just then my attention was distracted by a human apparition outside the garden fence walking under the pelting rain without an umbrella. I got up in a hurry to wipe the grime from the window and brought my face in close to get a better look. The man was running and quickly disappeared before I could be certain whether it was Ismail or someone else. What would he have been doing out in the rain? I drew away from the window, about to sit down again. But I decided instead to lie down on the bed. I kicked off my shoes and rested my head on the pillow. It felt good to close my eyes. Despite my extreme nervousness at Ismail's behaviour, it was nice to have a clean blanket and a warm room in such rainy, flood-like weather.

*

After his nap, the old man continued…

"Khojah Bahira wouldn't let Widad go with them to the wedding parties, which would sometimes last until the early morning hours. She would say that it wasn't the right time to give this young woman her debut or for the women to get to know her. Because Widad was scared of being alone in the Farafrah house, Bahira hired a servant named Fatima to stay with her whenever Bahira and the others were out. Fatima was in her forties, an Armenian woman who had lost her family during her terrifying flight from the genocide during the Great War. She made it to Aleppo with a group of young girls. She looked like she was their mother; at the time she was over thirty. Most of the girls were taken in by local merchants, but a scrap metal seller proposed to Fatima and made her his second wife. Her name was difficult to pronounce so the merchant called her Fatima, after his dead mother, and let her live in a small room that had once been a storehouse for his merchandise. He defended her against the ruthlessness of his first wife, who considered Fatima a personal servant for her and her children. Unfortunately for Fatima, the merchant died and left her in the custody of his wife, who used to beat her every day, until she was driven to run away. She simply packed her tattered clothes and some food in a bundle, flung open the door and left. She wanted to become a professional servant in the homes of the wealthy. It seems that fortune began to smile upon her when she entered the service of one of the good-natured Khojahs, and she began living in an atmosphere of happiness, dancing and song, getting to know most of the Khojahs in the city and many of the wives of notable men. She would simply leave the house of her master if she were ever insulted or confronted with an unkind word. Or she might receive a better offer and move to another house. This is exactly what happened when Bahira asked her to come work at her house. She agreed immediately despite the fact that she had no quarrel with the woman she was serving at the time.

"Although Fatima wasn't fluent in Arabic, she understood what was asked of her. She spoke her own private language, a mélange of Arabic, Armenian, Turkish and Kurdish, which made Widad laugh. She would spend the day sweeping, dusting and washing, and she went shopping for food at the nearby market, peeled the vegetables, and prepared all the meals. And because she had been brought to Bahira's house on account of Widad, she found that she was expected to take care of the young woman above anyone else in the house. She took this task seriously, to the extent that she refused to serve the other women whenever she was hurrying to take care of something Widad had asked her to do. This annoyed Suad, Farida and Aisha. Still, they found her pleasant even when she refused to do chores for them. Whenever the women went to work a wedding party or an engagement or some other occasion, Fatima would focus entirely on Widad, never leaving her side. Fatima would salt some watermelon seeds, and they would sit and chew on them beside the window in the wooden balcony, looking down and watching the people on the street, which was illuminated by a kerosene lamp the city administration had hung from a telephone pole in front of the house. She regaled Widad with wondrous stories. Even more wondrous was the fact that Widad could understand the tales Fatima told her in her unusual hybrid language. Widad actually understood so well that she became addicted to hearing them. She hoped Bahira and her friends would leave the house for parties so she could be alone with Fatima, who only felt like telling her stories when the two of them were alone.

"Fatima would make up stories for Widad. Believing that the young woman was afraid of the dark and of being alone, she tried to entertain her. She thought this was why Khojah Bahira had brought her there. The most beautiful story was about a young man who got into a fight with the son of the governor, wounding him seriously. But he didn't die, so the young man, whose name was Kurdo of the Mountain, had to flee into the mountains, where he became a professional bandit. Kurdo envied travellers and their wealth, so he would hold them up and steal their money. The beautiful thing about Kurdo of the Mountain was that he distinguished between rich and poor. He would steal from the rich and leave the poor alone, which was why the people loved him and were proud of him. They would help him and deceive the soldiers sent to kill him. Fatima told Widad many stories of the adventures of Kurdo of the Mountain. He fell in love and was beset with desire. He stole from the rich and helped the needy, killed soldiers but also helped those wounded fighting against him. Kurdo of the Mountain assembled a band of brave young men. Once there was a young Armenian woman who fell in love with him and followed him up into the mountains. He tried to make her return to her family, but she refused because of her love for him. She even saved his life once. Fatima turned the story of Kurdo of the Mountain and this Armenian girl into a sprawling epic with dozens of related stories. The main plotline was romantic love and heroism. In reality the soldiers had eventually managed to kill Kurdo and the Armenian girl, and to arrest the other members of his band. But Fatima refused to let her epic have an unhappy ending out of concern for Widad's feelings. Widad sympathised with the bandits. So Fatima continued inventing new adventures and stories about the indomitable Kurdo of the Mountain.

"Kurdo of the Mountain became a familiar figure in Widad's mind. She vividly pictured his handsome face and strapping body. He was intimidating and feared by his enemies; even his friends and the men in his gang were careful around him. Widad would ask Fatima to describe all of Kurdo's adventures in detail. How did Kurdo stand? How did he speak? Did he fight with restraint or did he open fire on his enemies with abandon?

"She tried to behave like the brave Armenian girl because she was in love with Kurdo. Whenever she dreamt about the adventures of Kurdo and his gang, she would picture herself alongside her hero. There were no wrinkles on his face. He was handsome and strong and he didn't resemble any of the men Widad actually knew. She couldn't think of anyone with his features. She loved Bayonet Abduh but he could never compete with Kurdo of the Mountain. Her affection for Abduh was nothing like her love for Kurdo, which was why Kurdo's face wasn't that well defined for her. She believed he might have looked like Captain Cevdet, to some degree, the man her mother had loved and for whom she had abandoned Bahira's house of music.

"The way Widad hung on Fatima and her stories made Khojah Bahira uncomfortable, and she thought seriously about kicking the servant out. She had intentionally hired an older woman who didn't speak Arabic very well in order to prevent any relationship from blossoming between her and Widad, but Fatima had managed to win Widad's heart and trust. The stories made her more solitary and reflective, and further removed from Bahira. So why had Bahira bothered to set her apart from other people? Ever since Widad's arrival, Bahira had been concerned about her. She forbade her from going out, afraid that a man might see her and fall in love with her. And since he would be prevented from approaching her, he might try to kidnap and run off with her.

"She was also concerned about women. Because of her work she was unable to be with her all the time, which was why she had brought Fatima the Armenian to take care of her and entertain her in the first place. But she had certainly not expected her to become fixated on the made-up stories that she would insist on hearing every night, even when Bahira was at home.

"Fatima instilled something unnerving in Widad's heart without realising that it was forbidden in Khojah Bahira's house. The stories made her dream about men, those terrifying creatures, mortal enemies of the Khojah. She had forbidden them from entering her house ever since Widad had arrived, out of concern for her, and now all of a sudden Fatima had brought them in with her stories about Kurdo of the Mountain. Once, Widad made the mistake of mentioning him affectionately as the women were sitting down for lunch. Widad giggled as she said that one day she wanted to marry a bandit and elope with him into the mountains. In that moment everything came to a standstill. All the women stopped chewing. Suad, Aisha and Farida turned around to see how Bahira would react. They all knew she was wait-ing for the right moment to discipline the young woman according to her fancy, to assert her control over her. Bahira chewed her food in silence, glaring at Fatima, who was stiff with fear. She knew well that she had put Widad into an impossible position with stories that had encouraged her to dream about boys. She had heard a great deal about Bahira and her love of women. Her feminine intuition told her that Widad was being groomed to become the older *ablaya*'s lover, which was why she would tell Widad not to bring up those stories with anyone, no matter who it might be.

"They finished lunch, but before Fatima could begin wash-ing the dishes Bahira called her into her room. Shutting the door behind her, she started to upbraid her:

"'What are you doing, Fatima?! I didn't bring you here to mistreat me like this.'

"Fatima responded in her particular dialect:

"'I done? You say… take care Widad… Fatima good girl.'

"'I didn't ask you to tell her about any bandits.'

"'I say once… love other time.'

"'You made her fall in love with a bandit… what's even worse is that she thinks about men now. That's off-limits in my house. I don't want her to trust men.'

"'But he's a girl.'

"'Yes, Fatima, Widad is a girl,' she said, adding with irri-tation, 'I didn't bring you here to explain that to me. Get out of here. Right now.'

"'Oh my God!'

"'I don't need a housemaid any more. I'll take care of Widad myself.'

"Fatima remained silent. She cared about Widad. She had arrived there to take care of and entertain her and now she was so attached to her that she might even beg the Khojah and kiss her hands and feet just so she could stay. For the first time in her life she might beg someone to let her stay.

"What happened?" I asked the old man. "Had she fallen in love with her?"

"No. Fatima wasn't like that. You might say she had a mother's feelings. Would you believe that Fatima had never had a child by the kind-hearted scrap metal seller? It hadn't bothered her at the time because she saw with her own two eyes how children were dying from hunger, getting sick and throwing up and being trampled underfoot. Her own mother had died mourning the little child she would leave behind, all alone in this terrible world. At that moment she wished never to have a child or become a mother herself. She never experienced that special feeling mothers have for their sons and daughters. When Khojah Bahira hired her to take care of Widad, she was overwhelmed by maternal feelings from the very first day. She took care of Widad the way a mother cares for her own daughter."

"That's nice. And Widad, how did she feel about it?"

"The young woman loved the servant because she had filled the void left by her mother, who had been buried in Maydan Ekbas," the old man said. "She missed her whenever she heard Fatima's stories. Often she would rest her head against Fatima's shoulder as she listened to her, her mind drifting through the worlds that were constructed in her imagination, the universe of those stories with Kurdo and the Armenian girl. Every instalment of the story, every sentence, would miraculously become images she watched in her head. Much of the time she would fall asleep as she breathed in the scent of her housemaid. After a while this smell became more familiar, odours became mixed together for Widad, and she could no longer tell the difference between the scent of her mother, Badia, or the smell of Fatima. The two scents merged, becoming one and the same thing."

"So did Fatima leave?" I asked, wanting to get back to what happened after Bahira tried to kick her out.

"She did.

"Widad was huddled in the corner weeping when Fatima came in to say goodbye. She was carrying her belongings, dressed and ready to go, and she had wrapped a scarf around her head. Widad stopped crying and got up to embrace her. Then she started to cry against Fatima's chest, heedless of the way her tears were soaking into Fatima's dress. She continued sobbing, and they remained like that for a while, until Widad calmed down.

"'I hate Khojah Bahira,' she whispered in Fatima's ear, as Fatima gently stroked her head.

"'Don't blame Khojah. He knows what best for you. She worried about you.'

"'Take me with you, Fatima.'

"'Too hard, Widad dear. I'm housemaid. You're important lady.'

"'So tell me, where are you going? I'll try to convince Khojah Bahira to bring you back.'

"'Khojah Bahira stubborn. Nothing you can do.'

"'I'll try anyway. Just tell me where you're going. Please.'

"'Fatima, he doesn't know.'

"'Promise me that you'll call and tell me where you are as soon as you get settled. I want to know what's going on with you.'

"'*Çok güzel.*'

"Just then Widad pulled her head away from Fatima. She held her, kissed her, and smiled. And what a smile amid her tears and red eyes and dripping nose. She was adorable. Fatima smiled back at her.

"'You're my mother now,' Widad found herself confessing. 'Let me call you mother.'

"Fatima liked that. She felt happy despite being thrown out of the house. She said goodbye and left. Widad followed her out into the courtyard. Aisha and Farida stood there beside the fountain, leaning against one another, and Suad stood near the living room. She could see Widad's pain as she followed her servant anxiously. Soon the door clicked shut. Widad rushed back to her room and closed the door behind her. Khojah Bahira watched all of this from her window onto the courtyard.

"Bahira loved Widad, passionately loved her. She found her adorable when she cried, with her eyes and nose inflamed. She used to call Widad's mother 'Caramel'. She deserved the name as much as her mother had, even more so.

"She was happy that God had sent her Widad, happy despite feeling that Widad had started to hate her after she'd kicked Fatima out, and that was why she had to do something, to take care of her even at the expense of her lifestyle and profession. To hell with the women's gatherings. To hell with all the ladies and their weddings. She would focus exclusively on her sweetheart.

"Bahira was jealous of Fatima's imaginary heroes. She was convinced that those characters would turn into flesh-and-blood men with names and bodies. She had allowed Widad to live there without exposing her feelings for her out of concern that she might leave. She gave her space so that she could get used to the house, its way of life. She didn't intend to reveal her feelings until later. She felt pleasure whenever Widad observed Aisha and Farida rubbing up against one another, unabashedly touching and exchanging kisses. Widad would laugh when she saw them doing that. She enjoyed watching even as Bahira stole furtive glances to track her reactions, monitoring her breathing, her blinking, the moistness of her lips, so that she could evaluate her level of readiness.

"Bahira's extreme caution with young girls began after an incident with Sabiha, who had run away from her family and joined the troupe as a prodigy singer. When Bahira invited her to join them she did so immediately. She was olive-skinned, her hair was black as night, and she had particularly soft features. There was nothing rough about her. By contrast, there were many women with rough shapes but smooth natures, including Khojah Bahira herself—a thin mouth, nose and eyes. She was happy, laughing all the time, even when she was singing. Bahira loved her from the moment she laid eyes on her, and her love for her grew steadily as she taught her how to sing. One day Bahira made a move, pulled her in close and started kissing her. This came as a great shock to Sabiha. She was shocked and she recoiled forcefully and pulled herself out of the Khojah's clasp. She was troubled. Her face turned bright-red and flustered, despite her eventual laugh as she regained her composure and pulled herself together.

But after that Bahira felt that this girl wasn't hers, that Sabiha would run away and return to her family. And that's exactly what happened. Bahira lost her love this time and became depressed. Her friends and performers had to console her for a long time before she could forget about the prodigy singer.

"Bahira was standing behind and to the side of her window so that the women in the courtyard couldn't see her. She was in tears, knowing full well that she had been cruel to Widad and Fatima because of her love, which she hadn't been able to express.

"Is it wrong to feel passion? To love? They would say she wasn't normal, that she was a *bint al-ishreh* who had to get married to a man to continue working at weddings, as many women in the profession had done before her. This wasn't right. She hated men. Every human being should be allowed to love however they pleased. What matters is that the beloved have a good heart and kind nature. God is beautiful and He loves beauty. Whether the beloved is a man or a woman shouldn't be important. Affection is what matters.

"She wasn't comfortable with men. She wasn't attracted to their rough, stubbly skin, their facial hair, their grunts and boisterous voices. God had created her this way—loving women. She loved soft skin and breasts. She loved the scent of a woman and detested the odour of a man. She had loved a great many women, one of whom was Badia. Now there was Widad.

"Through the windowpane she watched Aisha and Farida arm in arm as they sadly returned to the *iwan*. They were devastated to see Widad broken-hearted over her servant. The two of them sat down on the sofa. Aisha leant her back against the cushion and cradled Farida's head, stroking it as Farida rested against her chest. She wiped away the tears wetting her thin cheeks and sighed deeply. She loved that woman who looked like a man.

"The day Fatima left, Widad locked herself in her own room. It wasn't a work night so they all stayed home. A heavy silence fell over the courtyard, except for the sounds of footsteps whenever one of them stumbled here or there. Suad tried to enter Widad's room to bring her some food, but Widad made her leave the plates outside the door. Suad thought it would be better not to disturb her that day, although she found an inventive way to lighten the mood and actually speak to Widad. She picked up her *kamancheh* and stood by the door, serenading her with long selections from the songbooks of Muhammad Uthman, Dawud Husni and Mohammed Abdel Wahab.

"Widad listened to the doleful sound of the instrument. Suad was a talented player, and she made Widad forget her hatred for Bahira for a short time. Widad smiled at an upbeat section, at which point she felt hungry and started to eat. Suad kept playing for an entire hour, and then pushed open the door and looked inside. Widad was sitting on her bed, resting her head on her fist. She had eaten some of the food, so Suad smiled at her encouragingly and closed the door once again.

"Early the next morning, Bahira slipped into Widad's room. She stood beside her bed and regarded her sleeping beauty. Widad's elbows were folded and her hand was on the pillow, as though she were looking back at her. The blonde hair Bahira had curled herself was spread haphazardly, a small, solitary curl rested limply on a neck as white as snow.

She was so adorable while she slept. If Bahira hadn't been so concerned not to wake Widad, she would have reached out and caressed her.

"Her pale skin was even more alluring than the experienced Khojah had expected. Sleeping women seem more beautiful and paler than they do when they're awake. Her gown was hiked up to the middle of her thighs and wasn't clinging to her chest because her nipples had become so soft.

"The Khojah crouched down and rested her wrists on the bed. She continued to watch Widad sleeping there peacefully, scrutinising her forehead and the line of her nose, down to the tip as it curved around after that in a subtle arc towards her lips, full and crinkled, then the curve of the chin, the bend of her neck.

"It was here that Widad most resembled her mother Badia: in the curve of her chin and the bridge of her nose. But the corner of her closed eye looked strange to Bahira. Had she inherited that from her father, Captain Cevdet? Was he that handsome? If so, that meant she had also inherited from him those balanced and graceful movements that had captured Bahira's imagination, those unnamed and indescribable movements, which Raheel called a kind of uncommon dance.

"Widad shook her hand, which had fallen asleep and gone numb as it rested on the pillow in front of her. She opened her eyes and saw Bahira's face staring down at her from up close. Still suspended between sleep and wakefulness, she shuddered with fear, her pupils dilated. Sensing her disquiet, Bahira smiled at her, reached out and touched her cheek and neck. Widad relaxed once she realised it was Bahira, and closed her eyes again but didn't fall back asleep.

105

"'Good morning,' Bahira said in a soft and gentle voice. 'I just came to see how you're doing. I know you hate me right now but here I am anyway. I don't want to lose you the way I lost your mother. It doesn't matter how much I loved her. A man came along and stole her from me. He took her away to one of those border villages and made her live like a peasant woman. Then she sent you to me before she died so that I could take care of you. May God have mercy on her soul. She knew what a big mistake she had made, and she didn't want you to trust in men and soldiers and outlaws. I love you. I don't want to lose you. You may hate me now but someday you'll understand why I had to do this. It was for your protection.'

"Widad stared directly into Bahira's eyes, listening to what she was saying. She didn't like what she heard but she didn't hate Bahira either. She listened.

"'I won't leave you in anyone else's care ever again,' Bahira continued. 'You'll come with me wherever I go, to parties and weddings. You're my sweetheart and you're going to stay right by my side.'

"She smoothed Widad's hair and caressed her ear, sliding down to her neck. But Widad's resentment rose despite Bahia's gentleness.

"'I cared for Fatima,' Widad said harshly. 'She loved me the way my mother did. I even called her Mama.'

"Bahira remained silent as she listened, trembling.

"'I'm not going to run away with some nogoodnik the way my mother did with Captain Cevdet,' Widad continued.

"'I don't want you to get involved with any men at all.'

"'Why not? In Maydan Ekbas there were a lot of men. I didn't particularly like any of them except for Bayonet

Abduh, and I never thought about going off with him. I'm so pathetic…'

"'You can't trust men. They're all selfish. We women understand one another more fully. And if you do leave my home in order to shack up with a man, I wouldn't want you to become a slave to him.'

"'Of course not. I'd just as soon stay here. I love you, and I love Suad and Aisha and Farida.'

"'So you don't hate me…'

"'Of course not. I don't hate you. And I don't want you to hate Fatima. Ask her to come back and I'll give up on her stories.'

"'Forget about her. I'll be like a mother to you from now on.'

"Widad frowned. She wanted Fatima, and if she came back she'd love Bahira. She turned over. Behind her the Khojah exhaled. She wanted Widad as her own, all to herself. She wanted her to become a woman untainted by men, even from the world of make-believe.

"She gently touched her thigh and asked her to turn around, but the young woman wouldn't budge. Bahira was patient with her the way a lover waits for the beloved. They remained like that: Widad with her back turned and Bahira crouched beside the bed, hand touching Widad's thigh, then moving up to her waist. Bahira found that Widad wasn't going to prevent her, didn't push her hand away. She was accepting her touch, and it appeared that she had grown accustomed to these things because of how often she had seen it with Aisha and Farida when they were touching one another. She got up and sat on the bed, leaning against her and resting her elbow on the pillow in order to tousle Widad's hair. Now she began to stroke the girl's arm, then her shoulder, moving up to her neck. Widad's coquettishness and the feel of her skin were so pleasurable. Bahira's head was hovering directly over hers, and she noticed that Widad's eyes were open, staring firmly at an insect on the wall.

"'Do you know what love is? You're old enough to know something about it. It's when you get hung up on someone and can't bear to be apart from them. It's like a girl who loves her mother. But then again it isn't anything like that. Aisha and Farida love each other. God bestowed upon human beings the distinction of being able to love another. It's the opposite of hatred. As far as a woman's concerned, to love is to lose yourself in the one you love. Without any reason or purpose or benefit. Men love women because they're selfish. Women love only in order to give. A man can only take, he demands a woman's future for himself alone. He impregnates her so she'll bear his children for him, makes her serve him at home, cooking and cleaning and working for his well-being. Her comfort isn't important. When a woman loves another woman, the goal is love and love alone. Without children, the two of them cooperate and serve one another. It's the purest form of love. Our love is like the love of mystics.'

"Widad was listening to her closely, no longer just looking at the insect. They were so close that her heartbeat could be felt in Bahira's body. Bahira decided to confess to her. The time had come.

"She drew closer to her and whispered, 'I've started to have feelings of the purest love for you. I love you. I threw out Fatima because I was afraid you would fall in love with a man and not love me. I was afraid you would hate me for that.

Forgive me. A woman in love will kill for her love. Sometimes she'll behave badly.'

"Khojah Bahira fell silent. Widad was waiting for her to finish. She liked what she was saying. Eventually she turned around to look at her. Her face was only a hair's breadth away from Bahira's. Each of them could feel the other's breath. She was searching the Khojah's eyes for the words she was waiting for her to say. She found her staring back at her strangely. Bahira was fragile, desperate, sincere. There was something else she had noticed in Aisha and Farida's eyes. She wasn't sure what to call it, something that makes eyes heavy, warms the heart and parts moist lips.

"Bahira closed her eyes, letting her mouth fall onto Widad's lips."

CHAPTER THREE

How the Old Man's Servant Ismail Plotted to
Kill Me, or at Least Make Me Run Away

IT WASN'T VERY LATE, but I could tell that the old man
was exhausted from talking for hours on end. Ismail wasn't
around; possibly he'd gone to bed, or perhaps he was sitting in
a corner of the house plotting something unpleasant. I offered
to help the old man to his room and asked him to show me
the photographs hanging on the walls so I could see pictures
of the people in the story I had been listening to over the last
two days. I was certain that this dignified old man was one
of the characters in the story he had been telling me, or at
least that those characters had once been part of his world.

After uttering that racy sentence about Bahira kissing
Widad he stopped talking for a while. It seemed appropriate
for me to stand up and take a look outside. It was dark and
rain-washed. The sound of the downpour had grown more
intense ever since the old man had stopped talking. As I stood
there, I wiped away the grime from the window with my
handkerchief and pushed my face against the glass, cupping
my hands around my eyes in order to get a better look at the
darkness outside. It was difficult to see anything. The only
light was coming from the window, pooling on the ground,

expanding and then vanishing. The rain had created a shallow river near the window that was filled with bubbles, as if it were boiling. Imagining Ismail's face coming at me from out of the darkness, I was seized with panic that made me suddenly jerk away from the window.

I returned to the old man, who had settled down as though he had fallen asleep. I offered to help him back to his room.

"Don't trouble yourself," he said, lifting his head like someone who had just woken up. "I'm very tired, but I'll just wait for Ismail."

"There's no need for that. Besides, he may have gone off to sleep. Let me help you. I'd love to take a look at the photographs in your room, if you wouldn't mind."

When he reached out his hand towards me so that I could help him up the smooth marble staircase, I realised that he was inviting me to look at the photographs.

"What do you think?" he asked in a voice that seemed more restrained than necessary. I was sure he didn't want Ismail to hear him talking to me about the pictures. Once he was in bed, I tucked him in up to his neck. He watched me as I stood looking at each picture for a long time.

Do I need to describe all of the photos in his room? That would be impossible. There were more than a hundred pictures in a hundred frames. As I already mentioned, the old man was in most of them, more than fifty of them; most were black and white, some had yellowed with age. There were also some pictures that had become damaged because of improper preservation techniques before they were framed.

The images summarised phases of the old man's life. There were several pictures of him as a little boy, then as an adolescent and a young man, which is where the phases of the old man's life seemed to end because I didn't find any photos of him as an adult or an older man. If he were about eighty years old—and that's what I'd guess given his obvious frailty and the way his hands shook from Parkinson's and the wrinkles on his face and hands—there was a period of more than fifty years missing in the photos. Just as I was thinking about asking him why that should be, I looked over to discover that he was already asleep. I let him be, turning back the photos, this time with much more focus because I was doing so without supervision. Just then I noticed a picture frame hidden behind the dresser. There were actually several photos lined up in a column in the narrow space between the dresser and a window. The column of frames was concealed by the edge of the curtain, which had been bunched together and tied into a knot. The picture that had caught my attention was an old newspaper clipping showing a reception at Damascus Station in Aleppo to welcome back the national delegation from Paris in 1936; it was taken in front of the decorated engine. Members of the delegation were visible, flanking the French High Commissioner Monsieur de Martel. On either side of him were Hashim al-Atassi and Saadallah al-Jabiri and Fares al-Khoury and Mustafa al-Chehabi and Edmond Homsi and Jamil Mardam Bek. Behind them was a beautiful young peasant girl standing on the steps of the train car, holding a suitcase and staring dumbly at the camera.

So this was Widad. I leant in to scrutinise the image more carefully. I was pleased with this discovery, convinced that what I had heard from the old man were in fact true stories about a woman he had known when he was young. I tried to see what Widad looked like but the image captured in the newspaper only gave a vague idea of this young woman. Black-and-white splotches covered her face, which couldn't be made out so easily anyway since she was standing right behind the High Commissioner and the members of the delegation, who were the main subject of the photograph.

You might ask how I could tell she was beautiful from a blurry photograph. I have no good answer to that question. From the old man's story, I had imagined a beautiful image and what I saw confirmed what I had pictured. I began looking at the other frames for more pictures of Widad, those below and above the picture of the delegation, but I didn't find any. All the other photos were of other people, including the old man when he was younger, with a pudgy woman who was much younger than him.

I moved away from the column of frames and began to poke around on the other side of the window, an area that was more open and visible. After I had examined about a dozen frames, it became clear to me that this overweight woman was in a lot of pictures, whether standing by herself or alongside the old man, who was a young man back then; the two of them looked like a married couple. Finally I noticed that some of these photos had been taken in Paris, in front of the Eiffel Tower, to be precise.

I was hoping to find other frames with clearer pictures of Widad, or perhaps of Khojah Bahira, but something startled me. Ismail was standing by the door, angrily glaring at me. He was tense and silent. I tried to melt into the wall. If there had been an exit I would have run away, but there was no way out. The old man was asleep, softly snoring even as I could hear the sound of my rapid heartbeats.

"What are you doing in here?" Ismail demanded in a hushed voice, between gritted teeth. "There's no reason for you to be in this room…"

"The old man was tired. We thought you were already asleep. I offered to help him get up here, and he welcomed the assistance. I helped him to lie down and then tucked him in, as you can see."

"You're meddling in other people's business."

"You mean by looking at these pictures?"

"Yes."

"The old man said I could."

"The old man has never invited a stranger into his room. You're taking advantage of his kindness. I'm warning you, I've had about enough of this."

"But I haven't done anything. I just helped the old man up here and found these pictures."

"I should never have let you in the house that night. I didn't have to."

"So why did you, then?"

"I thought you were going to leave the next morning. You made the old man tell you stories that aren't true. You're wearing him out with these stories. Talking is exhausting for him. You have to leave in the morning."

"In the morning?"

"And before the old man gets up. I'm warning you, it's better if you just go."

He was quite insistent. And Ismail was threatening when he looked at me in that spiteful manner. I wished the old man would wake up because he was the only person who could help me in that moment.

"How are you going to explain my departure to the old man if I suddenly disappear without saying goodbye?" I asked.

"Shaykh Nafeh won't even remember you." So his name was Nafeh. I had learnt something new. "I'll give you an umbrella, a compass and a knife."

"Why would Shaykh Nafeh tell me his story in such detail if he were just going to forget all about me, as you say?"

"He's making all these stories up. Besides, I don't want you to hear any more of them."

I forgot about how frightened I was. Drawing closer to the edge of the curtain and pulling it back, I pointed at the High Commissioner and the members of the delegation and the picture of Widad.

"And who is she? He told me something about her that corresponds with this picture."

I didn't realise this would infuriate him further. I just thought I was arguing with him. His eyes were like those of a murderer and I became even more frightened, but still I found myself asking:

"Why don't you want me to hear these stories, or know anything about the history of these characters?"

He didn't respond, sternly ordering me instead to go back to my room. He told me to get out of there and then stepped aside so I could get past him to the door. I left the room without looking at him and hurried back to my room. Once inside, I closed the door and bolted the lock, leaning against the door and breathing heavily.

I lay down on the bed and wrapped myself in the blanket. The room was chilly, and raindrops were rapping against the windowpane, which only made me feel colder. I stayed awake for a long time thinking about what was happening, unable to sleep. I had to find a way to ignore Ismail's warning and threats, but what I couldn't stop thinking about was his insistence that everything the old man was saying was a delusion or confabulation, just like the stories Fatima the Armenian told Widad. I wasn't convinced, but still I had to muster up the courage to stay in the house if I was going to hear the rest of it. The stories were no longer just stories. They had become the history of a person I was living with and a puzzle concerning another person who wanted to prevent me from hearing them.

I hadn't expected to find the picture of Widad at the train station. But why was that the only picture of Widad? And who was that pudgy woman? The old man had never mentioned her. I presumed she was his wife, and that the two of them had travelled to France for their honeymoon. Did he meet Widad before or after he got married? Was she his mistress? I suspected she was one of his lovers because he had placed the newspaper clipping somewhere discreet so it couldn't be seen right away. But what would Ismail do if I refused to leave, if I stayed at the house and asked the old man to protect me, assuming that was even within his power?

I stood up again to make sure the door was locked. I was gripped with real terror at the thought that Ismail had been in my room the night before. Was there a secret entrance to this room? No way. The door was locked and the window was securely closed. There was a dresser and a mirror against the wall, a clothing rack and a painting above the bed of a few verses of poetry with the mountains of Bcharré in the background, in addition to two nightstands, one on either side of the bed with a lamp on each. That was everything in the room. There was also one bare wall covered with matte paint.

I thought about my wife Nadia and my son Hassan. Then I thought about my colleague Mr Tameem and the Land Rover driver. I hoped to God they were all right. What if they had told my wife and my boss that I was lost in the wilderness? Everyone would think that I had been eaten by wild dogs and hyenas. All of a sudden I shuddered. What if Ismail was thinking about taking advantage of the possibility in order to murder me and then dump my body far away from the house so that I would in fact become fodder for those wild animals? On more than one occasion, especially just now in the old man's room, I had seen in his eyes that he was capable of resorting to that kind of act to get rid of me. I got out of bed and started to pace back and forth. I was trying to think of a way to stay in the house without Ismail doing anything to me.

At first I thought it would be good for me to talk to Shaykh Nafeh, but the idea quickly fell flat. What could the old man do against his servant? Ismail appeared to be in his fifties, physically fit, and he wielded emotional and intellectual influence over his master because of his many years of service, but also because of their being cut off from the rest of the world, living together far out in the sticks. I also thought about the possibility of Ismail softening towards me. There was a small chance that we could become friends, but the idea seemed unlikely and implausible. He seemed to want to prevent the old man from talking to strangers or from telling his stories, and I wondered if he had convinced the old man to live out in this place, isolated from the rest of the world. As for why Ismail didn't want the old man's story to be spread around, that was a matter I had to consider more thoroughly. Perhaps the old man's story could unlock that riddle.

I was tired of bouncing around the room. I felt like I was getting dizzy, so I went back to bed, decided to sleep on it. As I struggled to get to sleep amid the rhythm of the raindrops cracking against every surface they encountered, I heard what sounded like someone trying to open the door to my room. I sat up in bed, transformed into a frozen statue with nothing but a sense of hearing. The natural light seeping in through the window allowed me to see the door handle jiggle down slightly as the door was pushed; but it wouldn't open because it was bolted shut. I jumped up and walked over towards the door on my tiptoes so as not to make a sound. I stood there, trying to figure out who was there, one hundred per cent sure, of course, that it was Ismail. I was only this courageous because I was confident that the deadbolt would protect me from that malevolent criminal. I thought he would go away once he realised how hard it would be for him to get inside. But as I watched, the bolt seem to disengage all by itself, as if there were another handle on the other side of the door. I wasn't even fully conscious, thankfully, as I rushed to the door and grabbed hold of the lock. You might have thought, dear reader, that I was going to use my weight to prevent the door from being opened, but that's not what happened. I pulled open the door with a quick movement and came face to face with a masked person holding a thick piece of wood. This person was surprised by my action, and perhaps he was as frightened as I was because he turned at once and ran away without a sound. I found myself chasing after him down the corridor and then down the stairs to the ground floor. I stopped in the middle of the staircase to catch my breath, watching as this person disappeared down another hallway. Then I heard the distant sound of a door being slammed shut. Everything was quiet, which could have been scary, but it was actually calming because of what had just happened. I sat down on the staircase, trying to slow my heart and breathe deeply. Then I stood up and walked back to my room, where I discovered the tool the person had been using to open the lock. It was the kind of implement train conductors use to open cabins and closets on a train: a metal handle with a Phillips-head on the front. I picked up the tool and examined where it hung on the wall, finding it strange that I hadn't noticed the metal implement before.

I went back into my room and locked the door once again, placing the chair against it so it would make a noise if that person tried to break in again. Then I lay down, feeling as if I had defeated Ismail this round, which was how I managed to sleep without interruption until morning.

I said "that person" because I wasn't certain that Ismail was the masked man who had tried to break into my room and kill me. I would have to be more careful. This was my life. It wasn't a game. If I were going to survive, I would have to take precautions. That person seemed spryer than Ismail who, I surmised, must have been in his fifties. That person might have been shorter than Ismail, or at least that's how he seemed to me in the darkness. The entire confrontation had happened as if in an action movie I had been watching, in which I already knew that the hero was going to emerge victorious in the end.

I woke up late the next day. I lay there for a few minutes with my eyes open before getting up to look outside. I thought the sun was coming out because I was in such a good mood, but unfortunately it was still raining hard, which made the world outside darker and still darker. In fact, I can't remember a storm like that during the entire time I had been working in the countryside. Wasn't it strange for it to be happening just then? Was it a coincidence, or was I being forced to listen to the old man's stories? Was the rain giving me an excuse to stay? Smiling to myself, I thanked God. I went into the bathroom and conducted my morning routine, shaved and started getting dressed.

Heading downstairs, I went straight to the hallway that leads to the front door. I wanted to find out how serious Ismail's threats were. I saw a kitchen knife, an umbrella and a military compass on the counter. So the man was dead-set on kicking me out. Examining the compass, I discovered that it was high quality and Russian-made, while the knife was laughable, albeit sharp; used for cutting meat.

Returning to the cosy living room, I found Shaykh Nafeh sitting next to the fireplace, gazing through the window at the rain falling outside. I said good morning to him and then took my seat once again. He asked me if I had eaten breakfast yet and I told him I had just woken up but wasn't hungry. He wasn't listening to me, though, and he reached out his hand to press an electric buzzer that I noticed for the first time because he hadn't had to use it in my presence before. It was a matter of seconds before Ismail came in.

"Ismail," he said, gesturing towards me, "please bring our guest something to eat for breakfast."

I looked over at Ismail. His intimidating and threatening eyes were locked on me. He was intense and mysterious, trying to ignore the events of the night before, but he also seemed to be warning me there'd be even worse consequences if I didn't obey his order for me to leave.

"I understand our guest would like to be on his way," he told the old man, without turning his eyes away from me. "Now that the rain's letting up…"

"Do you really want to go?" the old man asked, turning around, clearly confused by what his servant said.

"I had thought about going," I said. "If the rain stops or lets up somewhat then I'd rather go and look for the Land Rover, or try to make it back to Aleppo. I'm already very late in getting back. They're probably looking for me right now."

"But it's still pouring outside," the old man said. "You're not going anywhere."

I looked over at Ismail, as if to say to him, Nice try.

"I could escort him as far as the asphalt road," Ismail volunteered.

"Our guest is staying."

"But sir, they're looking all over for him even as we speak."

"Ismail, you'll run to the closest village with a telephone and call to let his family know he's all right."

I nearly burst out laughing at the sight of the servant when he heard his master's unambiguous decision. Ismail was silent, searching for the words that might get him out of this. He hadn't bargained on the old man becoming so fond of me, certainly not to the extent that he would be deployed to call my family.

"Can you give us a moment," he said, whirling around towards me. "I'd like to speak to the old man about a private matter."

I waited to hear the old man's reply, but he was stock-still. Perhaps he also wanted me to leave, so I got up.

"No problem," I said, stepping out of the living room and into the hallway.

I waited in the corridor for fifteen minutes. I tried to eavesdrop on their conversation but couldn't make out a thing. I did notice how loud Ismail was becoming while the old man's voice was softer, as if the servant had authority over his boss that he didn't want me to see. After a while Ismail came out, visibly holding back his fury, slammed the door behind him and stood right in front of me, preventing me from going back inside to join the old man.

"The old man wants you to stay."

"So I'll stay then."

"Listen, I don't think you should hear his stories. You're a puerile and insolent person, tricking the old man into trusting you like this. Ask him to talk about something else."

"What is it about these stories that gets you so worked up? It's just an ordinary tale…"

"None of your business. There are some things that are none of your business…"

"Does it have to do with Widad or Khojah Bahira?"

All of a sudden he grabbed me by the throat and squeezed until I felt like I was going to suffocate. "I'll cut out your tongue," he said, thrusting his face in close to mine, spraying spittle across my mouth. "You're going to forget whatever he's told you, you hear me? You've got to forget all about it!"

He let me go before I choked to death. I had trouble breathing, and as I was trying to catch my breath, he grabbed me by the hair and pulled my head up at a painful angle before continuing to threaten me.

"I pray to God the rain stops. Then you'll have to go, or else I'll stab you to death with the knife I left on the counter for you. I'll be gone for two hours. When I get back I'm going to say that your family didn't answer the phone. In the meantime, you can speak to the old man. You'd better not ask him to tell you any more of his made-up stories."

He yanked my head to one side and then let it go before walking off. I nearly toppled over as I backed away. I fell against the living-room door, struggling to catch my breath, waiting for the colour to return to my face.

"There's something I can't figure out about your servant Ismail, Shaykh Nafeh," I said later. "He doesn't seem to want me to hear the story about Widad."

"What I talk to my guests about is none of Ismail's business."

"Sure, but clearly he would prefer for this story to remain locked away in your memory vault. Sir, I also noticed how you go quiet whenever he walks in on us. It's come to the point that he wants me to leave."

"Let's forget about him and get back to Widad. Now, where were we?"

"Please, I have a question before we resume the story. Who is Ismail? Is he just your servant, or is he?…"

"He isn't a servant."

"Does he have something to do with the story? It seems like he has something…"

"You're getting ahead of things. Let me finish the story and you'll be able to figure it out for yourself."

I asked him to let me throw out a few more questions before Ismail got back from wherever he had gone. It was very important to me that I flesh out the picture of these characters in the story I had painted in my mind.

"What do you want to know?" he asked.

"Last night in your bedroom I found a picture of Widad at the train station in Aleppo."

"Yes, I held on to that. It's a photocopy of a newspaper clipping."

"Where did you find the newspaper?"

"I had to search for a long time before I was able to find it and buy a copy. It was at the National Archives in Aleppo."

"Do you remember the name of the newspaper?"

"I think it was the Aleppo newspaper *al-Shabab*, published by the late Muhammad Tlas."

I wrote down the name of the newspaper on a piece of paper I had been carrying around in my pocket so I could jot down notes I was afraid I would forget, then put it away once again. Ordinarily I carried a notepad around with me in order do quick sums or record passing thoughts about the agricultural harvests or the loan data, but I'd lost it while trudging through the rain on the way there.

"I had to skim all the issues of newspapers and magazines from September and October 1936," he continued.

"And is that issue of *al-Shabab* still there?"

"I'm not sure. That was thirty years ago. Why do you ask? Do you want a copy?"

"I do. The photocopy I found behind the curtain in your room doesn't give a clear impression of Widad. I think if I took a look at the original perhaps I'd be able to get a better picture. Also, do you have a picture of Khojah Bahira?"

"No, but somebody told me that there's a photographer who held on to a framed and enlarged portrait of Widad and Khojah Bahira in his studio. It was a beautiful photo, which was why he kept it, hung it up in his shop like an advertisement for his work."

"What's his name?"

"I think it's called Dunya Studio, in the Bab al-Nasr neighbourhood."

I took out the piece of paper again and wrote down the name of the studio.

"The name won't help you," he said. "I already went there, but it was too late. The photographer's died, and his wife cleaned out the studio. They told me that someone who emigrated to Brazil took all his equipment and his pictures with him. I spent a long time searching for him but now I'm an old man and I'm tired of looking."

"One last question. Have you ever told anyone this story before me?"

"I never saw the point in telling it after I came here with Ismail. What educated person in their right mind would follow all those roads and seek shelter with us, giving me the chance to tell the story? I thank God it's been raining for three days straight. I hope it continues until I've finished. But if you keep asking questions, I won't have time."

"So I'm the only person who knows this much?"

"Ismail knows the story, too, but he hates it. He's always asking me to stop talking about it. He's even tried to convince me that I'm making it all up, that I've confabulated these events because of how isolated we are here and because my mind is breaking down from Parkinson's."

"I understand…"

"And there's that other person…"

"Which person?"

"The doctor who loves to go hunting. He was on a hunting trip when he got lost in the woods. He was dying of thirst when he arrived on our doorstep. It was so hot outside. It must have been June. That was three years ago. We welcomed him here and I started telling him the story while we sat out on the veranda. We would stay up until dawn, which comes early in the summertime."

"Then what happened?"

"One day I woke up and sat down to wait for him. After waiting a long time I asked Ismail, and he told me that the doctor had left early that morning without saying goodbye, which made me very sad."

I shivered. My fear of Ismail returned. I imagine the circumstances under which the doctor had left. Either he had been killed or he had left under duress.

"How long did he stay with you?" I asked.

"Three days."

"Had he heard as much of the story from you as I have? More? Less?"

"I think he heard about the same amount. I can't remember."

"Do you remember the doctor's name?"

"Yes. I repeat his name whenever he comes to my mind. His name was Dr Waleed Fares."

Distressed, I bolted upright and walked over to the window, looking out at the world drowning in rain, thinking to myself that there was a strong possibility he was dead. If I were forced to leave I would come up with an excuse to return to hear the rest. Only death could prevent me from doing so. I became certain that the same thing that happened to Dr Waleed Fares was happening to me, and that whatever happened to him was going to happen to me as well. I also thought… this story might lead to my death.

Just then I saw Ismail standing there, about a hundred metres from the garden gate, unmoving beneath a blanket of rain. He was facing me. Perhaps he was staring at me through the ropes of rain. When the old man cleared his throat I tried not to think about what might happen and went back over to him, sat down and politely asked him to resume. Words cannot describe just how relieved he seemed when I asked him to do so.

CHAPTER FOUR

Good morning poplar branch standing upright
The flesh lives on
O day
While the bone must end standing upright
For the sake of the oppressed eyes may I reach my end standing upright
A slave awaiting the moment of command

A POEM OF ADMONITION KHOJAH BAHIRA SANG
TO WIDAD AT THE HAMMAM

"A s WIDAD SURRENDERED to Suad's hands while she put on the final pieces of jewellery, Khojah Bahira said:

"'Come on, we're late, it's already past twelve.'

"'Of course, *ablaya*, we're ready,' Widad replied, gazing in wonder at herself in the mirror.

"Bahira went out into the garden and began barking orders at Aisha and Faridah. The two women lined up the bags and the suitcases, which had been stuffed to the gills. Suad crouched in front of Widad. She was mesmerising, a woman unlike any other.

"'Soon you're going to be famous, Widad,' Bahira said, kissing her on the cheek. 'Everyone's going to know you as one of the most beautiful women in Aleppo. Women will gasp at your charms. Your name will be on everyone's lips.'

"Widad smiled as she examined herself a second time. The four women had taught her what it meant to be beautiful, what it was that made her so beautiful. Suad's cheek was still caressing hers, two faces joined together, imprinted on the surface of the mirror.

"'You're pretty, too,' Widad told Suad, trying to be nice.

"'Who, me?' Suad asked. 'I'm a dog compared to you. It doesn't bother me, though. Every gasp that escapes from a woman's mouth when she sees you is for all of us.'

"From the courtyard she could hear Bahira telling them to hurry up. Just then Widad kissed her and got up. Soon after that the carriage delivered the five women to the Balaban *hammam*.

"Now that her love had been well and truly accepted, Khojah Bahira decided that the time had come to bring Widad out of her forced isolation and present her to the women of Aleppan society. She no longer feared that someone was going to steal her away. Bahira had been nervous that Widad might get scared and possibly even run away if she confessed her love. But Widad accepted it with an open heart. When Bahira kissed her for the first time, she responded in kind.

"Bahira spent the entire day in Widad's room. They held one another in bed all day long. They cried together, too, their tears running together. The women always had something to cry about. Ever since Widad accepted her Khojah's advances, being apart from her had become difficult. Bahira wasn't satisfied with just embracing and kissing her sweetheart, and Suad was forced to bring their lunch and dinner to Widad's room on a serving tray so Bahira could feed Widad by hand. When Suad left the room she would report to Aisha and Faridah that things were going as well as possible. Joy spread through the Farafrah house. The women started playing cheerful music underneath the window that looked down on the courtyard. Aisha danced even as she banged out the rhythm. That night Bahira guided her sweetheart back to her room so that she could sleep in her bed with her, at which point Suad reclaimed her own room.

"At first Widad was embarrassed whenever Bahira stroked and kissed her in front of the other girls. But modesty cannot destroy passion, and since they all lived in the same house, freely entering each other's bedrooms, everyone had to accept public displays of affection. There was nothing more natural than seeing couples in a romantic situation, caressing. At first she was embarrassed whenever Suad would come into her room for whatever reason when the two of them were in bed together half naked, or, shall we say, with very little on. Bahira didn't like her body to be separated from Widad's smouldering body. She didn't see the need to move away from her if Suad or Aisha or Faridah walked in. She always had to sit next to Bahira whenever they were in the courtyard or some other room together. To sit beside her also meant touching her the same way Aisha and Faridah did right in front of her. Meanwhile Suad would go around serving all of them because she didn't have anyone.

"Within a few days everything began to feel normal to Widad. She started to appreciate the pleasure she and Bahira enjoyed, which only made her find Bahira even more beautiful and pleasing. She started to feel a lump in her throat if her *ablaya* neglected her for even a moment when she was engrossed in a conversation or busy with something else. As the days went by, Widad stopped feeling any shame when the two of them went into the bath together or came out at the same time. Bahira had become her *ablaya*, which, as we already mentioned, was the most natural of things in the Farafrah house.

"Widad was ready to move on to the women of Aleppo. She had become aware of her self-worth and the extent of her beauty and gracefulness. Even more important, she had learnt how to show it all off naturally, without going too far or not far enough. She learnt how to speak and laugh properly, how to style her unruly hair, how to walk in high heels without falling, and how to touch her face without ruining her makeup. In Aleppo high society she would meet elegant and privileged women from the upper crust who were beloved for their musical talents and their passion. Daughters of *pashas* and *beys* and *aghas* and *effendis*. Wives of merchants and factory-owners and large landowners and distinguished bureaucrats. She might come into contact with the wives of the governor or the mayor, the head of the Chamber of Industry or Commerce, government officials or judges and court employees. For all of these reasons, Khojah Bahira was careful not to let Widad mix with the people until she was fully put together. She also wanted to detonate this secret weapon in the faces of all those other women when she revealed to them that she was her new *abalaya*.

Bahira had reserved the Balaban *hammam* for precisely this purpose, sending invitations to all the women who would be interested, especially women of a certain disposition. Suad attended to Widad's makeup while someone else took care of the food and sweets that would be on offer at the *hammam*. Apparently word about Widad had already spread among the women, and tongues wagged in telling the tale of a dangerously beautiful woman whom the Khojah had taken as her new lover. Curiosity was at its peak by the time invitations to see Widad actually arrived. On the appointed day, cars and buses, both public and private, started to deposit women at the *hammam*, clogging the streets leading to Bab al-Hadid and the Serail near the citadel. Some women had to walk a great distance on foot. Other Khojahs were also invited. Of course, Khojah Samah, Bahira's rival in music and in love, was among those invited. Bahira wanted to make it clear Widad belonged to her, and there was no point in trying to win or steal her away from her.

"So that's why Khojah Bahira had that party?" I asked the old man.

"Exactly. Her aim was to have a reception, to invite all her friends and clients, most of whom were also *banat al-ishreh*, in order to introduce her new girlfriend, who at that point was as unknown to the community as the community was to her. Presenting Widad was a little bit like announcing an engagement."

"Were all the women present necessarily of the same... orientation?"

"For the most part. There would have been quite a few women who hung out with them but who weren't *banat al-ishreh* themselves. They would have found a certain pleasure in that, even if they had no *zdeeqa* themselves."

"A *zdeeqa* is a kind of girlfriend, right?"

"Correct. The invitation would be addressed to the *ablaya* and her *zdeeqa*. You'd see them sitting two by two."

"But why have it at the *hammam*? Why wouldn't she invite them over to her house?"

"It had become customary to hold such gatherings in the public *hammam*. Things happened more organically in those spaces, without disturbing children and husbands, many of whom would have had no idea that their wives might be going to the *hammam* for reasons other than to bathe. There's another important reason as far as the *banat al-ishreh* are concerned. It's totally natural at the *hammam* for a woman to take off some or all of her clothes and to wrap herself in a towel. This was a preferable situation since it made it easier for them to caress one another."

"Please, continue," I encouraged the old man.

"When the bus with Khojah Bahira and her women reached the edge of the government building, the road from there to the Balaban *hammam* was totally cleared of other buses and cars so that their vehicle was able to drive right up to the door of the bathhouse. As as it came to a stop, Suad and Aisha and Faridah hurried inside carrying the packages and musical instruments while Bahira and Widad waited in the bus for a sign to follow them inside.

"The outer courtyard of the *hammam* was full of women, seated two by two on cushions lined up on benches or on the floor, which had been covered with cloths. They took off some of their clothes or stripped down naked and wrapped themselves up in towels. Some of the women there had fancy titles with particular rings and echoes to them:

"Fadila Khanum, wife of Nu'man Beyk, who had inherited from his father 6,000 hectares and a spacious *konak* in the village where he would spend most of his time in spite of Fadila's hatred of the village and her particular love of living in Aleppo. Her *zdeeqa* Waheeba Khanum, the respectable woman married to the head of the lawyers' guild who dreamt of being elected to Parliament. Fadwa, wife of Professor Nazem, the *litterateur* and poet who taught Arabic literature. Umm Saadeddine, wife of the Board of Directors of the Ghazal cotton and spinning company of Aleppo. The wife of the district governor of Minbaj. Adeela, wife of the personal translator for the French High Commissioner Comte Damien de Martel, and her *ablaya*. Saadiyeh, wife of the editor-in-chief of *Voice of the North* magazine. Umm Umar, wife of the esteemed head of the Syria Social Club who brags about his wife's relationship with the wife of the governor. Sumaya, wife of the governor. Amina Khanum, wife of the president of the association of literary clubs in Aleppo, and eloquent spokesperson simultaneously both for and against the French, depending on the circumstances; her girlfriend, the very skinny daughter of the assistant to the head of customs. Umm As'ad and her *ablaya* Dalal. Mounira Khanum, wife of the owner of the Phoenicia Glass Works, well known for her good looks and her high morals. Miss Yusra, wife of the owner of Sarah's Scents Workshop for all kinds of colognes and face creams and hair-styling products. The wife of the owner of the National Factory for Shirts and Socks, and her girlfriend Iftikar, wife of the owner of the Imperial Sawfar Hotel. And other wives of high-society men, in addition to Khojah Samah and her new Jewish *ablaya* Raheel.

"Joyful, chattering, giggling and singing, some leant against one another and others clung to the woman next to them. They flirted with their girlfriends, affirming their affection. When the attendant opened the door, Suad and her two friends appeared, and the *hammam* sprang to life with ululations, the mood becoming more and more excited. These three women took up their designated place next to their friend Bahiya, the heavy-set *oud* player who had arrived there before them and started to play a medley in the style of Ali Darwish. The women all knew that the time had come for Khojah Bahira to arrive with her fresh discovery. All eyes were staring at the door. It was only a matter of minutes before the door swung open and Khojah Bahira swept in holding Widad's hand.

"What happened was more like magic than reality. Suddenly all the idle chatter ceased, the musicians stopped playing, and not a sound could be heard. Everyone watched the two women as they strode towards their designated spot, which was adorned with roses and furnished with satin. It never occurred to the women to cheer. They just stood there, frozen. It was simple: all eyes were locked on Widad's extremely sweet face, which exuded youth and innocence.

"Seeing confusion in the eyes of all the women present, Khojah Bahira felt the thrill of victory. Silence was an even surer sign of her success. Meanwhile, Widad shyly watched what was going on. It was the first time her beauty was being put on display before women who were experts in matters of female beauty: the *banat al-ishreh* have a greater passion for women's beauty than men; they celebrate and lust after a beautiful woman. She took strength from Suad's eyes and her smile, letting go of her embarrassment entirely. When the two of them sat down in their special place, like a bride and groom, Khojah Bahira lifted her hand, signalling for Suad to strike up the music. At that moment the women returned to their senses and began chattering once again.

"They cheered the music enthusiastically as it began again, applauding at every opportunity. Then Raheel stood up and approached Bahira and Widad, kissed them both, showered them with blessings, and, standing in the middle of the room, started to dance. She wanted to demonstrate her friendship for her old *ablaya* in spite of everything that had happened; also for simple Widad, who couldn't be faulted for having taken her spot in Bahira's bed. Raheel danced joyfully. Bahira silently watched her dance, holding Widad's hand.

"After leaving Bahira's, Raheel had joined Khojah Samah's group. She started dancing at parties organised by her new Khojah. Samah invited her to live in her house in the al-Jumayliyya neighbourhood near the train station. Samah dumped her *ablaya* as soon as Raheel arrived to replace her in the beautiful Khojah's bedroom. Nobody ever shed a tear for women who dumped each other like that. It was like a little light sweeping. Anyone could take another's spot in those *ablaya*s' lives, their bedrooms and their families. The whole thing wasn't much more than temporary jealousy, which would dissipate as soon as the jilted lover became involved in a new passion. When Raheel became Samah's *ablaya* she told her all about Widad and how beautiful she was. For some strange reason Raheel didn't detest Widad; she would talk about her and her beauty with admiration. And because Samah was one of Bahira's fiercest rivals, she asked Raheel all about Widad: whom did she look like, what did she look like, what colour were her hair and her eyes, how did she walk, what were her talents? And so on and so forth. She was so consumed by curiosity that she even dreamt about a young lady who looked like Widad. This all took place without Raheel becoming envious at all. When the invitation to the *hammam* came from Khojah Bahira, Samah was delighted because it would afford her the opportunity to meet Widad face to face. To be clear, let me just say that Raheel did feel some passing jealousy when she saw Samah scrutinising Widad with her discerning eyes. At that point some of the guests cast inquisitive glances at Raheel because they realised that Widad had taken her place with Bahira. Which is why, as I said, she got up and congratulated the two women before proceeding to dance.

"In such an atmosphere, Khojah Samah had to be on her best behaviour. She had won Raheel but now felt jealous that her ex-lover now had a more beautiful *ablaya* than her. She stood up and wrapped the towel around her beautiful womanly body once again. She had been reclining in her seat, having loosened the towel to reveal her milky-white breasts and thighs, exposing herself at one and the same time to Widad and Raheel, who by that point was dancing seductively. Samah picked up the bag she had brought with her and walked back towards her ex-lover's group. Samah's movement got the women all riled up. Her stories with Bahira were legendary. She climbed up on the dais and kissed Bahira on the cheeks and embraced her with exaggerated affection, before sending Widad a powerful glance.

"'I'm Khojah Samah,' she said. 'Maybe you've heard of me, maybe you haven't. Whatever the case, you'll be hearing a lot about me from this day forward. Let me give you a kiss.'

"After planting this kiss on her, she embraced her, trying to pull Widad's body closer, kissing her on the neck and then moving away. This all took place within earshot and in view of Khojah Bahira and the other guests. Widad's face turned beet-red as she looked over at Bahira, who winked at her to indicate that everything was fine. Samah opened her small purse, pulled out a gold necklace encrusted with emeralds, and held it up high for everyone to see. At that point she came up behind Widad and fastened it around her neck. She congratulated them both and then stepped off the dais and returned to her seat.

"Raheel watched Samah overstepping the boundaries. Supposedly they were there to celebrate Widad and Bahira in the forthright announcement of their relationship, an event meant to warn other women against getting involved with either of those two *ablaya*s from that day forward. The women were chatting loudly in overlapping conversations about what they had seen when Samah brushed past Raheel. Now the audience's attention turned towards them as they awaited Raheel's reaction. Jealousy among the *banat al-ishreh* was lethal. Raheel continued her mysterious dance as she crossed the distance to her *ablaya* and started to undulate in front of her. Her body was twisting like a snake, her arms waving like those of an octopus. Her upper body leant in, as if she were about to pounce, as if she wanted to sting her. Samah was standing upright, hands on her hips. She could feel Raheel's jealousy, took pleasure in it. Things went on like this between the two of them for a while. Then what happened, you ask? All the women were in suspense about what Samah might do to her *ablaya*. She pulled her in close, planting a long kiss on her lips that slowed down her mysterious dance. The women cheered for a long time. Samah eventually peeled herself away from Raheel and guided her back to their dais.

"Then the mood started to heat up. The band was playing a dance number by Sayyid Darwish, and lots of women stepped away from their girlfriends to dance alongside the band. Samah and Raheel had stirred up desire among the women.

They stopped caring about what was going on as each became more interested in her girlfriend, either dancing for her or else caressing and kissing her. Bahira noticed that the women's attention had shifted away from her and Widad. There was now more than one dancer on the floor, so she flashed Suad a signal to stop playing for a few minutes, and this made the women stop what they had been doing. Bahira whispered something in Widad's ear, then stood and went down to the living room. The group went back to playing, 'I Never Meant to Hurt You/Why'd You Leave Me?' by Mohammed Abdel Wahab. Widad knew that song well from living in Bahira's house. She knew how to dance to its rhythm properly. But then she started moving in a way that could not be described as dancing. It was more like movements that thrilled the heart with their tenderness and affection. The women froze and followed every move she made, every flick of her eyes. She was a bashful angel, as soft as a breeze. The resounding music drowned out the cries escaping the women's mouths despite all their attempts to control themselves.

"The *hammam* party continued well into the evening. Bahira sang a few odes to Widad. Then Samah sang a bawdy song. They ate and they drank, they sang, they danced and they ululated. Then they competed to be first to present Widad with their gifts. On that one day she took possession of gold necklaces and rings as well as Ottoman and French coins, which catapulted her to the ranks of the elite."

When we heard the thud of the storm door as it closed, the old man fell silent. Ismail was back from his imaginary errand to get in touch with my family. The old man clammed up because he knew full well that Ismail was dead set against his telling the story, which is to say: the old man was now colluding with me in order to satisfy my desire to hear it. I didn't tell him about what had happened the night before, how Ismail had threatened me and asked me to leave. I didn't want to spoil their relationship. It would have fallen entirely on me to find a solution to any bad blood between them.

We heard light footsteps, then the living-room door opened and Ismail walked in. He was sopping wet from head to toe. I had seen him standing out in the rain so that he could convince the old man that he had actually gone to a nearby village to call my family. I already knew the outcome of his errand in advance. Ismail glared at me resentfully. Because he was making a puddle on the floor, he stood away from the rug so it wouldn't get wet. The old man lifted his eyes, waiting to find out what happened.

"Nobody picked up," Ismail said in a scornful voice. "I went to all that trouble for nothing."

"What do you mean 'nobody picked up'?" the old man asked, looking at me and then looking at him. "You should have tried calling more than once."

"I tried twenty times. The rain must have knocked out the phone lines."

A convincing argument. The old man nodded and then asked me:

"You should have given Ismail your address so he could send a telegram."

"You're right, my good sir. That never occurred to me."

I glanced at Ismail, whose displeased eyes were staring back at me. I spontaneously tried to reassure the old man.

140

"Tomorrow I'll go with Brother Ismail to do whatever has to be done."

Ismail was none too pleased with the idea.

"I'll get lunch started," he said, casting another spiteful glare my way before turning to leave.

Once Ismail was gone, the old man said, "Ismail has a good heart. Don't take it personally if he seems not to like you. He doesn't care for strangers much. I don't know why exactly, but I can assure you, he's harmless."

"He knows you're still telling me the story. That's just provoking him."

"Let's keep our voices down until lunch is ready."

"Khojah Bahira started receiving lots of invitations to host weddings and private parties. All the women in the city heard about her after the *hammam* party, and it seemed as though every last one wanted to see Widad. The women believed she had become the sole property of Khojah Bahira ever since it was announced that she was her *ablaya*. But it didn't prevent them from watching her perform and appreciating her beauty. This was why they fell over themselves to invite the pair to their homes, whether for coffee, a party or simply to participate in other gatherings of the *banat al-ishreh* like the one at the Balaban *hammam*.

"Bahira begged off invitations to visit other people's homes. Nobody knew why. I would venture to guess that at first she didn't want Widad to get a look at her friends' houses. She wanted her to be familiar with only one house in the city: hers, in the Farafrah neighbourhood. She had brought her into the music group as a dancer, and Widad began accompanying her to weddings where Bahira would sing and Widad would dance. The women of the city had become accustomed to dancers wearing special costumes. Widad would wear a long, frilly white silk dress that extended down to her ankles, and the frills would glide along her shapely body, sending the women's hearts aflutter. It was as if they were seeing a brand-new kind of dance for the very first time. To be honest, none of them were interested in dance or its technical aspects when Widad was dancing. She hypnotised them with a mysterious and unfamiliar power, which was actually a sort of vulnerability mixed with grace and sweetness. The movements were often barely more than her body folding and vibrating to the rhythm, and stroking her temple with her finger as she held the back of her hand with her other hand. When Bahira asked Widad to descend from the dais to move closer to the women, they could really appreciate Widad's sweetness and exceptional grace, her shy smile and rosy face.

"When the groom showed up, the dancer would strut ahead of him and guide him to where his bride would be seated, although she would often hop up to get him herself. Widad found the whole performance quite taxing. She wasn't accustomed to dancing in front of men. But from that point on she had to participate in the wedding when it was time for the groom and bride to leave together. From the first wedding party at the Orange Café, it was clear that all the women had fallen under Widad's spell, so much so that some would completely forget to ululate. Everything was going very well. Widad loved it, and became ever more rapt in her dancing. Once she leant in close to her Khojah and whispered how much she loved weddings, how much she loved dancing at

142

them. Just then voices rang out announcing the arrival of the
groom. This caused quite a commotion throughout the room
as most of the women, apart from the groom's mother and
sisters, of course, hurried to put on their headscarves. Widad
stopped dancing and sat down to watch it all. This was her
first time at an Aleppo wedding. The groom's mother asked
Bahira to have Widad dance for her son when he got there,
but Widad refused out of modesty. To show she was serious,
she stood by the living-room door, watching as the ululations
reached a deafening volume. The groom was an eighteen-
year-old boy with a pencil-thin moustache. He arrived in a
daze, reeking of sweat: his friends had got him drunk. Widad
began walking ahead of him, guiding him towards the bride,
whose female relatives had all refused to come down and greet
him, when her foot slipped from embarrassment and lack of
familiarity. She might have taken a tumble had it not been
for the groom's steadying hand. But then, woozy from all the
drinking, he fell down and took her with him. All the women
rushed over to pick him up along with Widad, who danced
away from them, weeping. He followed after her and for some
unknown reason tried to get hold of her again. But Bahira,
who had stopped singing, blocked his path. Suad managed to
guide Widad into the other room so she could cry in private.

"The women needed to calm the Khojah and apologise to
her if they were going to keep her and her band from walking
out on the wedding. As they all tried to seat the tipsy groom
next to his bride, ululations began to ring out once more. But
a row had already broken out between the groom's and the
bride's families because of the young man's lack of decorum.
The groom's family chided the girl for her failure to get up

143

and welcome the groom even as the bride's family expressed their annoyance at the groom's immature behaviour. The hubbub escalated into a heated argument. On both sides, women with cooler heads tried to calm things down as they got closer to insults. A few members of the groom's family continued cheering, and an unassuming woman from the bride's family shouted at them:

"'What's going on here? Are you ladies celebrating the fact that your boy is smashed tonight?'

"Those words detonated like a grenade in that atmosphere. The groom's family exploded in anger, and a fight erupted after one woman pulled another's hair. Things deteriorated quickly into slapping and biting. Some of the gold jewellery on the brawling women went flying. Khojah Bahira tried singing at the top of her lungs to calm the situation but the women paid no attention. They kept on fighting or joined in if they hadn't already. Just then the mother of the bride jumped up on the dais and grabbed her daughter by the hand to announce that the wedding had been cancelled: her daughter wasn't ready to get married. Then the bride's aunt stood up and slapped the tipsy groom square in the face. The women stormed out of the hall, followed by their relatives."

I laughed long and hard as I contemplated these events. The old man let me laugh even as a smile flickered on his lips. In a good mood, I asked him:

"Widad must have been mortified that evening, right?"

"Very much so, but once they got back to the house, Suad and Bahira made her feel much better. The Khojah promised she would never make her dance in front of a groom again. Bahira cared about Widad more than anything else, so she made an arrangement with a professional dancer named Malak, who would perform whenever a groom was present, and would take care of the wedding party festivities for both bride and groom."

"I would think that Widad's unusual dance couldn't totally spoil the mood of wedding parties."

"That's true. The impact of her dance, which immersed you in sweetness and light, couldn't be fully appreciated without paying close attention. She required participation and harmony. Khojah Bahira was clever enough to know that the mayhem caused by the groom's entrance and the accompanying whirlwind of ululations called for a professional and more traditional dance."

"She didn't offer the job to Raheel?"

"She knew Raheel would have said no anyway. As I mentioned, she had started working for Khojah Samah, and since she was a jilted *ablaya*, she would have refused no matter what."

"Did Widad see any other fights?"

"Fights were always breaking out at weddings. But as you know, one shouldn't get the impression that our weddings are nothing but disagreements and fights. Anyone who works weddings, though, is bound to come across them."

"Of course, I understand, old man…"

"Widad would dance until the groom arrived. When he showed up, she would sit down to watch as Malak the hired dancer emerged and put on her show, always decked out in her traditional costume. This solution satisfied everyone, including the wedding organisers. Malak did a fine job performing her duties. Widad would watch the other women hurriedly throw on their veils to conceal their semi-nudity, which would otherwise be revealed in their wedding clothes. The groom would peek through the living-room door until he made his entrance. Malak would dance her way in front of him, through the storms of cheering, all the way to her seat. The young women then started dancing—weddings were an opportunity for single women to strut their stuff in front of the mothers of the bride and groom who were hosting the reception. But things didn't always go according to plan. Simply put, Widad became quite familiar with a lot of noise as well.

"Some people believe that if the bride stomps on the groom's foot on their wedding night she'll always have the upper hand in the marital home. Some would take part in that silly custom ironically while others took it seriously. At one wedding, a rather plump bride was dead set on the idea. She stepped down so hard on her groom's foot that Widad, who was watching, thought she might have broken his foot. The groom yelped in pain, lifted his foot and grabbed his bride, hopping on one foot as he fought against tears. The music stopped abruptly and Malak stopped dancing. The women's ululations came to a halt. Nothing could be heard except the sound of the groom whimpering in pain, then cursing and chastising the bride, and then his vow to divorce her. The young man railed against his wife's clumsiness. He had signed a marriage contract with her without having set eyes on her. He went to sit in his place, all red in the face, and refused to let his bride sit by his side.

"Chaos broke out as the women struck up a debate. The bride's relatives tried to calm the groom down, but to no avail. His mind was made up. He was going to divorce her. In order to prove how serious he was, he went over to Widad, asking her in an audible voice to marry him on the spot. The young woman froze in horror, ready to leap up and run away, but Bahira intervened, instructing him as firmly as possible to get away from her. The bride was in a sorry state, crying inconsolably over losing her groom right before her very eyes and ears. Tears, black from the kohl she wore around her eyes, streamed down her face and as she wiped them away, her face became monstrous.

"The groom got up once again and asked the young women still at the wedding which of them would like to marry him. He didn't want to waste the money he had already spent on the party. And lo and behold a woman emerged from the bickering crowd, holding the hand of her daughter, who was barely thirteen years old. She walked up to the dais and presented the groom with her daughter, saying:

"'This is my daughter Aisha. I consent to your marrying her right now.'

"The groom sized up the little girl. All the other women fell silent, holding their breath while they awaited his decision. He seemed to be looking back and forth at the little one and at his overweight wife, whose face was smudged with eyeshadow, comparing one to the other. He told his mother that Aisha was more appropriate for him. They had to find a suitable dress for her. All the relatives of the overweight bride stormed out in anger and tears, asking the *shaykh* to conclude a new marriage contract. Bahira had to ask for a larger fee because she would be forced to remain a little later."

I chuckled as Ismail came in to set the table for lunch in the dining area off the living room. When he saw me laughing, he threw me a spiteful glance and went about his work. Just

147

then the old man fell silent. I got up to stand by the window, staring up at the rainy sky in order to avoid making eye contact with Ismail.

After lunch I felt a sharp pain in my stomach and rushed out of my room towards the bathroom at the end of the hall. It was still siesta time. When I sat down on the toilet I was surprised by explosive diarrhoea with an unnatural colour and stench. I cleaned myself up and dried my hands before walking back out. It occurred to me that I might have been poisoned by wicked Ismail. My head was pounding and feverish, and I became overwhelmed by extreme concern for my health and for my very life. I went back to sit down on the toilet without dropping my pants and tried to think. *Had Ismail laced my food with poison?* I didn't feel like making myself throw up, and I tried to avoid rushing to judge Ismail.

I struggled to recall the symptoms of poisoning from cases I had witnessed myself or read about. I felt I would need to pull down my trousers and sit on the toilet because I was sure to have explosive diarrhoea. Perhaps I'd feel slightly dizzy and my heart would start pounding violently. I could hear my voice ringing in my ears:

"It's burning… Ismail poisoned me."

Apparently the sound of my own voice convinced me that I had been poisoned. I was instantaneously overcome with panic as I realised that I would have to purge myself right away.

Ingesting a poisonous mushroom in the countryside or in the middle of the forest, far from hospitals and ambulances, was the worst thing that could possibly happen to someone like me. If you pass out, you may die. But if you know you've been poisoned and you manage to stay conscious, you have to shove your hand down your throat, press your finger as far down as it can go and make yourself throw up. Then you have to drink a gallon of water and repeat this forced vomiting several times, until your digestive tract is rid of the poisonous substance.

By the third round of my purging process, I saw that I was only throwing up water, which allowed me to relax. I stayed on the toilet in order to catch my breath. The process was so painful, I felt as if my digestive tract was going to come surging out of my body. Once I had calmed down completely I stood up and washed my yellow face, dried it off and opened the door to go out, which was when I bumped into Ismail.

He was just standing there, as if he had been pressed up against the bathroom door. He was blocking my path, fixing me with a wolfish stare. He knew full well what was going on inside of me. With a hint of sarcasm, he said:

"I hope you're feeling all right, sir."

"May God protect you."

"Your face is a bit yellow, though. You were throwing up, were you? I could hear you all the way downstairs."

I didn't want to appear weak in his presence, so I didn't mention the poisoning.

"It seems I've come down with some kind of a bug, or maybe I ate too much at lunch and my stomach couldn't handle it."

"I know what it is."

"What's that?"

"I added some wild herbs to the old man's food. You pampered city folk are allergic."

"To herbs?" I asked in bewilderment.

149

NIHAD SIREES

"There are various herbs that grow in these parts," he said, threateningly. "Including poisonous ones, of course. Thank God you just had an allergic reaction this time."

So that bastard had poisoned me after all. I was staring him straight in the face, unsure what to do.

"What's your decision?" he asked me.

"What do you mean?"

"Why don't you just go home so you can be nourished by your wife's reliable home cooking and the warmth of her bed?"

"I'll go when the old man says it's time for me to go."

"As you wish, sir," he said, as if saddling me with the responsibility for whatever might happen.

I started to walk towards my room but stopped and wheeled round to see him staring at me disapprovingly. I moved in close so I could whisper, as he had.

"Why can't we be friends?" I asked him in a gentle tone full of goodwill.

"But we are friends."

"Friends? You've been threatening me nonstop. Listen, let's make a deal. I'm in good shape. My work often brings me out to the countryside, into the wild. I know how to flush out poison and how to take care of someone trying to break into my room at night with an oak switch. Anyway, I'm really stubborn and I'm always up for an adventure." I was lying about this; I'm as skittish as a bunny rabbit. "Just leave me alone, and we can remain friends."

"How about you just leave, and then we can remain friends, *inshallah.*"

"Is this because of the story?"

"Yes."

150

"Why don't you want me to hear it? What's the worst that could happen to you?"

He walked away without responding, down to the ground floor. I followed after him. If he wasn't going to tell me what the whole thing had to do with him, I hoped I could at least get him to give something away. I grabbed his arm to prevent him from going downstairs.

"It's just the old man's life story. It doesn't have anything to do with you, as far as I can tell."

He moved two steps back up, coming within a hair's breadth of me. He was visibly upset. He could have taken a bite out of my nose just by opening his mouth.

"Listen up, adventure-lover," he snarled, breathing into my face. "Don't forget that you stumbled out of a broken-down car and got lost in the wilderness on a rainy night full of hyenas and wild dogs. I swear I'm going to get rid of you."

He clenched his teeth as he spat out that last sentence, then wheeled around and started down the stairs. I stood there for a moment before heading back to my room. I needed to think. I stood next to the window, looking out at the grey sky and the torrent of water pouring from dark clouds. I was vehemently against the idea of leaving. I was hooked on the story and couldn't see a way around it or Ismail at that moment. If I left then, without hearing the rest of the story, I knew I'd regret it for the rest of my life. I was going to stay and wrangle with Ismail.

I heard a door close downstairs, and then the house was silent. I expected to see Ismail walking around the side of the house so I looked out the window at the backyard but didn't see anything. I waited for five minutes and when he didn't appear, I felt the need to lie down on my stomach to

151

ease the pain of the forced vomiting. Because I make the bed every morning I had to pull back the blanket. When I did, I froze. Right there, on top of the white sheet, was a scorpion as big as my hand. Its tail was curled high above its body, as if it were about to strike. I was paralysed with fear. I had seen my share of scorpions out in the wild, but I had never seen such a gargantuan one. It was reddish brown, though its tail was yellowish and its stinger was white. If that creature had stung me, I'd have been a goner. Thankfully I'd pulled the covers back and seen it before lying down.

It took a long time for me to come up with such a vivid description of the scorpion because I was dumbfounded in the moment, my mind inert. The scorpion spun around and disappeared under the blanket. When it vanished from my sight I snapped out of it and attacked the spot where it was hiding, raining blows down on it, trying to smash it with my shoe. I continued to pound away until I was exhausted. I moved away from the bed and with two fingers I yanked back the blanket to see what had happened. Strangely, I found no trace of it. I pulled the blanket all the way back but the scorpion had escaped and must have been long gone. I searched for it in the folds of the bed, clutching my shoe, but I couldn't find it anywhere. My fear grew. If I didn't find it, I'd be staying in a scorpion-infested room. I was in a daze. I couldn't stop looking at my foot, my hand, my shoulder. I was convinced that the scorpion was creeping up on me. I'd jump suddenly. Finally I retreated to the corner and crouched down, so I'd have a full view of the floor.

I could feel panicked heartbeats pounding against my knees, which were pressed up against my chest. Ismail was seriously trying to kill me, I thought, and I was getting close to giving up. Then I imagined myself fleeing the house, carrying Shaykh Nafeh with me, taking him to my house in Aleppo where we could enjoy the kind of peace and quiet that would allow me to hear the rest of the story without scorpions or poison. We'd be pampered by my dear wife Nadia instead.

Just then I heard the sound of something falling, like a box of matches hitting the bare floor. The scorpion had dropped from underneath the bed and it was now heading towards me, making a scratching sound, its tail curled up, its pincers at the ready. I may come across as a coward but when I find myself up against mortal danger I can be quite courageous; at least, that's what's happened in every exceptional situation I've ever been in. I crawled towards it on my knees, clutching my shoe, and at just the right moment I swung it down and smashed the creature. I heard a crunch. Yellow fluid came seeping out of its crushed shell—the poison with which Ismail intended to kill me.

I swept up the mangled scorpion and wiped away the fluid with a paper towel before heading downstairs to toss it in the garbage. When I was done I washed my hands with soap and water. The kitchen was tidy and clean, smelling of strong disinfectant. There was a set of shelves along the wall and a long block of shiny marble with another row of cabinets over the countertop. There was a huge refrigerator and a rectangular table against the wall, with a chair on each side. A hand towel hung there. I smelt it: it was clean and smelt of laundry detergent.

I opened a cupboard and discovered that it was full of tin cans. I opened another to find that it was for clean plates.

Ismail was very neat, I thought to myself. A stranger like me could feel a kind of calm in this kitchen. I stood there for a moment and then turned to leave when I noticed that the open door concealed another door behind it. I had to close the kitchen door in order to see the other door, and that's just what I did. The second door was quite narrow, no wider than sixty centimetres, and it didn't have a doorknob. An old photograph of the Aleppo citadel hung at eye level. I assumed the door would be locked but I mustered up some courage and pushed. It swung inwards, just like that.

So this was Ismail's room. The daylight illuminated it to reveal a carefully made bed and a bookcase with hundreds of books in Arabic, English and French. There was a large armoire and several smaller cabinets. I couldn't imagine what they contained. I walked over to the bookcase. If it was strange to see so many books in one place, I found it even stranger that they should be in Ismail's room, in particular. Apparently he could read three languages. He was educated, the bastard. At the side of the bed was a nightstand with a lamp and a book Ismail had been reading, with an ostrich feather as a bookmark. It was *Déscription de l'Égypte*, written during the Napoleonic campaign against Egypt in 1798. I opened it at the bookmarked page: here was a chapter in which the author described the Egyptian bridal procession, specifically the female dancers who would walk out in front. I returned the book to its place, exactly the way it had been positioned, so that when Ismail returned he wouldn't suspect anyone had been there. I went over to the bookcase to examine the other titles. I was surprised to learn that he read about Egypt and dance and wedding ceremonies. The shelves contained works of history as well as nineteenth-century French and English novels by Flaubert, Stendahl, Balzac, Dickens, Conrad and others. There were historical books by Durant and Shaykh Kamel al-Ghazzi, the memoirs of Naum Bakhkhash, books about home gardening, a book about toxins, another about fighting snakes and another about mushrooms, and a copy of *The Tribes of Syria* by Ahmad Wasfi Zakaraya.

I had to squat in order to read the titles on a lower shelf. It seemed that he wanted those books always to be within reach. Most of them were about the arts: *The Egyptian Singer*, published in 1912 by the Gramophone Limited Company in Egypt, *Diwan al-Ataba al-Sharqiyyah*, and *My Life* by the American dancer Isadora Duncan. There was one book that particularly resonated with me: *Voyage to Egypt and the Land of the Nubians*. The book is a travel narrative set between 1805 and 1828 in Egypt and the Nubian region, and it was dedicated to the Russian tsar. Flipping through it, I discovered drawings of a number of dancers from the region as well as a number of images depicting the lives of the inhabitants.

I had to think through several things right away, the most important being what connected Egypt, dance and Ismail. Did it have something to do with his slightly Egyptian accent? I'd have to postpone my questions until later. Time was short, and Ismail could come back any minute and find me in his room. He would kill me for sure. Walking away from the bookcase, I opened his wardrobe, its chaos in total contrast to the neatness I'd found in the kitchen and his bedroom. There were all sorts of clothes: a Bedouin robe, Arab *dishdasha*s and *keffiyeh*s and other things. As I pushed away a higgledy-piggledy stack of clothes, my hand touched cold metal. Tossing the clothes aside, I saw the barrel of a hunting rifle. It was unloaded. I pulled it out, held it in my hands, and moved to the window to get a closer look. A French model. The two barrels didn't smell of burnt powder, suggesting that it hadn't been fired for some time. I noticed a Latin inscription on the wooden butt. I shivered as I brought it into the light: Dr Waleed Fares. Just then I was overcome with incapacitating terror. Fear made me consider getting out of that room immediately, but it also drove me to search among the piles of clothes for rifle cartridges. Maybe he had stashed them here as well. Rummaging around in a hurry, I found a cartridge full of red plastic-tipped bullets. I made sure everything appeared to be back to normal, at least the way I remembered it, and then left the room. I went back to my room, hid the rifle and the cartridges under my bed, and sat down to take a few laboured breaths, nervous about what Ismail would do if he caught me poking around in his room. Some time later I heard the front door close. He had returned.

I sat by the fireplace in the living room, waiting for the old man to come down from his nap. He was taking a long time, so Ismail went up to look for him. I stood up to watch the rain. Where could Ismail have gone in this weather? Where was he hiding out? Maybe there was a shack nearby, or a secret entrance to another room where he was plotting to kill me.

I was confused by everything I had found in his room off the kitchen. But what really disturbed me was the fact that I'd found Dr Waleed Fares's hunting rifle. The old man had told me that his one-time guest had disappeared after three days without saying goodbye to him or hearing the end of the story. I doubted that Ismail had forced him to leave. It seemed much more likely that he had murdered him and disposed of the body. Today I confirmed that he had been killed. If he had left, he would have taken his rifle with him, since he would have needed it out in the wilderness. The most likely scenario was that Ismail had killed the doctor with his own hunting rifle and then buried him in the garden.

I felt like I had fallen into a trap. I tried to understand how Ismail could hate the story so much that he would threaten to kill anyone who heard it. I felt incapable of making sense of it by way of the books in his library, since I had still only heard a portion of the old man's tale. There had to be some connection between the story and the subject of dance, which Ismail read so much about. He seemed to mark the chapters that discussed dance. The copy of *My Life* by the dancer Isadora Duncan and published in the Fifties by the Arab Awakening Publishing House in Damascus, had been read more than any other. And why read so much about Egypt? Had the women in the story travelled there? It wouldn't have been so strange since they were performers.

Of course, there was the possibility that the library belonged to the old man, rather than Ismail. He clearly had a personal interest in those Khojahs, which could have led him to read widely about traditional song and dance. But this hypothesis fell apart since it was Ismail who was reading the book beside his bed. There were also those pages marked with ostrich feathers that dealt with dance and other rituals. Besides, if the library belonged to the old man, why wasn't it in his room? Why was it in Ismail's secret room?

I was convinced the old man could read foreign languages because I had seen pictures of him in Paris; that would seem to confirm that the books were his, and that he had perhaps asked Ismail to move the library into his room so he would have space to decorate the walls of his bedroom with his pictures. But then why wouldn't he have placed the books on the shelves in the living room instead of filling them with all those curios and the ceramics and china?

All of a sudden I had a terrifying thought that gave me the urge to piss. What if the old man was part of this trap—a strange estate out in the middle of nowhere—and they could use his story to lure in strangers or people who got lost and took shelter with them until Ismail murdered them? I'd heard a peculiar story—I can't remember where or from whom—that was very similar to the situation I found myself in, and which I'm now relating to you.

Once there was a man driving along a mountain road in the middle of a heavy rainstorm. Quite a coincidence. It was after midnight and dark outside. The windscreen wipers were on the highest setting but the man was still having trouble seeing anything. Things suddenly took a turn for the worse as the car skidded off the asphalt and crashed into a boulder. The man was dazed. The place was isolated, it was pitch-black, and he decided to stay in the car and wait until another car passed so he could ask for help. A long time passed and he started feeling cold. He was wet and the engine was still on when he decided to get out and start walking through the darkness in search of shelter. After a while he saw some light through the trees. He set out in that direction, plunging into the forest. He made it to a house that had been designed by a mountain architect to resemble an ancient castle. He rang the doorbell and an elderly manservant opened the door. He asked if he could come in or use the phone to call his family for help. The butler showed him in and asked him to wait by the fire until his master could join him. The place was full of stuffed animals: heads of bears, deer and wolves hung on the walls. The place was creepy and the man felt uncomfortable. A few minutes later a middle-aged man came in, welcomed him, and invited him to stay the night, after which he would drive him in whichever direction he was travelling. The two of them sat by the fireplace, savouring the warmth and hot drinks the manservant offered them. The important thing is that the master suggested that they play a game to pass the time before going to bed. The guest warmly agreed.

The master took out some playing cards and explained the rules of the game. It was like bridge, although the rules were somewhat vague, and the master had to repeatedly explain the possible moves to this man, who was not accustomed to playing cards. At first things proceeded smoothly and the man almost began to understand some of the rules, but the master mysteriously changed the rules so that his cards always beat those of his opponent. The man seemed to be constantly losing. He was always expected to wager whatever he had, no matter how meagre. He felt he should be gracious to his host, and went along with whatever he said, until finally the master won all of the man's cards, which ended the game. At that point he declared that the rules of the game stipulated that when one player loses all of his cards he must do whatever the winner asks of him. The master's request was for the guest to work in the house for an undisclosed period of time. If he wanted to win back his freedom he would have to play the same game with the master, with the same rules, until he was able to beat him. But if the man refused or tried to run away, the servant would shoot him. Just then the servant came out with a rifle aimed at the man.

The story goes that the two men continued playing the game until one day the master again changed the rules. You might think that what happened to me wasn't comparable to what happened to that other guy, but I find many things in common, including the fact that the man was the prisoner of a game whose rules went on changing, whereas I found myself the prisoner of a story that stretched on and on—and might never end.

The sky was starting to darken when I heard footsteps. I turned around immediately, expecting to see the old man coming down from his room, but instead I saw Ismail, alone, and glaring at me with an alarmingly hateful look on his face. I suspected that he had discovered the rifle and bullets in my room, or at least knew I'd found the scorpion and squashed it. He stood in front of me for a long time, shrouded in inky darkness. I was standing by the window, and he could see me more clearly than I could see him. The lights hadn't come on yet.

"Now look at what you've done to the old man, you piece of shit," he said to me, as if he were surprised I was still alive. "He's exhausted and can't come down."

"What's the matter with him?"

"It's all your fault. Too much talking has worn him out. If anything happens to him, I'll kill you right away. I told you to leave but you rudely refused. The problem now is that the old man is asking for you to go up to his room. We'll figure something out. As friends, like I told you. Now get up there and talk to the old man."

"What should I say to him?"

"Say whatever you want, you son of a bitch. Tell him a story. But don't let him open his mouth. I don't want you to hear any more. I'll be right there to make sure my orders are carried out exactly. Got it?"

"Got it."

"You're a bastard and a loser. I'll be watching you tonight, too. Tomorrow morning I'm going to take you to the main road so you can get the hell out of here and never come back. I want you to erase from your mind everything you've heard here. If I ever find out that you talked about it, I swear to God I'll track you down in Aleppo and kill you. Got it?"

"I just want to ask: why must this kindly old man be denied kindness? You're so insistent that I have to go. Apparently you were planning something for Dr Waleed Fares before I got here but then he ran away. Shame on you. The old man is just trying to enjoy himself."

"Did he tell you about the hunter?"

"He did."

"Seems to me you've heard a lot already. It's none of your business. Take a look at yourself. You're healthy. You've got your whole life ahead of you. You should live it. I'm not sure you've got nine lives left in you."

"Clearly you only want the best for me."

"Come on, go and tell him about your work at the Agricultural Bank. I'll be along in a bit."

We could no longer see each other in the darkening gloom. He was standing by the door, and I had to pass him to go into the living room.

"I don't think I'll have dinner tonight," I said, pausing

161

there. "I don't feel like being poisoned. Don't charge me for tonight's meal."

I felt like he was smiling at me but I might have been mistaken. When I tried to get past him, he caught at my arm so violently, it felt like a hunter's trap.

"Calm down. Everything's going to be fine, just as long as you do what I tell you. But if I come up there and hear him telling you that story, I'm going to hurt you. If you refuse to leave in the morning, I'll kill you. So you can be sure of my intentions, I encourage you to inspect your room. There might just happen to be a poisonous scorpion sitting between your sheets."

"Thanks for the heads up, but I already found and killed it."

I couldn't see the look on his face as I pulled my arm away and left the living room, but I heard him snort. I walked up to the second floor and turned towards the old man's room. I knocked on the door and heard his invitation to enter.

He was leaning against the headboard, covered with a heavy sheet and a Spanish blanket. His face was yellow, and he was clasping his trembling hands. I felt affection for him and pity for his failing health, and I felt guilty for having exhausted him with storytelling. But the man seemed lonely whenever I wasn't around. He needed me, and there I was in his room. I had come to entertain him, just as he had requested.

The light in the room was weak, which only made his face look thinner. He was of a more advanced age than I had realised, perhaps ninety years old. He had begun to resemble my own father during his last days. He allowed me to stare at his face even as he struggled to control his shaking hands. He was gazing at the pictures hanging on the wall across from him, photos from his youth. I was totally convinced that his tale was a part of his life. I hurried over to the window where the photo of Widad at the train station hung behind the curtain. I took down the frame and moved back towards the light.

I took a better look at her face, trying unsuccessfully to find some common features between Widad and the old man. But Widad's face started to look more familiar to me. Where had I seen it before? Seriously, I started to feel as though I knew someone who looked like her, or maybe I knew the woman herself. Bullshit, I thought. It must simply be that I was seeing the picture for a second time, or maybe I had dreamt about it the night before. I put the photo down somewhere hidden, so Ismail wouldn't see it if he came in all of a sudden. I looked back at the old man, who was waiting for me so he could continue the story. Maybe it wouldn't be finished that day or the next. Ismail had ordered me to keep the old man silent. The house was full of mysteries, and it seemed the story might explain some of them. Perhaps it would only make them more mysterious. I couldn't forget that Ismail had tried to kill me, or at least harm me and force me to leave. I found myself telling the old man honestly about my fears.

"I can see that the story isn't going to be over any time soon, but I'm afraid I'll have to leave before I hear the end."

"I beg you not to go. I'll try to finish within the next three days. Tomorrow you can go with Ismail to the nearest telephone and let your family know that you're fine."

"But Ismail himself is the problem. He threatened me. He wants me to leave. He doesn't want me to hear the rest of the story."

"Don't worry about him. He's like this with anyone who knocks on our door. The doctor also complained about Ismail's threats before he left."

"Did he actually leave, or did he disappear? Personally, I think he disappeared."

"What do you mean?"

"I found a rifle hidden in the house."

"Ismail got that as a present the first day he arrived here. He received it in my presence. Ismail's a good person. He just doesn't want me to tell this to anyone, which is why we're out here in the sticks, cut off from the world."

These last few words confused me, and I scrambled around in my warren of thoughts. So where was Dr Waleed, then? Was I to understand that Ismail was unwilling to kill him because he had been given the rifle as a present? It wasn't true that Ismail was a good person. Maybe he was merciful because he hadn't killed the old man yet. But what did he mean when he said that the two of them were isolated out there in the sticks because Ismail didn't want him to tell anyone? That would mean that the servant had some kind of leverage over the old man, that he was able to keep him cut off from the world in this remote place.

"Ismail tried to break into my room last night," I told the old man. "He wanted to prove that he's capable of hurting me. Then he tried to poison me. Apparently he put something in my food. And finally, I found a poisonous scorpion in my bed."

The old man didn't react, just kept staring at the designs on his blanket. He was mulling over what I'd just told him. We stayed like that for a while. I stared at him and he stared at the blanket.

"What would you say to going to the city with me?" I asked him. "I'll take you away from here. I could carry you. You could finish telling me your story in Aleppo without anyone interrupting you."

He turned his face towards me and gazed into my eyes. It seemed he had already been thinking about the possibility of running away, because after a little while he started shaking his head to indicate he didn't like the idea. Probably he was imagining being carried on my back as I helped him to escape. Just then I heard Ismail's footsteps approaching the bedroom door.

Before Ismail came in the old man warned me about something of the utmost importance.

"There are poisonous plants out here in this part of the country. A person should take care not to…"

The servant overheard some of what the old man was saying as he walked in. He glared at us, and I stared right back at him. He knew that our conversation had been about poisonous plants, but that could be the case whenever two men find themselves together in a cosy house on a rainy day. He shut the door and sat down on a rocking chair, his head hidden by the closet. All I could see of him was his jaw, his nose and his forehead. He had come to spy on us, to listen in on our conversation. The old man continued talking as if his servant weren't there.

"These plants are all around us. People come to think of them as familiar and they nurture them regularly, but they are poisonous, sometimes even lethal."

"I'm familiar with some of them," I said. "Some of our colleagues at the Agricultural Bank are agricultural engineers and they're always mentioning their Latin names, but I tend to quickly forget them. I'm better at remembering numbers and statistics and the value of loans given out to the peasants.

"Haven't you ever heard them talk about the oleander plant? It's very common around Aleppo."

"Oleander, what else?"

"Yes, *Oleander nerium*. Every part of it is poisonous. It's a stimulant that causes vomiting and heart palpitations, paralysis in the respiratory system, and then death. You need to be careful. Its poison is extremely lethal. Once these hunters ate some birds that had been eating oleander branches."

"And what happened to them?"

"Some of them were poisoned and died. A number of beautiful flowers are also thought to be poisonous, such as Sitt al-Husn or 'Bella Donna', which causes fever and hallucinations if ingested by a human being. It can result in sudden cardiac arrest. There are also Datura plants that are extremely poisonous to livestock and human beings alike. Consuming just seven grams of its leaves can lead to death. Flowers of the nightshade plant, also known as 'the drunkard', can provoke an accelerated heart rate. Consuming a large amount of it can cause insanity, even death. I could rattle off other names such as hyacinth, dieffenbachia, larkspur and the ricin found in castor beans."

"How will I know if I've been poisoned by one of them?"

"You've got to keep track of your pupils; most likely they'll become dilated from the atropine."

I wanted to find out what Ismail had put in my food that had made me feel I'd been poisoned.

"Once after eating I had intense diarrhoea and felt suspicious about what had happened to me," I told the old man, staring at where Ismail was sitting.

"Maybe you ate some poison ivy leaves. It can cause symptoms like that. If it had been a large quantity, your nerves would have violently seized up, and you would have had trouble breathing."

Had I seen poison ivy creeping along the side of the house? I had arrived at night and hadn't noticed any branches climbing up the wall. I tried to remember: maybe there was some on the walls looking out on the back garden. In the long silence Ismail looked over at me. From his stare I became convinced that he had actually poisoned me with poison ivy.

We stopped talking, the old man and I, because we weren't very good at this game of trying to fool Ismail. Time was passing, and the silence was all-encompassing, except for the rain hitting the window and the sound of water gushing from the gutters outside. How was I going to trick Ismail into leaving us alone until it was time to go to sleep? I exhaled in growing frustration and stood up. I decided to do something. I apologised to the old man as if I were apologising to Ismail.

"Excuse me, old man, I have to go to the bathroom. I'll be back in five minutes."

The old man nodded permission, and I turned to see Ismail staring at me intently. As soon as I closed the old man's bedroom door behind me, I could hear the servant starting a conversation, but I hurried to the bathroom instead of stopping to listen. I opened and then closed the door without going in, then tiptoed back to my room. I switched on the lights, lifted up the mattress and pulled out the rifle and ammunition.

I flipped open the gun, loaded it with two bullets and closed it again, preparing to head back when something suddenly stopped me. A snake—black, shiny, and terrifying—was slithering out from under my bed. I stiffened and froze on the spot. It was headed right for me, its eyes big and beady, its body thick as a loaf cake. It slithered towards me and raised its head. As it got closer, I had to move or else it would strike me. In a surprising move—more surprising to me than to the snake, to be sure—I lowered the butt of the rifle and brought it down hard on the snake's head. Its body writhed from side to side. Then I raised the rifle up high and brought it crashing down on it until its head was smashed. I didn't wait for the rest of the body to stop quivering, but moved away and started trembling as the blood returned to my face, making me unbearably warm. Staring into the mirror, I saw my face turning red and my lips going blue. I switched off the light, gently closed the door, and hurried back towards the old man's room. I knocked on the door and held the rifle up, ready to open fire. When I heard the weak voice of the old man calling out to me, I went inside. In a single bound I found myself face to face with Ismail, himself now frozen in shock.

I aimed the rifle at his head in an awkward way I'd learnt from the movies.

"Now, you're going to get the hell out of here, Ismail. You're going to leave the two of us in peace," I told him, sucking my teeth in order to let him know I was ready to kill him if he didn't do as I said.

"You're nuts," he said. "Put the gun down."

"No. Did you hear me? I'm warning you, don't come near me."

"All this for a story?"

"Yep, all this for a story."

I let him see my finger on the trigger and he stood up. He stared hard at me in anger and spite, almost spewing poison. I backed away from him slightly so that he wouldn't be able to come at me suddenly and grab the rifle, and nodded towards the door. He turned and headed out.

"Can't you see what your guest is up to?" he asked the old man, who had gone all yellow and was shaking miserably.

"Leave the old man alone," I commanded. "Get out."

He left. I inched my way forward without lowering the rifle, ordering him to shut the door behind him. He took hold of the handle and looked at me with an expression I can't quite describe. But before closing the door, he spat at me; spittle sprayed into my face, and the door was slammed shut. I wasn't bothered by his phlegm as it dripped down my face, and I hurried instead to secure the lock and rotate my chair so I'd be able to sit there and monitor the door and the window at the same time.

This all happened quickly, and in a way that stunned me more than it seemed to have affected the old man or Ismail. I had to explain to the old man exactly what I had done. His hands started to shake violently. Meanwhile, as I've said, his smiling face looked yellow and skinnier somehow.

"Please forgive me, sir. I had to do that. Now you've seen for yourself that he's trying to keep me from hearing your story. Let's not waste any more time talking about poisonous plants. Once again, I beg your pardon. Please, get back to the story. I really want to hear the rest of it. It's riveting. I'll do anything to hear it."

CHAPTER FIVE

From the Train Station to the Roxy Cinema

"A S FRUSTRATED AS I AM with Ismail," the old man said, once he had calmed down and his face had returned to a more natural colour, "I can't blame you for reacting like this. The story has to be told somehow. Now we've reached the part that has to do with me in particular."

"With you?" I asked him, breathless. "I'm dying to hear this. This whole time I've been wondering what connects you to Widad's story. Also, I'd really like to figure out the mystery of Ismail."

"He's no mystery. But I simply will not begin the story from the end. I mean, I won't tell it backwards. If I did that, you wouldn't be able to understand, and you'd ask me to start again and tell it the right way."

"I'm so eager to hear it, sir. I hope you won't pay any attention to Ismail if he tries to disturb us."

"Let me begin with the story of my uncle Ibrahim Pasha," the old man said, "and his fat wife and daughter…

"I used to live with Uncle Ibrahim Pasha. My uncle wasn't a *pasha* the way some might think. The word *pasha* just stuck to him for some reason, like a badge that everyone got accustomed to using. The first person to use it was my father. I don't know why. My uncle loved it when people added that extra adjective to his name. Most likely my father, who was five years older than my uncle, was trying to flatter him by using the honorific title *pasha*, and then he just got used to calling him that. My father started to use the word even when he wasn't around. Whenever Uncle Ibrahim telephoned he would identity him by using that name, which was how he came to be known that way all over town.

"My mother and father were going to travel to Paris by steamer, and they wanted to take me with them. They even recorded my name on the travel papers, but two weeks before the ship was set to depart, I came down with typhoid and was bedridden. My body was frail, very frail. When I got sick my mother wished that she could die in my place, or at least along with me. I was her only son. Typhoid was very dangerous and only the strongest men survived it. A scrawny little boy like me didn't stand a chance. This is how our relatives started to talk, and their chattering eventually found its way to my mother's ears.

"Because she knew me and realised how weak I had become, she believed all those prognostications and broke down completely. They had to take care of her and me at the same time. But I proved all the gossip and the advice wrong. I didn't die. Even the Jewish doctor who oversaw my treatment—or to be more precise: who oversaw my decay and my slide towards death—was astounded when I returned to health. He had been convinced that a recovery was impossible, certain I was going to die, which is why he spent more time caring for my mother than he did attending to me. When my fever broke and I came out of the coma, he pursed his lips and shrugged his shoulders in wonder, even as my mother's blood pressure hit its lowest ebb. He couldn't heal her. She couldn't get out of bed. It was only when I slowly approached her bedside that her blood pressure would return to normal and she would smile.

"My father paid the Jewish Dr Behar well, concluding that I was out of harm's way thanks to his care. He paid him double for me and my mother, even though the doctor had no hand in either of our cases. Nevertheless, the doctor offered my father some medical advice that was well worth his payment, and even more... hundreds of times more. He recommended that I shouldn't travel to France with them as my health might deteriorate even further, which would no doubt result in the typhoid killing me.

"The two of them had to travel so that my mother could be treated by superior physicians in France. She suffered from chronic low blood pressure and depression. Because they had managed to get permission to travel from the French Mandate authorities, and since their steamship was set to depart in two days' time, they decided to go without me, leaving me with my uncle until they returned. But they didn't come back. The ship sank somewhere between Beirut and Marseille, which is how I managed to stay alive, thanks to typhoid and the advice of a Jewish doctor.

"I had moved into my uncle's house along with our servant Khadija. At the time I was only twelve years old. Khadija was twenty-five. She was an incomparable woman, married to a man who used to beat her savagely, until her body was black and blue. The problem was that she hadn't borne him any children. This terrible catastrophe led to her having to endure

172

the ferocity and abuse of her husband. Despite her impassioned pleas—she was as gentle as a bird—he refused to divorce her. She was relieved when he finally married another woman, hopeful that his new wife would distract him from her, especially when, a few months after their marriage, her stomach started to swell. But Khadija was deluded. Her husband continued to beat her. His other wife only helped him do it. When she came over to our house for the first time, her face and body were bruised from the beating. My father nearly went to her house to confront her husband. My mother wept at the sight of her, giving her work on the spot. And that's how she came to live with us, despite the threats her husband shouted at her from the pavement outside our house.

"Khadija became my father's personal crusade. He offered her husband a substantial sum if he agreed to divorce her, but the man refused, so my father sent a police officer who threatened to throw him in jail. Nothing came of this, however. One day Khadija casually glanced across the street to where her husband usually camped out all day on the pavement, but didn't see him there. Several days passed without her seeing him. Khadija was worried about him—just imagine! Had something unfortunate happened to him? It seemed she couldn't be at peace until she made sure that her husband—who used to beat her with the strength of a horse—was all right. Khadija begged my father to send someone to look into the matter. My father chuckled at this behaviour, at her kind-heartedness. What kind of a woman was she? She truly was both strange and a good person. But we were shocked to discover, through my father's investigation, that Khadija's husband was dead. That's right, dead. His new wife had murdered him in a fit of rage, burying a kitchen knife in his chest. The killer went to jail and was sentenced to death. Her older brother took custody of her two children, one of whom was still breastfeeding at the time, and they nailed the door of her house shut.

"Khadija mourned her husband for a long time, remaining in seclusion for the entire period stipulated, without receiving my father or any other man. She lived in our house with us as if she were part of the family. The truth is that she didn't have anywhere else to go. When my mother and father drowned she totally fell apart, and when she managed to pull herself together, she said, 'I don't have anyone else in the world except for you.'

"One week after the tragedy, my uncle called me to say that he wanted to speak with me in private. As I sat across from him, I avoided looking him directly in the eye. I was afraid of him. I can't recall ever caring for the man. This is the first time I've admitted that. I never even told Khadija, who was so good at keeping and manufacturing secrets. Still, she instinctively knew somehow, as soon as I got back to our room from that meeting.

"My father and my uncle owned an artisanal soap work-shop they had inherited from their father, that is, from my grandfather, who died before his time. It was one of the most important and best-known workshops in the country. The quality of their soap was renowned as far as away as Cairo and Istanbul. It was said that people would check inside the boxes of bay leaf soap in search of the stamp imprinted with our family's name, al-Aghyurli.

"The workshop was in an ancient airy building divided into three sections. One for storing raw materials before production; another, for cooking the soap, with an enormous vat that had a giant burner underneath—from the vat, the soap would be poured and then left to cool before being cut into equal-sized cubes; and, finally, the section where the bars would be stacked on top of each other in a pyramid, leaving gaps for the soap to breathe and dry well. At that point the soap was ready to be sold.

"It used to make me very happy when my father took me to the workshop with him. I loved to inhale the smell of bay leaf that hung in the air. I was even more amazed by the sight of those soap pyramids as I walked around them. I never tired of looking up at them. I would knock over those structures all the time. But my favourite activity was stamping the bars of soap before the pyramids were even built. I would insist on helping to stamp them, despite how weak I was. Strong arms were required to bring down the heavy press hard enough on the surface of the soap bar. When I grew up and became a man, I realised how spoilt I'd been by my father and his employees. They always used to humour me, gladly giving me the stamp even though they wound up having to try and sell bars of soap marked with indecipherable designs. Everything changed whenever my uncle Ibrahim Pasha was at the workshop, and I would sit there in silence, not daring to move a muscle. He used to shout at the workers. He despised children, and he thought of me as a parasite and an idiot.

"When my grandfather got sick, my father and my uncle vowed not to sell off the workshop, to keep it within the family for ever. It would be a struggle for the two of them, one that would require all the means at their disposal. In order to control the succession of the inheritance, they would have to marry two sisters and give birth to boys as well as girls in order to marry them to one another… and so on and so forth for several generations. One of them would have to give birth only to males while the other would have to have females. But if they gave birth to the same sex, whether male or female, they would both have to get married all over again, again to two sisters. In other words, they had to move heaven and earth in order for the workshop to remain in the al-Aghyurli line and to hold on to the distinguished soap brand, the one I got a thrill from whenever I stamped the fresh bars of soap.

"And just as my grandfather had hoped, my mother gave birth to a boy, and my uncle's wife Hamideh Khanum had a girl, whom she called Jalila. Despite the fact that my mother and my uncle's wife were sisters, the two of them couldn't have been more fundamentally different. Whereas my mother was slim and emotional and good-natured, her sister was heavy-set and emotionless and not so bright. She weighed more than two hundred pounds, and in the days when Khadija and I lived with them she might have weighed as much as two-fifty.

"Because she was so fat, she moved very slowly, and couldn't walk without someone else's help. She preferred to remain seated to avoid exerting too much energy. They built a custom-made seat for her, one that was strong enough for her tremendous weight. Anyway, she used to wheeze whenever she tried to drag her arse from one place to another. And when she had to get up to use the bathroom or go to bed, she would call for my uncle Ibrahim Pasha or the servant to help her. But my uncle stopped taking the risk of picking her up or even supporting her in case he slipped a disc. He already suffered from back pain. And because there was a constant exodus of maids who fled after just one week of working in my uncle's house, they were forced to constantly search for new staff to work for them and take care of the house. My uncle had to employ several maids at once, two to tend to his wife and another one to tend to the rest of the house.

"Ayyoush and Ammoun, Hamideh Khanum's two private maidservants, were strong and accustomed to hard work. For example, Ammoun worked in a quarry. Both of them stayed by her side from the time she woke up in the morning until the moment she went to sleep, at which point they would tuck her into bed and return to their own homes.

"That fat blob needed someone to help her bathe and dry herself off, to get dressed and brush her hair. Once I became part of the household, I took great pleasure in watching my paternal uncle's wife, who also happened to be my mother's sister and looked like a mountain of jiggling white flesh. One time I saw the two servants helping her put on her underwear. She couldn't do it by herself because she was unable to bend over to grab hold of it. But what really disgusted me was when I happened to see her sitting on the kind of toilet that children sit on when they're potty trained. She struggled to get up. I examined the bowl later and discovered that it was quite large. I concluded that my uncle must have ordered a custom-made model to the specifications of his wife's rear end.

"Everyone who ever saw her found it hard to imagine how such a creature could have given birth to Jalila. Her thighs were so large they stuck together. How had she given birth at all? I often wondered this myself after learning that babies don't come out of their mothers' belly buttons, as Khadija told me when I nagged her to explain. Actually, I also heard some of my uncle's wife's friends laughing at her when they asked the same question. The mystery becomes even greater and stranger when you see Jalila, my uncle's daughter and my fiancée. She was eight years younger than me, meaning she was four years old while I was living with them. Like her mother, Jalila was overweight, meaning that she was set to be just like her in future, if not even heavier. She was also lazy and an overeater, consuming prodigious amounts of food in a single meal. She neither moved nor played, and was always looking for somewhere to sit down. What's worse, she was as stupid and callous as her mother. The thing that infuriated me most was that I only seemed to bump into her when she was sitting on her special toilet, struggling, all red in the face. Another thing she inherited from her mother was chronic constipation.

"My uncle's wife Hamideh Khanum did have one positive attribute: she loved music. I don't know where this love came from, but she had as good an ear as the country's most famous ladies at that time. Maybe she was just emulating them for the sake of it, but she really did like to listen to and play music, and shimmy and sway to good Arabic music.

"My uncle had one of the most beautiful houses in the entire city. My grandfather had built it for the whole family to live in but he passed away before it was finished. It had two storeys connected by an elegant staircase. The rooms on the ground floor were large and private: three bedrooms, two bathrooms and a kitchen. Wooden doors as large as the wall separated the rooms from one another, and when they were folded back all the way the three rooms could be converted into a large living room for entertaining. Usually most of those doors remained shut, and the family would only use the front room near the entrance and the three bedrooms; to be clear, right across from my uncle's wife's bedroom. A lot of the time, or perhaps even most of the time, I could see what was going on in her bedroom while I was sitting in the living room. She would always leave her door wide open, closing it only when she went to bed. The upper floor was totally neglected because Hamideh Khanum wasn't able to climb up there. They gave me my own room directly above my uncle's room, and which looked down on both the garden and the street. Because the upper floor had been completely forgotten, they let Khadija take the room adjacent to mine.

"The house had large balconies facing in all directions, with especially good views of the front yard and the street. In the summertime my uncle and his wife liked to sit in the shade of the cypresses, oleanders and chinaberries, their leaves crinkling in the breeze and blocking them from the sight of anyone on the street. In that season the westerly winds were pleasant but they also inspired sorrow in people's hearts.

"My uncle Ibrahim Pasha was sitting on the far side of the table when I walked into the living room. I sat down across from him. To my left, the door was wide open and I could see my uncle's wife in her room. It was late on Friday afternoon. Typically my uncle wouldn't go to the soap workshop on Fridays. He would stay at home after getting back from prayer, and relatives might drop by to say hello. A week had passed since we had received the disastrous news of my mother's and father's ship sinking. I was discombobulated and inconsolable. The idea that I would have to live my whole life in that house made me even sadder. So did my knowledge that, with that cruel twist of fate, my slim and tender mother had been replaced by my uncle's wife, a fat and vulgar woman.

Up until that day I hadn't been able to accept what had happened. Not even Khadija's bitter tears confirmed for me that the telegram my uncle had received informing us of the ship's sinking was true. But I had lost my mother for ever. She used to say she wanted to die with me or instead of me if I came down with a fever. That was why, when I sat down across from my uncle, I expected him to tell me that the news wasn't true and to apologise on behalf of the telegraphic service, especially when I saw him holding an envelope and staring at me as he waited for me to come in and sit down. So as to prevent my imagination from rushing to unrealistic expectations, he addressed me in his croaky and hushed voice, drowning out the orderly tick-tock of the grandfather clock that was taller than I was.

"'You know very well, nephew, what happened to your mother and father, God rest their souls.'

"He paused in order to add the necessary gravitas to what he was saying. I acknowledged this silence. He had taken away all my hope. I realised I was going to be an orphan for ever. His pause gave me the chance to reconsider my expectations. Because I hated them all so much, I had been hoping he would tell me they were kicking me and Khadija out of their house and that we would have to go and live alone in my parents' house, which was now mine. But he went on mercilessly:

"'It's time to read you your father's will.'

"He took out his glasses and placed them on his nose. They didn't have arms to go over his ears the way glasses are made today. He read out the will as I listened in silence.

"The only thing I understood was that I was going to have to live in my uncle's house until I got older, and that I would have to marry Jalila so that not a single share of the soap workshop would go to anyone outside the family. My uncle would be trustee over me and my property, which was half of the soap workshop and my father's house. If I refused to marry Jalila I wouldn't inherit anything at all.

"They bequeathed Jalila to me. That's what had happened. My uncle finished speaking, took off his glasses, and returned the will to its envelope. Then he stood up to place it on the table beside the grandfather clock. I remained speechless, staring at his empty chair. I was devastated. But I had a habit of not showing how upset I was, something I'd inherited from my mother, so I didn't express how much I hated my uncle and his wife and his daughter Jalila. Something to my left caught my attention and I calmly turned around. Jalila was sitting on her chamber pot trying to shit. She was staring right at me. I looked at her red and bloated face. Her mother was sitting behind her on her low-slung chair, shaking as she laughed at something one of her servants had said to her.

"Through a narrow window just below the ceiling you could see the last few stairs leading to the upper floor. Anyone walking downstairs would be able to see what was going on in the living room from there, and anyone looking from below would be able to see the person going upstairs. I was trying to look out the window so I wouldn't have to look at Jalila. I saw Khadija there. I wanted to gaze into her tender eyes. She looked back at me. It was the first time she came through for me. There she was, leaning over the guardrail, trying to offer me support with her tearful eyes.

181

"My uncle and I left the room. When I got upstairs, Khadija embraced me and held me close. In my room, I started crying and repeating, 'I hate him… I hate them all.' She tried her best to cover my mouth.

"The tragedy unfolded smoothly; at least for me it did. I was young. As I told you, I wasn't yet twelve years old. Whenever she started crying, I would squeeze Khadija tight. She liked me to call her Khaddouj. I knew she was crying over the death of her employers, who had both been very good to her. I would draw close and hold her, and she would reciprocate by holding me the way I liked to be held: with both arms, resting my head on her shoulder as my face brushed against her neck. She would cry for a bit longer before calming down. We'd stay like that for a long time.

"I loved the way she smelt. Not even my mother had a smell like hers. A scent like cloves. Even today, I still can't figure out how to explain that smell. Whenever she hugged me, I would feel at peace, calm and still. There wasn't anything quite like Khaddouj's smell to take me away from thinking about the loss of my mother. There was no place on earth that could make me feel as peaceful as I did when my face was nestled between her shoulder and her neck. She'd lean her shoulders against me, wrap her arms around me, and caress my scrawny chest.

"She hadn't embraced me when we were at home. She never once did that. My mother didn't either. She'd let me rest my head in her lap and I would lie on my back as she freely tousled my hair and stroked my forehead with a tender hand. Whenever Khadija had me in that position, she'd laugh and call me a spoilt brat. In her opinion, an only child is bound to be spoilt by both parents, and that's the child's right. She hugged me for the first time the day after I'd spoken to my uncle. Rather than staying out on the staircase, she pulled me inside my room and then sat down to place me in her lap, squishing my face against that throne between her shoulder and her neck. We were both in tears. When we finally stopped crying I felt a tremendous calm, a peace that eliminated all of my dejection and my hatred for my uncle and his family. I was filled with tender and incomprehensible feelings whenever my chest nestled against her breasts. At first she would try to keep them away from me. Whenever I drew closer she would pull back, then she'd forget herself and turn back towards me. I would fondle her breasts once again. She tried to pull away, but in the end she stopped noticing when her breasts rested against my chest.

"That was the day I discovered the scent of cloves and sweet figs that lingered on her skin.

"She had a toned body, tall and barley-coloured. She was neither skinny like my mother nor fat like my uncle's wife. I would describe her as being full. When she hugged me to calm me down, I would run my hands over her forearms and her shoulders and her back. I couldn't feel her bones. They were covered by a thin layer of pillowy and comfortable flesh. I would cling to her so that her breasts were close to me.

"That familiar and pliable body silently used to take beatings from her husband before he passed away. I hated him from the instant I laid eyes on those blue and wine-coloured bruises all over her face and her neck. I believe that at the *hammam* she showed my mother the bruises all over the rest of her body. Maybe that's why I felt such powerful

183

sympathy for her body, just as she felt sympathy for my sudden orphanhood.

"We didn't speak much. That's just the way I was. My uncle would start to worry about my psychological well-being when he noticed my long silences, which could last for days on end. He would see me here and there, at various places in the cavernous house, looking around at everything and interacting with everyone in absolute silence. Khaddouj found a kind of eloquence in that silence, as she told me when I got older. Because of my distaste for my uncle's family, I shrank away from them, finding my only refuge in solitude and in being close to Khadija.

"After a while, I started becoming afraid of being away from her, especially at night. I would have strange nightmares about oceans, drowning, suffocation and then death. I would wake up mewling like a kitten, my body as stiff as a board, terrified of what I had seen in the dream, without the strength to toss away the blanket and get up to shake off what had scared me so badly. One time, when Khadija was singing me to sleep, I told her, 'I'm afraid of the night. I've even started getting scared of the dark.'

"She stopped moving, brought her face in close to mine, and asked me in a whisper, 'What are you afraid of? You haven't always been like this.'

"'I have bad dreams.'

"'Like what?'

"'Oceans and boats and caves. Drowning and people dying.'

"She shook her head. She understood that my parents' drowning was causing these nightmares.

"'There's no need for this,' she said encouragingly. 'You used to sleep in your room all by yourself.'

"I continued to be silent and sad. I really wanted her to sleep next to me. I couldn't stand being alone. She looked over and saw how despondent I was. The way I was looking drove her to ask, 'Do you want me to sleep in here with you?'

"I nodded unenthusiastically. She smiled at me. Maybe she considered me a brat for not jumping for joy at her offer, because she started tickling and kissing me, and we tumbled around on the bed laughing.

"She switched off the light and got into bed next to me. I wasn't right next to her, but up against the wall. She patted me and invited me to snuggle up next to her. She placed her hand under my head and pulled me in close. Then she fell asleep.

"For a while I couldn't move. I breathed in her strange odour, my face under her chin. I didn't want to upset her. The whole thing was pretty strange, obviously. I was too nervous to move, which could have made her move away from me or to turn onto her other side. I woke up in the same position. I didn't have nightmares that night. Her soft and warm presence, her tangy smell kept the nightmares at bay. In the morning she was happy to hear how well I had slept beside her, and she promised to sleep next to me that night as well.

"I started to look forward to nightfall all throughout the day. Whereas I had once hated the night, I began to love it, to anticipate its arrival. When it finally arrived, I would find myself in such a good mood I'd begin to hum a popular tune unintentionally. Khadija would smile and stroke my hair as she got the bed ready and then invited me to get in. She did so cheerfully, maybe with a little smile on her face as well. She would leave the light on and then get into bed next to me.

I would curl up next to her, and as I brought my face in close to her neck, she would move it out of the way so I could get in nice and close.

"The first time my skinny frame pressed up against her full and fleshy body, she didn't get upset. She began to play with my hair instead. She would run her fingers through it and then brush it down to the side with her hand. Then she would plunge her fingers into my thick hair and do the same thing all over again.

"'You heard about your beloved father's will. Are you sad about it?' she whispered.

"'Yes', I replied, relishing the scent of cloves. 'I'm sad about it. Nobody ever told me I was going to have to marry Jalila when I grow up.'

"'Don't worry about it too much. She's going to grow up to be very beautiful.'

"'But I don't love her, Khaddouj. She's so serious, so fat. I really hate all of them.'

"She scolded me by squeezing my head and squishing my nose under her armpit. She snorted once before saying, 'Don't you dare say anything like that ever again. He's your uncle, your father's brother.'

"'But I hate him. I feel like he doesn't even like me. I'm scared of him when his eyes get big and wide.'

"At first she remained silent. Then she sighed. Her chest rose and fell. Even though she was wearing a cotton night-gown, her left breast brushed across my ear. I lifted my arm and her supple belly found its way under my hand. Her head moved. I guessed that she was trying to look at me but all she could see was my hair. My face was still buried in her armpit.

186

"Some time passed. Maybe she was trying to figure out why I had done that. Why would I cling to her and dare to touch her belly button? She gently took my hand and returned it to my side, then drew a hair's breadth away from me, leaving my head where it rested. It must have made her uncomfortable.

"The next day she looked at me through different eyes. Several times I caught her sending probing glances my way. She was trying to discover whether I was staring at her whenever she turned away or bent over. Was I spying on her? She was obsessed, the poor girl. I felt a little bit guilty. I wasn't sure what I was doing exactly. I felt like I had committed an adolescent trespass, like being difficult or too serious. I was suspicious of my own reasons for being like that. It seemed to make her uncomfortable, so I didn't push. One reason for that was how happy I was whenever I touched her body. As far as I was concerned, she represented something maternal, the woman the little boy in me wanted to be near.

"I was sad about what happened. I had been comfortable with the way she looked at me but I started to avoid it, especially after she stopped going to the bathroom with me to help me bathe. She would take me in there instead and explain how I was to wash myself. She told me I was old enough to take care of myself. I would start crying whenever I took a bath. My tears flowed into the warm water I poured over my head with a copper pot. The first time I knocked on the door asking for a towel, she thought the redness in my eyes was from the soap. But when she found out I was sad, she would hug me the way she always did. She held me, without letting me cling to her in return.

"On the orders of my uncle, Khadija took me to register at the neighbourhood school. I had to re-enroll after nearly a month out of school. It was too difficult to get to my old school. We'd lived far from my uncle's house. My old school was two buildings away from my father's house.

"The arrival of the telegram about the ship going down made us forget all about school. I would gaze down through the window at the street and watch the other kids walking by in their black uniforms, carrying their bags as they scampered off to school or headed home afterwards, without feeling any urge to be one of them. I was comfortable with being lazy, until my uncle Ibrahim Pasha found me sitting with the women, listening to their idle chatter, and he mentioned that school could take me away from all of that. By the way, I found everything they were talking about very interesting.

"The teacher enrolled me in his class and asked me to follow him. I had to let go of Khadija's warm hand as I secretly cursed the school and my uncle, who had brought it up in the first place. But I quickly came to like it. It was very different to my old school, much calmer. It had a large courtyard lined with classrooms. There was a single class for each grade. Most of the time they would combine students from two grades in the same room with a single teacher, but there weren't that many students there compared to my old school. God only knew how many classes or how many students that school had. When we were let out of class, in between periods, it was like Judgement Day. The boys were naughtier. What really made me despise that old school was one of those boys in particular. He was enormous, even though he was only one year older than me. From the moment he laid eyes on me he started to bully me. If I didn't give him my lunch and whatever money I had, he would beat me up. I had to be very sneaky in order to avoid his wrath.

"At my new school I didn't encounter anyone as bad as that devilish bully. Perhaps there were other boys who picked on the weaker ones but I didn't run into any, thankfully. There was a boy in my fifth-grade class who was a lot like me. He was calm and skinny but bashful somehow. Whenever he spoke his face turned red, just like me. But he also had some strange tics which I loved to watch and have a laugh at whenever he was around. His name was Malek, and when I learnt that the name for heron in Arabic is Malek al-Hazeen, or Sad Malek, I started using that as a nickname for him.

"The best thing about that school was my teacher. He was old and wore a red fez to hide his baldness. He wouldn't leave his seat until the bell rang. He used to make the pupils do their homework in the classroom to fill time while he groomed himself, which he never seemed to stop doing. He would pull out a compact mirror and a pair of scissors, and start plucking the little black hairs from his ears. He never grew tired of this. I'd forget all about myself and my homework whenever he took out his mirror and I'd sit there staring at him. My seat was right in front of his desk, with only a single chair between us. He would catch me watching him a lot of the time, and I would look away, immediately fearing some kind of punishment. Then I would go right back to watching him as soon as he returned to the busy work with his ears. Sometimes I was even able to make out a tiny hair that had evaded his scissors and mirror. I imagined pointing it out to him.

189

"1936 was an important year, with a flavour all its own. I turned twenty and Jalila turned twelve. I finished my bachelor's degree. Although I wanted to travel to Damascus to continue my studies, my uncle thought I should stop with just the one degree so I could take over the books at the soap workshop. He wanted me to go straight to work and learn how to manage the business. I would eventually become the owner, once my uncle passed away, along with Jalila, who would become my wife.

"I spent my days at the soap workshop waiting for my Jalila to call. In the evenings Sad Malek and I would go to the Dunya or the Eastern to watch Mohammed Abdel Wahab films. We'd also take part in demonstrations and other anti-French Mandate events organised by the National Bloc. One day in September, Malek came to see me at the soap workshop. He whispered in my ear that the delegation that had travelled to Paris at the beginning of the year to negotiate with the French government for independence was arriving in Aleppo that day. They were returning after a victory in the negotiations. The Bloc called on the people to give the delegation a welcome worthy of heroes returning from a glorious battle. I asked my uncle for permission to go, and as he had actually donated some money to the office of the National Bloc he let me. We hurried off to the train station.

"The train was packed that day with people who had come to greet them. First and foremost was Monsieur de Martel and the other members of the Aleppo Government. A brass band played as we chanted slogans in favour of an independent Syria. Apparently they had also added an additional slogan celebrating Syrian-French brotherhood. We began to chant it, overjoyed by the successful negotiations. As the train approached, the people grew increasingly excited and the music more frenetic. By the time the music stopped, some of the most excited people had nearly fainted. Station agents were stopping the enthusiastic masses from falling off the platform and onto the tracks. It was only by the grace of God that dozens of people didn't become victims of the Treaty, crushed under the wheels of the train.

"The delegation descended from the train, with Mr Hashim al-Atassi at the front, followed by Saadallah al-Jabiri and all the rest. Monsieur de Martel kissed each one of them on the cheeks and the grandees gathered there to greet them did the same. When they had all lined up in front of the train to have their photo taken for posterity, a young peasant woman whose beauty surpassed anything I'd ever seen before appeared at the door of the train. She stood there in shock. She wondered if she had done something inappropriate because the masses had stopped chanting and shouting. The brass band had also stopped playing. Everyone was staring at her, finding her presence on the train quite strange. As for me, I was in love. I loved her from that moment. I wanted to know her story and what she was doing there. She recoiled in embarrassment, especially when the camera flash bulb went off and released smoke into the air. She placed her hand over her face, covering her eyes, seemingly blinded by the flash.

"The poor thing said something to the delegation and to Monsieur de Martel before she descended the carriage steps and stepped onto the platform. The chanting started back up again and the marching music resumed. The people forgot all about her, especially when the delegation and their welcome party moved towards the exit. But I didn't forget about her, even as the huge torrent of people forcefully pushed me along. I was trying to find her, but I couldn't even get my own bearings as the people shoved me ouside the station, into the street, and far away from the building. I knew I had lost her. I returned to chanting slogans along with everyone else, holding Sad Malek's hand.

"The next day I scanned the newspapers for coverage of the delegation's arrival and I found the photo with her in it. I bought two copies of the paper, one of which I stashed in my room. The other I placed in my pocket so as to keep it close by while I was at the soap workshop. I would take it out in order to regard the young lady's beauty. In the evening Sad Malek and I went to a café where I showed him the picture. It seemed that he liked her as well, and she became the girl of our dreams, my friend Sad Malek and I.

"We began to talk about her every day. We wondered what her name was, who she was, where she might be at that moment. We started making up stories about her. We wished we would run into her on the street, which was why we continually wandered around the city neighbourhoods, checking the faces of veiled and unveiled women. One time we came across a woman who looked liked her, so we followed her. When we caught up with her and looked her in the face, we discovered it wasn't the one we were looking for. But she was young and beautiful. Malek fell in love and followed after her to find out where she lived. From that day forward he no longer shared my love for the woman from the newspaper.

*

Now that I had been introduced to the first link in the connection between him and Widad, I asked the old man, "Did you ever speak with Khadija about the young woman in the newspaper?"

"I began to stay alone in my bedroom. I'd take out the newspaper and gaze at her face. I wanted the paper to give me a clue about where she might be hiding, but it was useless. Isolation made me think too much. Khadija grew nervous. Once she anxiously said that I had begun to stray and that I was getting more and more distracted. I tried not to respond because I wasn't sure if she would laugh if I told her I was in love with a young woman I didn't know anything about, apart from her picture in the paper."

"But you told her in the end, right?"

"Of course. One night we were sitting in my room just before bedtime. She was knitting me a pair of woollen gloves for the coming winter and I was looking at an open book but couldn't focus enough to read. I was desperate to talk to her about the girl in the newspaper. When I showed her the picture in the newspaper, she thought I was pointing at the French officer or other members of the delegation. I pointed out the young woman who was standing behind them on the steps of the train carriage. I told her I loved that woman."

"What did she say?"

"She started laughing at me. Then she warned me not to fall in love with anyone because I was just going to have to marry Jalila, my uncle's daughter. When I said I was serious, she realised she couldn't see very well or make out anything in the picture apart from the delegation. I promised I'd buy her some glasses. But Khadija did begin to listen as I told her about that young woman. I relaxed. She gradually realised that the whole thing was merely the fantasy of a young man."

"Where did you meet Widad after that?"

"I'll tell you in due course. But I'm worried about Ismail right now. I don't hear a sound from downstairs."

"Don't worry about him. I'll check on him as soon as you finish the story."

"I told you my uncle's wife Hamideh Khanum loved music and concerts. She often tried to emulate high society women and considered herself one of them. But since her extreme obesity prevented her from leaving the house, she would host parties in the living room several times over the course of a year, although she spread word that she held a private salon on the first Monday of every month called the Hamideh Khanum Salon.

"I could tell by the preparations going on in the house whether there was an event the following Monday. All the seats would be moved into the living room, and more chairs would be rented from a private company. I would help move the dining-room table into a far corner. I took pity on sweet Khadija, who had been instructed to set up the three rooms with the doors wide open, expanding the space to accommo-date a hundred or so women in addition to the Khojah and her girls. We arranged the rows of chairs in a semicircle around where the musicians would sit. According to my uncle's wife's instructions, we left space for the dancer to move around. My uncle's wife would talk excitedly about the dancer with her visiting friends. I would hear them whispering about her extraordinary beauty. One of them hinted at a romantic relationship between the dancer and Khojah Bahira, whom I had seen before at my uncle's wife's salon.

"Whenever the Monday parties convened I would always be sure to spy on the women. I would sit with Khadija on the landing and look down on the living room. Khojah Bahira was on my mind, with her manly look and masculine clothes. When I was thirteen years old I began to take more pleasure in watching the women play music and dance and kiss one another. Then I noticed how some of them would ask for sheets or blankets, according to custom, and place them over their thighs. I could see the outline of their hands as they writhed and rubbed against each other under the blankets. They were *banat al-ishreh*. They caressed one another in view of the other women. Khadija warned me not to look at such things but I didn't pay any attention to what she said.

"On this particular Monday I was in my spot by the window on the stairs leading upstairs. So that nobody could see me I had left the small curtain sewn by Khadija closed. I would draw it back a little with my finger and look out. The living room was filled to capacity with women, friends of my uncle's wife. Hamideh Khanum was sitting in her chair in the front row. To either side of her were her closest friends, whom I knew well from their visits to the house. They were chatting and laughing with one another. My uncle's wife's servants and Khadija were performing their duties. I noticed that all the women had curled their hair. They were also chewing gum. Those who were well-known lovers of women would cling to their *ablaya*. Because I was looking over the musicians from up on the landing I could see things that were concealed from the others. I would see one

195

of them caress her girlfriend's ear with her fingertips while another one leant her head back and rested her neck in her girlfriend's hand. I also saw rapid kisses as they whispered in each other's ears.

"Then the Khojah came in, followed by her performers. The Khojah greeted my uncle's wife by kissing her on both cheeks and then did the same thing with a number of other invited guests. Everyone took their seats facing the performers. The Khojah's voice was gruff and the way she moved and sat was masculine. Apparently Hamideh Khanum had inquired about the dancer. Bahira said that she was changing her clothes and would be there shortly, just as soon as the mood warmed up.

"Mohammed Abdel Wahab was all the rage in those days. The all-female troupe started to play one of his songs from a film with Warda, 'His Eyelid Teaches Love'. Placing a fez on her head, the Khojah started singing. She was mimicking Abdel Wahab. The women were playing, snapping their fingers as they started to sway. The *kamancheh* player stunned me. She was very pretty. I also saw a woman holding her girlfriend who was sitting on the floor beside her. Then she plunged her hand in between her thighs in order to stroke her down there. Both of them were in the second row, which allowed them to hide from prying eyes. Her girlfriend surrendered. She rested her head on her shoulders, closed her eyes and smiled as if in a dream. A little while later I saw the women looking behind them. A young woman dressed in a *gallabiya* made from embroidered white silk *saya* came forward and stood in front of Khojah Bahira so the women could admire her height and her beauty.

"All the women were staring at her, as if they had been bewitched by some kind of magic spell. Even the woman who had been caressing between her girlfriend's thighs removed her hand, mesmerised by this young woman. The band was on to their second song, 'Why Do You Tease Me?' by Mounira Mahdiya. Khojah Bahira hadn't started singing yet. I looked over at her. The magic spread to me as well. I became completely still. Even my breathing slowed down. It was the young woman from the station.

"I pulled the curtain back all the way and pushed my face up against the glass. I forgot about trying to stay hidden. What good was that caution in the presence of such magic? Just then she started to dance. My movement had attracted her attention and she was staring up at me, smiling sweetly. Her smile calmed me. What was this dance that so captivated all the women and me? It wasn't a dance, more like effortless movements to the rhythm of the music. My heart was pounding. My entire body was quivering because of my long-lost love; now, all of a sudden, I saw her dancing right before my eyes. Khojah Bahira also saw me but she didn't pay me any mind. I received another look, then a third, then a fourth. Whenever she looked over in my direction, she would smile. Later on she would tell me that she had been smiling at the hilarious sight of me, with my face distorted against the window pane.

"I didn't realise what I was doing until I had walked down the stairs and was approaching the living-room door. I was burning up with love and my desire to see her up close. I also wanted her to see me. My love had no meaning if she didn't notice me, didn't recognise me. The path between the rows of chairs began at the living-room door and ended where the

197

musicians were. I stood by the door, unconcerned with the anger my presence might stir up among those women who were accustomed to covering themselves whenever men were around. In those days, I was more confident than most men. I stood there without taking my eyes off of her. From time to time she would look at me and our eyes would meet. She was so gorgeous. Without even being aware of it, I started to move through the chairs in her direction. When Khojah Bahira noticed how mesmerised I was by her dancer's beauty, she frowned even as she kept on singing. I stood in the middle of the space; Widad looked at me while she danced. It seemed as though she were dancing for me and me alone.

"The Khojah finished singing and the dancer stopped dancing. We were face to face. For some strange reason the women didn't seem to notice me at all. They were too taken by the dancer, as well as the soft ambience all around her.

"'What's a man doing at a women's party?' Khojah Bahira demanded, angrily gesturing at me.

"The women needed a few seconds to extricate themselves from the grip of the dancer and absorb what Bahira had just said. I was gazing into the eyes of my enchantress, and she was gazing right back at me. All of a sudden a maelstrom of judgements and ululations broke out as the women realised they would have to conceal their feelings as well as their chests and their legs. Many of them noticed that their hands were in places they shouldn't be. When I looked over at my uncle's wife, I saw her whining as she pointed towards the door. Just then I felt myself being shoved by my aunt's servants and by Khadija. I was so mesmerised that I didn't even notice what was happening. I collapsed outside the living room. Khadija brought me to my senses and started pushing me upstairs to my room. I cast one backward glance at the dancer and saw her doubled over in laughter at what was going on all around her.

As I was being prodded upstairs by Khadija's two powerful hands, I heard Khojah Bahira introducing her dancer after everyone had calmed down. She said her name was Widad…'"

"So you had been searching all over town for your sweetheart, and you ended up meeting her inside your own house?" I asked the kindly old man.

"That's right. It never occurred to me that I might see her at our place, especially because I saw her for the first time as a young woman arriving from the countryside. The second time I saw her she had been transformed into a well-known and much-loved dancer."

"Weren't you a little bit disappointed to discover that she had become a dancer?"

"On the contrary. She was so attractive. You might say that her beauty was extraordinary. And the way she moved, it was as though she were doling out tenderness to each and every person. That's what made her seem a sorceress. My love for her only grew."

"Then what happened?"

"Everyone at the party thought I was acting strangely. Hamideh Khanum complained about me to my uncle Ibrahim Pasha. He called for me that night and started shouting: 'We try so hard to provide for you, you little ingrate, but you're never going to grow up!' He told me he couldn't understand why I would walk in on those honourable women while they were unveiled. He said he was going to punish me for it."

"Well, did he?"

"The truth is that he was convinced the dancer had hyp-notised me just as she enchanted everyone else. He decided to keep me out of the house during the next party."

The old man was smiling calmly. He had forgotten all about Ismail. The memory of his first encounter with Widad had put him in a good mood. But I found the whole thing rather strange. I was sitting there with a loaded rifle in my hands, constantly watching the window, or looking over towards the door, then over at Shaykh Nafeh lying in bed. It was so odd that I should be defending his memories with a gun and trying to keep Ismail, a man still incomprehensible to me, from putting a stop to our conversation. I cautiously stood up, as if I were racing from one trench to another, and picked up the framed photograph I had hidden from Ismail's view. I gazed at Widad, standing on the stairs of the train, just above the head of Monsieur de Martel.

"I spent the next few days totally confused about what to do," the old man said. "I had found the young woman from the station but she was still so remote from me. Sometimes I was ecstatic, sometimes I was sad. Love had found me but there were still many difficulties. Should I just go and talk to her? What would I do if I found myself face to face with her? What could I possibly say to her? Should I tell her I was in love with her? Would Khojah Bahira let me talk to her? Hundreds of questions were running through my head and I didn't have the answer to a single one. I was fed up with the vow to marry my cousin. That is, the vow made by my dead father, who had linked my inheritance to my marrying overweight Jalila. Then there was the fact that Widad had become a dancer. I was sure she had more admirers than there were hairs on my head. And finally there was the intimate relationship she had with her Khojah, which I'd heard about while eavesdropping on my aunt and her friends. Did my love for her have any hope?

"Khadija could sense what I was up to. She noticed I was always distracted and sighing. Sleep didn't come easy for me. I started asking her to leave me alone so I could stay up late with the newspaper. She could tell what my problem was without knowing specifically that the dancer was the same woman I had fallen in love with at the train station. She thought I was a strange young man who fell in love with every young woman he met. That's what she said when she invited me to tell her what was bothering me. One time, after everyone had gone to bed, she said, 'We're alone now. Nobody can hear us. Tell me, Nafeh, are you in love with the dancer?'

"She whispered this, as if someone were pressing their ear against my door.

"'Yes, I love her, Khaddouj,' I replied. 'I'm so clueless when it comes to affairs of the heart.'

"'When will you stop falling for young girls? They're a dime a dozen. Besides, it isn't healthy to fall in love with every woman you see.'

"I looked right at her. She was right to say that. But she didn't realise that the girl at the station was also Widad the dancer.

"'It's her,' I said with a sigh.

"'What do you mean?'

"'I mean, I finally found the girl from the station. It's Widad.'

"Khadija needed some time to process what I was saying. She repeated to herself several times: *Is she the same person?*

201

Is she the same person? I nodded at her, and she leant forward on her knees and stood up. She began to pace around the room silently, picking up a few things here and there. She was thinking. Then she came back and sat down next to me.

"'But she's a dancer and a *bint al-ishreh*', she whispered.

"'I don't care,' I said, slightly irritated. 'If I never get the chance to see her again and speak to her, I'll just die.'

"'You won't die if you don't get another chance to talk to her. Now your uncle Ibrahim Pasha, he'll kill you if he finds out about this.'

"'Please, tell me how I can meet her. I don't know what's come over me since the day I first saw her. Help me figure out what to do next.'

"'Khojah Bahira will never let you near her. She's a woman hunter. Everybody in town knows that. Now that Widad's her *ablaya*, she'll bare her fangs to defend Widad, if necessary.'

"'Where does Khojah Bahira live?' I asked without regard for the Khojah's fangs.

"Khadija stood up and moved towards the door. The poor dear was worried about me in my lovestruck mood.

"She paused and whispered, 'I'll find out tomorrow. But God forbid…'

"Then she walked out and shut the door behind her. I stayed awake until morning.

"Two days later I was standing outside Khojah Bahira's house. It was late afternoon. I hadn't been able to come up with an excuse to leave the soap workshop until later in the day. I told my uncle I had a stomach ache and diarrhoea, so he let me go. I didn't go home, though. I went straight to the Farafrah neighbourhood instead. That morning I had made up my mind. I put on my finest clothes, knotted an elegant tie around my neck under my starched white collar, and styled my hair with scented lotion. I was perfectly presentable standing there at the door. Nevertheless, I checked my hair to make sure that everything was perfect. I had thought about bringing a bouquet of flowers but I hadn't been able to find any on the way, and I didn't want to lose time by going home first.

"The neighbourhood was quiet. There were some people walking past, a little boy playing in the street. I was nervous of what would happen when I knocked on the door. I envied the little boy his innocence and his lack of involvement in romantic affairs. I placed my hand on my heart and found it beating more quickly than usual. I thought my face must have turned yellow; it might even have gone blood red. I waited there for an infinitely long time, standing and thinking. Then I heard Khadija's voice urging me on. When I turned around to look for her, I realised I had been hearing things. I pumped myself up, telling myself that whatever was going to happen was going to happen, that they weren't going to kill me. Then I gave a short prayer, walked up the stairs, and knocked on the door.

"The woman who had been playing *kamancheh* at the salon opened the door. She was kind but confused and asked me delicately, 'Yes? Can I help you?'

"She was smiling sweetly, which encouraged me to open my mouth and stammer, 'Khojah Bahira's house, please?'

"'This is Khojah Bahira's house. What do you want?'

"'I would like to see Miss Widad.'

"She stared at me with great curiosity, scrutinising my face, my shiny hair and my clothes. She was confused but she stayed calm, becoming even a bit more so. Apparently I had impressed her.

"'Who wants to see her?'

"'Nafeh Effendi, Hamideh Khanum's nephew,' I said, introducing myself.

"'Ahhhh...' she said, nodding her head to indicate that she recognised me.

"'You're the one who showed up at the women's party...'

"'Yes, ma'am. May I...'

"'What do you want with Miss Widad?'

"What could I say? I should have prepared myself for questions like that.

"'It's just that... I'd like to see her,' I said simply.

"She nodded to indicate that she understood, then calmed me with a smile that seemed to indicate sympathy with my awkward situation. She invited me inside and led me down a dark hallway. She was wearing a pink summer dress, and because we were walking towards daylight, I imagined I could see the outlines of her body through the diaphanous material, so I looked away. She pointed towards a simple couch in the *iwan* and asked me to sit down. Then she went into one of the bedrooms.

"I sat on the edge of the couch, pulled my knees in close, and folded my hands in my lap. That's the way I'd sit sometimes when I was in someone else's house. I felt as though the earth were shaking under my feet, then under the couch I was sitting on. I soon realised that the whole world seemed to be shaking because of my overactive heartbeat. I looked up to see two women staring down at me from the upstairs bedroom. I recognised them from my aunt's party as the percussionist and the *qanun* player. The *qanun* player was leaning against the shoulder of the percussionist. They were both smiling as they whispered to one another. As soon as I looked away from them, I heard movement in the two downstairs rooms that were separated by opposing staircases. The *kamancheh* player who had let me in disappeared into one of those rooms. Instinctively I looked up to see Khojah Bahira poking her head out from one of those rooms to size me up. I could tell she wasn't happy to see me in her house. She pulled her head back inside before I could look away. I noticed that the two staircases had beautiful wrought-iron banisters leading up to a platform connecting the two rooms. I could hear whispering coming from the room. The Khojah's raspy voice grew louder but the conversation remained inaudible to me.

"My anxiety grew. Maybe she was asking the *kamancheh* player to kick me out. A long time passed like that. I amused myself by looking at the plant climbing along the length of the wall, musing that it probably grew up and over the wall, towards the street. I heard laughter coming from upstairs, then a door opening and soft footsteps. I turned around to find Widad standing on the landing, holding on to the banister: beautiful, elegant, bashful. Her eyes were all enchantment. She was wearing a plain housedress that hung down to her knees. I carefully stood up to greet her. I wasn't sure I wouldn't collapse to the ground. She smiled at me, then looked away and came down the steps, walked over to the *iwan* and stood right there in front of me. She extended her hand to shake mine. I was trembling. She welcomed me and sat down on the couch. I sat down next to her.

"Time went by. I didn't know what to say. We sat there in silence. From time to time I would look over at her to find her twiddling her thumbs, just as I was. I looked up and saw Khojah Bahira and the *kamancheh* player staring down at us from the bedroom. Craning my head, I saw the other two women looking down on us from upstairs as well. What kind of a visit was this? How was I going to speak to her?"

"But you must have said something…" I told the kindly old man. "To introduce yourself to her, I mean."

"Finally I managed to force myself to say something. There were five pairs of eyes staring at me."

"What did you say?"

"I said, 'My name's Nafeh and we met at my aunt Hamideh Khanum's salon the previous Monday.' She nodded and told me she knew that. Then we had a conversation in something like a whisper.

"'I saw you once before, a long time ago.'

"'Where?'

"'At the train station. We were welcoming back the delegation coming from Paris.'

"'Ahhh, that's right! I was just arriving in Aleppo.'

"'But I lost sight of you in the crowd. Ever since that day I've been looking for you.'

"'Why?'

"'I don't know what to say exactly. I was smitten. Then I bought a newspaper. They had run that photo, the one with you in the background, behind the delegation, above the head of Monsieur de Martel.'

"'I was in the photo?'

"'I have two copies. I'll give you one.'

"'Thank you.'

"'Your name's Widad.'

"'Yes.'

"'I'm Nafeh.'

"'I know. You just told me that.'

"'Ahhh, right. Can we go out sometime? We could go to the park for a picnic, for example, or to the cinema, if you prefer. They're showing a new Mohammed Abdel Wahab film.'

"'I don't know. I don't think Khojah Bahira would approve.'

"'Let me speak to her.'

"We fell silent. We sat there, looking away from one other, the conversation at an end. I could feel her looking up at my face. When I looked over to do the same, our eyes locked. Time went by. I considered getting up to leave but she stopped me by asking in a hushed voice, 'Why did you want to see me?'

"My answer this time was quick and direct: 'Because I love you.'

"I continued gazing into her eyes. I really did love her. I would have died for her. She was flummoxed by my answer, by my confession of my love for her. Her face turned red and she tried to look away, but continued gazing right back at me. I felt she was happy to hear about my love for her, that she wanted to accept it.

"We were both startled when we heard Suad the *kamancheh* player hurrying downstairs to ask us if we'd like some tea. I said, 'No thank you,' and asked to speak with Khojah Bahira before I left. Suad stopped. Instead of going to the kitchen, she went over to the *iwan*. She was very sweet, and seemed to be enjoying this event. Still, she was worried about what the Khojah might do to me; the way she looked at me told me so.

"'Why do you want to see Khojah Bahira?' the *kamancheh* player asked in a whisper.

"'I need to ask for her permission,' I replied, my courage renewed.

"'What do you mean?'

"'To take Miss Widad to the cinema.'

"'I sensed there was some danger in what I was asking the *kamancheh* player. She turned around in a hurry and glanced towards the banister. Through the crack in her bedroom door, I could see the Khojah pacing and watching us agitatedly.

"'Right now?' the musician asked me.

"As I looked over at Widad, I could tell she wanted me to do this.

"'Not right now. Some other day.'

"'Go now, then,' she said, as though she had found the perfect solution. 'We'll come up with a way to make it happen. The Khojah doesn't have to know about it. She despises men.'

"I walked back towards the foyer with the two women behind me. I opened the door and asked Suad, 'When should I come back?'

"'We'll find a way to get in touch with you. Don't come back until then. Goodbye.'

"I grabbed Widad's hand under the pretence of shaking and saying goodbye. Her hands were moist with sweat. She seemed to agree with everything I said. She was hooked on me. I pulled away and left. When the door closed, I leant against the wall to gather my strength. I'd used all my strength to make my first and last adventure a success.

"The nearby voice of the muezzin was calling out the dusk prayer, tender and reassuring. I looked up at the sky and said,

'O Lord.' I saw the climbing vines of ivy. They had tumbled over to the outside wall, just as I suspected. I wiped the sweat from my brow and started walking home slowly."

The old man fell silent. He closed his eyes and remained quiet. As far as I could tell, he was trying to pinpoint the exact moment in his memory. He was breathing heavily. Some of the wrinkles in his face were trembling. I looked at the photograph for the last time and returned the frame to its place behind the curtain. The rain was loud, creating a regular and pleasing rhythm. Just then it occurred to me to look at my watch. It was past twelve. A new problem floated to the surface of my mind. How was I going to feed Shaykh Nafeh? I stood up and pressed my ear to the door. I thought perhaps I had heard voices downstairs. The strange thing was that Ismail hadn't moved since I'd kicked him out of the bedroom by threatening him with the rifle. I continued to listen for a moment but didn't hear a thing. I drew away from the door and turned towards the window. I tried to look out through the blinds. The inky darkness prevented me from seeing the back garden. I moved away from the window. I was nervous. The old man was snoring softly, his mouth open. Suddenly I had the urge to go back to the window because I sensed something unusual. Maybe the light reflecting on the glass had kept me from seeing out. I switched off the lights and hurried over to it. I would have shouted from fright had I not thrown my hand over my mouth. There was a head there, just below the window, blocking out the natural light. Two white orbs were looking right at me through the two slats. I was sure it was Ismail. Apparently he had got a wooden ladder and was climbing up in the rain to spy on me. Before he could see me in the darkness of the room, I threw open the window and his head vanished. I pushed aside the window frame and looked down. There he was, Ismail, trying to scurry down quickly. I pointed the rifle at him and shouted at him to freeze.

Ismail stopped where he was and looked up at me. He was glistening from the rain that soaked him, sopping wet and hurling spite towards me. If the rifle had been in his hands instead of mine, he would have shot me right then and there.

"You're spying on us, you son of a bitch!" I spat—but I whispered so as not to bother Shaykh Nafeh. "Aren't you at all afraid that I might kill you?"

"Kill me?" He paused a beat before continuing, "You're a motherfucking coward. You couldn't even kill another dog like you."

"I swear to God. I'll kill you if you don't stop pushing me."

He let out a short, derisive snort. As he climbed back up two steps I could see him more clearly.

"What are you trying to get out of all this?" he asked me. "Why don't you just get out of here? Leave us alone. I swear I'll let you go in peace."

"Don't start with me. I'm going to stay here with the old man. He needs me."

"For the story?"

"He needs to get it out. I'm helping him by listening."

"How long are you going to stay? Until he's finished?"

"None of your business."

"It's not worth it. I'm going to kill you before you can leave."

"I'm the one with the rifle. It's aimed at your head as we speak. Let me hear the rest of the story in peace. When it's over, I'll be on my way."

"I don't want you to hear the end of the story. Even if you do, you'll be dead before you have the chance to take it with you back to the city."

"But why?"

"Because the city has forgotten all about it. I don't want people to start talking again."

"But it's the story of the old man's life."

"And my own life, you goddamned homewrecker."

So that was it. Ismail had some important connection to the story. He was a part of it. I had been expecting that.

"It won't be long before the old man passes away. He's had a long and full life," he went on, but with a much more intense edge than before. "At that point, I'll go back to Aleppo. I don't want the story to get there before me. I'm going to live out my life there. I'll defend my reputation and my dignity with every fibre of my being. If you think this rifle is the only weapon in the house, you've got another thing coming. The problem is I don't want to kill you in front of the old man. You do realise that you were in the crosshairs of my pistol just a little while ago. The old man is the problem."

The rifle wobbled in my hand. It was no longer aimed at his head. So he had a weapon. He reached down to his waist, pulled it out, and held it up for me to see. He smiled wickedly as he slid it back under his waistband. He seemed to be saying something else but I couldn't understand him. I was hung up on the matter of weapons. Ismail was dangling there by my mercy as I gripped the hunting rifle. I knew it was out of ammo, but I didn't have the heart to use it anyway. Like he said, I'm a motherfucking coward. I didn't want to kill anybody, even if it was Ismail, who was just waiting for the chance to get rid of me the same way he'd got rid of Dr Fares, as far as I could tell. Meanwhile, he had a pistol, but he wouldn't use it against me as long as I was protected by the old man. But what if the old man were to die? The thought terrified me. This meant that my life was bound up with the old man's. I would have to protect him.

My upper torso was sticking out the window. Rain was pouring down on me, but it didn't bother me at all. My only concern was the old man, and how to keep him fed.

"The old man has to eat," I told Ismail gently.

"The old man's gonna die, O Great Master, all for the sake of your stupid story. And you know what's going to happen to you if anything happens to him." Then he added, "Why don't you just let me come in and feed him?"

"You know I'm not going to let you inside. You'll bring the food at the appointed times, and I'll take care of the rest."

"Come on, go back to your room and we can all get back to our normal lives."

He was trying to lure me away from the old man's room so he could carry out his plot against me. I refused.

"You knew full well that I'd say no way," I said. "I also love life."

"Are you afraid I'm going to kill you?"

"Absolutely. You're going to kill me as soon as I'm away from the old man."

"Aren't you afraid I might poison you?"

"You're going to bring the same food. You won't give me a special plate. I'm going to eat the same thing you give Shaykh Nafeh."

He was silent for a few moments while he thought the matter over. It seemed he didn't have any other choice. Through gritted teeth he grunted how much he hated me, how I wouldn't get out of there alive. Then he climbed all the way down the ladder. I watched him walk away, cursing me nonstop until he disappeared on the other side of the garden. I shut the window, switched the light back on, and dried myself off. I took off my wet clothes and borrowed a shirt from the old man's closet. After half an hour I heard Ismail's footsteps walking down the hall. He placed something on the ground, tapped on the door, and then drew away. When I opened the door he was standing by the staircase. He spat and then went back downstairs. There was a serving tray with a number of plates, some drinking water, and the old man's medication. I carried the tray inside and locked the door once again. After waking the old man, I fed him and gave him his medication. I placed the tray back in the hallway, then crawled into bed beside him and fell asleep, cradling the rifle.

In the morning the old man roused me with a gentle nudge. At first I was disoriented to find myself in his bed, but after a few seconds I recalled the events of the previous day. The rifle was on the floor beside the bed. The first thing he asked after waking me up was to go to the bathroom.

"The bathroom?" I asked, yet another chore that was required when taking care of him. I also needed to use the bathroom. I stood up, grabbed the rifle, and hurried over to the window. The rain was still coming down. The garden was peaceful. I looked for Ismail but didn't see him. Even the wooden ladder had disappeared. I backed away from the window and stood in front of the bed, clutching the rifle as I considered the best way to get to the bathroom without running into Ismail. Apparently I was a funny sight because the old man was smiling, and then he burst out laughing.

"You look like a moron who's kidnapped someone and then finds himself in a tough spot."

"So that's what you think of me, huh?"

"Precisely. You've got try to understand where Ismail's coming from. If you knew the reason why he doesn't want you to hear this story, you'd forgive him. Anyway, I'm happy to see you fighting so hard for this. If you keep it up, I'll stand with you. We'll find a way to work things out with Ismail. I just ask that you think kindly of him despite his actions. Come on, let's go to the bathroom."

I helped him get up and put on his robe. I slid back the bolt and opened the door. The breakfast tray was sitting right there. The old man and I smiled. Ismail had done his job to perfection. We walked the five paces to the bathroom. I was listening intently, trying my best to hear any movement Ismail might make to announce his presence.

"Ismail told me that this story is his story as well, the story of his life."

"Yes," the old man said, not looking at me. "That's true."

"What did he mean by that?" I asked as he opened the bathroom door.

"You'll understand everything once the story is finished. Are you or aren't you patient enough?"

I told him I'd be patient. Then I helped him into the bathroom, took off his robe, and left, shutting the door behind me. I moved towards the staircase and crouched down in a fighting posture, rifle at the ready.

The ground floor was quiet. Everything was as it should have been, clean and organised. Where was Ismail? What was he up to? What did he have in store for me? I heard a sound coming from my bedroom. I stood up and pointed the rifle at the door. I walked without making a sound, and when I reached the door I pressed my ear up against it. No sound. I pulled back. I was afraid. I was the one with the rifle, but I wasn't going to be able to use it. I didn't have the right to do so. The old man had just asked me to think kindly of Ismail, to try and understand where he was coming from. The story was his story, too. I never thought I would become so obsessed with a story about a person like Ismail. It was his own past he hated so much. I heard another noise coming from my room. I was certain it was Ismail. Maybe I was wrong. I retreated to the bathroom door and waited there until the old man was ready. I went in when he called out for me. I helped him with his robe and he left me there to clean up myself. He told me he was going to wait outside until I was finished. He was my only protection then, not the rifle.

After we'd had breakfast and sat down on the couch, the old man said:

"The following days passed extremely slowly. Every time there was a knock on the door, I expected it would be Widad, or someone with news from Widad. I spent those nights in real anguish. Sleep abandoned me, and I became more and more distracted. I started being able to recognise Widad's sweet facial features in the photographs more easily after having met her in person. I would place the photograph directly under the light and begin drifting off with the idea of her until morning. After a week had passed without their calling me as Suad had promised, I became increasingly anxious, increasingly suspicious that Khojah Bahira had forbidden them from getting in touch. She must have really hated me. I would ask my uncle Ibrahim Pasha for permission to leave the soap workshop to hurry over to the Khojah's street, which wasn't far from work. I'd just stand there staring at the door, waiting for Widad to look out. Then just as abruptly I'd head back to work when I grew tired of waiting for another chance to ask for the Khojah's permission, and on and on.

"Inside Khojah Bahira's house what actually happened was exactly what I suspected. Much later Widad told me everything. I had been on her mind ever since I had wandered into the women's gathering at my uncle's house. I had impressed her. I was the spitting image of the heroes in those tales her housemaid Fatima used to tell her. Widad would confide in Suad, talking to her about me at times. Suad was able to confirm that I was Hamideh Khanum's son, and Widad learnt that I was an orphan, just like her. Apparently this commonality made her care about me even more. There's something else I have to mention that also helped me win this round against Khojah Bahira. I was a handsome and elegant young man in his twenties, brimming with vitality and sophistication, whereas the Khojah was nearly fifty-five. The truth of the matter was that Suad herself preferred the company of men, and she began to encourage Widad's desires. The two of them would talk about me whenever they were alone together. But the Khojah, her *ablaya*, could sense that her sweetheart's mind was elsewhere. She asked her about

216

it, but Widad hid her feelings for me from the Khojah. Suad warned her not to talk openly about me for fear of stirring up Bahira's jealousy. On the day I went to visit them, when Suad informed her of my arrival, her cheeks turned all red and she started crying.

"The Khojah tried to forbid Widad from seeing me. She asked Suad to kick me out at once. But the *kamancheh* player convinced her it wasn't such a bad idea for Widad to spend time with me because I was the nephew of Hamideh Khanum, one of their most important clients. She argued that there was nothing to fear from Widad spending time with someone of my social class. After I left, Bahira had felt, with the expert and subtle intuition of a woman, that this love story might have been developing. She became irritable, perpetually on edge and began to forbid Widad from going out except when she was with her. She would constantly talk to her about the savage men who took women by force and tore them limb from limb—like feral dogs, wild animals. They didn't know anything about love but would seize a woman and destroy her virginity, impregnate her and force her to have their children. They planted impurity at the core of women, who then demanded ritual cleansing. They insisted that women wash their feet. If they got sick, women had to become their nursemaids. If they grew tired of a woman, they would kick her out and replace her with someone else.

"But all that talk couldn't convince Widad to hate me or stop thinking about me. She would simply listen to her *ablaya* and nod her head. Yet she would be thinking about the day when we could be together. Suad told her to be patient. But what could I do in the meantime?

"One day our chance came. I was sitting on the veranda looking out onto the street when I saw a boy approaching our building. He stopped at the garden gate and tried to find a way to knock on the door. At first he didn't see me, so I stood up so that he could. My heart told me he had a message for me, just as Suad had promised. I went down to meet him at the gate. He told me that I should go to the Roxy Cinema at once. He handed me a ticket for the three o'clock screening as well as a handwritten note from Suad asking me to come in only after the film had already started, so that it would be dark and nobody would be able to see me. I gave the boy a respectable tip and hurried back upstairs. I put on some nicer clothes, slapped on some cologne, greased my hair until it was shiny and then styled it. I placed a white rose in my coat pocket and raced over to Baron Street. I stood at the entrance to the cinema, listening to the brass band playing while people filed inside. The film was a French tragedy. I didn't happen to notice the title, and I couldn't understand why the two women had arranged for us to meet at the screening of a depressing foreign film. As soon as they announced that the film had begun, I handed my ticket to the attendant and went inside. The usher escorted me to a private box for families. He led me inside and then left, drawing a curtain aside for me. The film was showing a woman weeping over the dead body of her husband or beloved. As I stood there in the box, my own beloved Widad and her friend Suad were sitting right in front of me. Both of them turned towards me. In the glow of the screen I could see both of them smiling at me encouragingly. I was perhaps a confusing sight. Or maybe I looked funny with my shiny hair and the rose jammed into my coat pocket.

Suad gestured towards the empty seat beside Widad, and I sat down. We sat there in silence watching what was happening on the screen in front of us. Neither of us knew what to do. I had to offer the first word but I had forgotten everything I had planned to say. Finally we bridged the gap by turning to look into each other's eyes.

"Widad was exceedingly beautiful in the darkness and the glow of the screen. In that moment I knew I was in love with her, that I would do whatever it took to win her love, no matter what it cost me. I also knew that she loved me. She would smile whenever we locked eyes. I cautiously reached out my hand, asking for hers. As she turned back towards the screen, she held my hand. It was warm; her touch gave me indescribable feelings. I could feel her soft and regular pulse. I squeezed her hand gently and she reciprocated. She became increasingly soft and pliant. After a while, her hand started to sweat. I took out my handkerchief and dabbed at her hand.

"'This is the second time my hand has started sweating when we've seen each other,' she whispered, leaning her head towards mine.

"'Don't worry. I'll dry it off with my handkerchief.'

"'But you'll miss the film.'

"'I'm here to see you and you alone.' I felt myself bursting with words as I whispered, 'I'm so happy I found you. I'm even happier that you love me back. Do you have any idea what's going on inside my heart?'

"She stared back at me, as if to ask what was going on in my heart.

"'I'm yours. I'll do whatever it takes to be with you. I want you to love me as much as I love you.'

"'I...'

Her hand, still in mine, had started to sweat again and I dried it once more. She really did love me.

"'I want to marry you,' I said.

"She continued to stare at me. She squeezed my hand. She said she wanted the same thing, but then she corrected herself, 'I have a problem. And you have a problem, too.'

"She was right. I had a serious problem in my cousin Jalila, and the matter of the inheritance. Her problem was Khojah Bahira.

"'Khojah Bahira?' I asked her.

"'That's right.'

"'I'm going to give up the inheritance, and you're going to run away from the Khojah. Isn't that what you want?'

"She gazed into my eyes for a long time, unable to respond. She continued watching the film. 'Isn't that what you want?' I asked her a second time, but she didn't answer. I just left her damp hand resting in mine. What I understood in that moment was how difficult the whole thing seemed to her. We remained in that position until I heard Suad ask me to leave before the film was over. She told me she would send the boy again with a new card and a new appointment. Then she said goodbye. The promise of another appointment put me at ease. Widad stared into my eyes and squeezed my hand one more time. She took the rose from my coat pocket, then raised it to her lips and kissed it. I said goodbye, stood up and left. As I closed the curtain behind me, they watched me go. Once I had left the cinema, I couldn't go home right away. I wandered around the citadel, breathing in the smell of her sweat on my handkerchief. At home, too, my nose was filled with her scent. I was so happy that I forgot all about the hardships that lay ahead of us.

"We met up several times in the private box at the Roxy Cinema. The more we came to love one another, the bolder we became. The last time she let her head rest on my shoulder, her hand in mine, as we watched the film. We attended many screenings together and often didn't remember a thing about the films themselves. But *Widad* with Umm Kulthum was one of my favourites because it had the same name as my beloved. The heroine Widad was a slavegirl with an angelic voice in the time of the Mamluks. Baher the merchant was her master, and he loved her very much but had to sell her after he lost all his money when bandits raided his caravan. We cried for the two lovers separated by fate. And oh how we cheered along with the audience when Baher was able to recoup his money and bring back his sweetheart. I saw that film several times, either by myself or with my friend Sad Malek. When we watched the film together, my Widad told me I was like Baher, the film's hero. I told her I was ready to spend all of my inheritance on her if Khojah Bahira were willing to sell her. We were both very moved by Umm Kulthum's singing. We memorised all the songs, especially 'You Like the Way I Love You'. Often Widad would whisper the opening line of that song in order to express her pure affection. I used to sing the song out loud when I was alone in my room. It was a way to call out for my sweetheart.

"We saw *The White Rose* with Mohammed Abdel Wahab three times together because the cinema extended its run for several weeks. We would sing along with Galal Effendi, a man forced to be apart from his love, Raga, played by the fresh-faced Samira Kholoussy, songs like 'O Rose of Pure Love' and 'My Moaning Makes You Sad' and 'My Pain, My Unhappiness'. I went to see the well-known film *Long Live Love* by myself a year and a half later. At that time I was in very bad shape, psychologically speaking.

"We also saw *Anthem of the Heart* by George Abyad, which was about a European dancer who drove a husband to leave his wife. We didn't like that one very much because the dancer was a bad person, whereas my beloved dancer was amazing and mind-blowing. But together we watched the films of Naguib el-Rihani, in which he played a character called Kashkash Bey. That was an indispensable opportunity for us to forget about the world altogether. We would laugh from deep in our hearts at the adventures of Kashkash Bey. We saw *Kashkash Bey, His Majesty and Yaqout Effendi* and *The Adventures of Kashkash Bey*. The last Naguib el-Rihani film we saw together was *He Wants to Get Married*, and we laughed so hard, tears streamed down our cheeks.

"I told you how I would hold her clammy hand all the time. Every time we met, I would pull a new handkerchief from my pocket and soak it with the sweat from her hand. Then, when I got home, I would hide it somewhere cool so it would stay damp and retain her sweat and its smell for as long as possible. Eventually I had about a dozen of those handkerchiefs. I still have all of them to this day."

That last sentence really struck me, so I jumped up.

"Do you really still have all those handkerchiefs?" I asked, interrupting him.

"Yes, I kept them all."

"May I see them?"

He nodded for me to go over to the dresser. I hopped over there, opened it and peered inside. He gestured towards the top shelf where there was a wooden box inlaid with pearl. I brought it down and took it over to him. He asked me to open it. There were several things inside: some old silver currency; an ornamental sash that dancers used to wear around their waist in the olden days, women's barrettes; a lock of blonde hair; folded-up papers that looked like notes; a large number of torn Roxy Cinema ticket stubs stamped with identical numbers; a plastic bag with a dozen white handkerchiefs folded carefully; and a few other small inconsequential things.

I took a handkerchief out of the plastic bag and held it to my nose, searching for Widad's smell. I imagined I could detect the delicate smell of feminine sweat, mostly evaporated over the years. I didn't smell soap or detergent, which meant that the smell on the handkerchief, whatever it was, was the smell of Widad. I pressed the cloth against my nose for a moment, until I had memorised the smell, and then returned everything to its place and closed the dresser.

I sat back down near the old man. We needed a few moments' silence: for him to remember that smell, and for me to inscribe it in my memory. Without my prodding him, Shaykh Nafeh began again:

"We were very happy during those innocent trysts under the guardianship of Suad, who chaperoned us and whom we loved, under protection of the darkness of the cinema, until the day we had feared and always knew would come. Khojah Bahira found out about our meetings."

I detected a cloud of sadness rolling over Shaykh Nafeh's face.

223

"How did she find out?" I asked him. "Who told her? Did someone catch you there, God forbid?"

"Nobody ever saw us together. We continued to take the same precautions whenever I was at the Roxy Cinema. I would come out, as I explained to you, before the end of the film, that is, before the lights went up."

"So how did that bitch manage to find you out?"

"The boy who used to deliver the tickets and the messages ratted on us."

"My God…" I said. I was surprised.

The old man was silent for a moment before explaining to me how it all came to pass.

"Bahira could feel Widad growing distant from her. She noticed that she was becoming distracted all the time. She no longer responded to caresses or kisses. She asked to be left alone, and spent time with Suad in a bedroom or on the roof-top. They would gossip with one another for long stretches of time. Khojah Bahira would ask Widad to join her at the *hammam* when she bathed. She began to notice how Widad would shrink away from her *ablaya*'s ageing female body. Widad would even avoid going to the *hammam* with her. In bed she would yawn and pretend to be asleep whenever Bahira tried to get intimate with her. When the Khojah asked why her sweetheart was drawing away from her in body and in spirit, Widad responded that everything was totally fine—she was tired—or she gave some other excuse. Bahira also asked Suad about it, but she would only ever say that she had no idea about Widad's state of mind. She allowed Suad to accompany Widad to the cinema to try to keep her happy. She was a young woman who had always adored love stories. She loved films. And although Bahira had refused at first, she eventually relented when she saw how sad Widad had become. The two young women would go to see a film every week and then tell Bahira the plot of whatever they had seen. As soon as they got back from the cinema, Widad would ask Suad and Aisha and Faridah to play for her so she could dance. Dancing to their music put her in a good mood, one befitting a woman who had just come back from a rendezvous with her sweetheart. At the end of the night, once she had danced and laughed to her heart's content, she would evade Bahira's caresses and kisses and advances. If her *ablaya* tried to embrace her once they were in bed together, she would ask her to leave her in peace so she could sleep. Widad was becoming happier and more beautiful but also more distant. Bahira sensed this right away because of how much she loved her and how jealous she could be. Nobody likes to see their significant other so affected by experiences they have nothing to do with. One time she sent Bahiya, the *oud* player married to the pimp, to follow them and find out whether they were actually going to see films together. Did they go inside together and come out together? Bahiya reported that there was nothing to be suspicious of. But with Widad's continuous and inexplicable coolness, Bahira started to monitor her more closely. Finally she noticed how the baker's employee who delivered their bread every day would speak to Suad for a long time. The last time, after Suad and Widad had left for the cinema, the Khojah summoned the young man and told him he should tell her everything because she already knew what was going on anyway. She threatened to report him to his boss if he didn't tell her the truth. If he told her what she wanted to hear, she would reward him with a silver *majidi* coin. The young man spilt the beans. He told her all about the tickets and the messages he delivered to a young man named Nafeh. And immediately Bahira knew it was me. My visit to her house was unforgettable.

"Khojah Bahira was a clever and experienced woman. She had learnt how to handle her sweetheart in a situation like this. She welcomed Suad and Widad as if everything were normal when they returned from the cinema. She even enjoyed Widad's dancing, her laughter and coquettishness. She praised her more than any previous night. The next day she went over to Hamideh Khanum's house and told her what was going on between Widad and me. She convinced my aunt that I was smitten by Widad's dancing, that Widad knew my soft spots and was taking advantage of me so I would marry her. Bahira left our place before I got home, having sown fears for her daughter's future and that of the soap workshop in Hamideh Khanum's heart.

"Hamideh Khanum told my uncle everything. I was in my room trying to write some poetry to my beloved when my uncle called me into the living room. When I got there, he asked me to close the door. As I did so, I spotted Hamideh Khanum and Jalila staring at me and scowling. I didn't understand what was happening until my uncle Ibrahim Pasha opened his yellowish mouth, which was quivering with anger. He cursed me and then hit me with an ashtray. He hurled every possible insult at me. He told me I was worthless, lost, a blind adolescent who didn't know what was best for him. He said everyone would speak ill of the family. Then he said something about cheap dancers and I understood at once. I was frozen in place, in shock. How had he found out? Then he made up his mind. There was no going back. He had to protect the inheritance from my thoughtless behaviour. I was grounded from that point forward. I was not to leave the house unless accompanied by him. I wasn't to go to the soap workshop ever again. I would remain like that until his daughter was one year older, at which point I would have to marry her.

"'Now get out of my face, you miserable piece of shit,' my uncle roared at me. 'You're to stay in your room until the wedding. It's the end of the al-Aghyurli family when a boy comes along and falls in love with a dancer. Hah!'

"I kept my mouth shut and walked out of the living room in a daze. The world had gone black. For a few moments I considered killing myself. My uncle's wife was gloating and Jalila was crying, but I couldn't figure out what she was crying about. Was it out of sadness for me, or fear of losing me? Khadija marched me up to my room. She was the one crying, not me. She knew all about Widad and our meetings at the Roxy Cinema. Before I could ask her, she wept and swore she hadn't said a word, and that Khojah Bahira had visited Hamideh Khanum that day. I knew the gig was up.

"Yes, it was over. I was stuck in my uncle's house. I had to stay in my room. I was forbidden from leaving the house under any circumstance. Khadija attended to me in my room. She fed me there. If I wandered around the house at all, only when my uncle Ibrahim was at the soap workshop, I was met with spiteful stares from Hamideh Khanum and her pudgy daughter. So I preferred to stay in my room anyway. I would lie in bed thinking, despairing of the world. I cried a lot, especially at night, after Khadija had gone to bed. How could

I be so unlucky in love? I was despondent. As I mentioned, I even thought about killing myself.

"I began to hate life itself. What kind of an existence was one without Widad? And what had happened to her? What was Khojah Bahira doing to her?

"I imagined that she was forbidden from leaving her house, too. Was she crying about it? She had been so happy when we first fell in love. She so looked forward to our meetings at the Roxy Cinema, she told me, so she could place her sweaty hand in mine. She once told me that she had begun see life as easy, as beautiful. But now she had to perform for wealthy women in their salons, at weddings, put up with the attentions of vile Khojah Bahira. The very idea filled me with bile and a hatred of life. The image of them in bed together drove me mad. I believed Widad would no longer accept the advances of her *ablaya*, but how could I know for sure? The Khojah was trying to make her forget about me. Meanwhile, I was devastated, and my crisis was only getting worse.

"The truth is that Khojah Bahira concealed what she was up to. She let the two women go to the movies every week as usual. The boy from the bakery would take the ticket, the message and the *baksheesh* from Suad but he stopped coming to see me to deliver the goods and instead went straight to the Khojah and gave her whatever Suad had asked him to give me. The first time I didn't show up, Widad found it strange. But in the weeks that followed the whole thing became even more disturbing. She grew very sad. At first she thought I might be sick. Once they tried wandering around my neighbourhood and in front of my house on the off chance that I might appear. But at the time I was in bed, despairing of the world. I couldn't even get up to go out onto the veranda looking over the street. Suad went to the soap workshop. My uncle didn't know who she was. She told him she wanted to buy some soap. Suad left the soap workshop even more confused by not finding me there either. They two of them were wondering what could have happened to me, just as I wondered about Widad.

"At home Widad was becoming increasingly irritable. The Khojah was monitoring her, and knew the reason for her irritation. She wanted to keep control of her. I was a man. All men steal away women from her, so she had to stand up to them, to get in their face. Even if this irritated Widad temporarily, she would eventually get over it. The Khojah didn't want to relive the story of Widad's mother Badia, whom the Yuzbashi Cevdet had desired so madly and whom she'd lost for all eternity.

"The Khojah watched Widad while she sighed. She was burning up. She didn't know what could have made me stay away from her. She lay down in bed next to her *ablaya*. She let her do whatever she wanted, and when the Khojah was finished she would turn her back and stay awake until morning. The Khojah could hear her sighs. Her heart ached for Widad, but she was looking out for number one. Widad no longer asked the women to play so that she could dance when she and Suad got home from the cinema. At home her pain only grew worse. Bahira could read it all over her face. As soon as they got home she would disappear into her room, take off her clothes and immediately get into bed. She might cry for a bit as well. Bahira would try to cheer her up with gifts or with new plans for a party, but to no avail. Whenever she danced at a wedding or a women's salon, she did so with a mask of sadness on her face. Maybe that was why she had an even greater effect on the women than before. This layer of sadness made her ever more attractive and enchanting. That's women for you, always so romantic. Widad began to hate going to the cinema. Mohammed Abdel Wahab and Kashkash Bey, Naguib el-Rihani and Umm Kulthum, George Abyad and Bishara Wakim no longer meant anything to her.

"Khojah Bahira informed Suad that there was going to be a wedding party at Hamideh Khanum's house soon and that they were going to work it. This started Suad's mind churning. Could it be the wedding of the man who seemed to be on the verge of passing out from the intensity of his infatuation with Widad when they sat there together in the darkness of the cinema? Had he forgotten all about his love for her and decided to marry his pudgy cousin all because of the inheritance? But then why would he have sworn that he was ready to give up his share of the soap workshop if that was the price he had to pay to be rid of Jalila? Suad couldn't bear to advise Widad to just forget about me.

"So I was imprisoned in my own bedroom. On my uncle Ibrahim Pasha's orders I had to wait there for Jalila to reach the age of female maturity so I could marry her. She was twelve years old. Every morning they would check her dress for splotches of blood so they could announce her wedding. My uncle was mapping out my future in his mind. As soon as his daughter came of age, he would marry her off to me and send us to study in Paris. I didn't know the entirety of his plan. I presumed I was going to marry her and then go back to the soap workshop. Because I hated it there so much, I despaired of my life and despised living. I loved one person and one person only, and she was the one I wanted to marry. But once they had prevented me from seeing her, perhaps she had started to hate me, and so I preferred to bury myself in my room.

"My beard was getting long. I neglected the hair on my head and started to hate bathing altogether. My body had atrophied. I cried and moaned all the time. I no longer had any appetite for food or drink or reading. All I did was take out the things that reminded me of her. I reread her letters and her brief handwritten notes. I'd stare at the ticket stubs, smell again the handkerchiefs scented with her sweat. Khadija had begun to fear for me and my mental health. I wasn't well. If I'd carried on that way I might have died, or at least wound up going insane. She would come in to check on me, sit down on the edge of the bed, and drown in a wave of silent weeping. Where was Nafeh? What had become of him? She started begging my uncle and his wife to do something to save me. But they were unmoved by her warnings. All she heard my uncle say in return was that nothing was going to happen to his brother's son; she didn't need to be afraid and should just worry about keeping me fed. But I refused to eat. In tears, she would beg me to eat, and when I saw her beseeching me like that I'd force down a few small morsels.

"Khadija started to despise them. She started to hate my uncle Ibrahim Pasha and his wife and daughter. In everything that was happening to me, she saw injustice against the son she never had. Since becoming an orphan I had been like a son to her. It seemed to her that my death wouldn't come down like a lightning bolt on my uncle's head because he didn't seem to care whether I lived or died. In fact, if I died, he would get his

231

hands on my inheritance. That would solve the problem of the soap workshop once and for all. Khadija started encouraging me to run away. She even went back to the house where she had once lived with her husband before he died, pulled out all the nails boarding it up and went inside. She cleaned it and got it organised. If my condition got any worse, Khadija planned to take me from my uncle's house to save me.

"My uncle had called Dr Behar several times. He prescribed some sedatives and growth hormones for me, and told my uncle how important it was for me to change my lifestyle. He recommended taking me to a mountain resort for some fresh air. But did my uncle have any interest in taking me up there? After a while he started to forget about me altogether. He grew bored of thinking about my condition. But Khadija never stopped thinking about ways to help me. She knew what was ailing me and how it could be treated. One day she suggested to my aunt that she bring in a healing lady to pray for me and to exorcise any demons that had possessed me. Hamideh Khanum yawned and then agreed. She told Khadija to go and fetch one for me. She too had grown bored of me, my sickness and demons. Khadija asked for directions to Khojah Bahira's house. This all happened without my knowledge. I was laid up in bed, dead to the world, totally despondent. When Khadija went to the Khojah's house and knocked, Suad came to the door. Khadija introduced herself as my servant and said she wanted to speak with Suad or with Miss Widad about a very important matter. An hour later they were all at Khadija's house.

"Khadija told Suad and Widad the whole story. She told them that ever since I had been imprisoned by my uncle and his wife, I was slowly dying in my room because of the separation and from the intensity of my love for her. She told them everything, about the inheritance and the requirement that I marry Jalila, who had not yet reached the age of maturity, and about the depth of my hatred for her. Widad broke down in tears. She never dreamt that I might die because of my love for her. She still loved me despite everything the Khojah had done to turn her away from me. But how were the two of us ever going to be able to meet? Khadija told them that she had everything figured out. All Widad had to do was put on some of Khadija's old clothes and make herself look like a pious old woman who went around praying for the sick and exorcising their demons, especially the female demons men fall in love with and who possess them. The only way they can be cured is through special rituals. Widad agreed to this plan. She was burning to see me and to heal me. The two of them helped her get dressed. Despite those old clothes, her beauty and her body still gave her away. My beloved was a consummate angel.

"Khadija and Widad left. Suad stayed behind at Khadija's house to wait for them. Twenty minutes later my servant was guiding Widad, I mean, some poor ascetic old woman with a hunchback, into my uncle's house. After informing Hamideh Khanum that the old woman had arrived, she immediately led her upstairs without anyone seeing her. She brought her into my room. She pointed at one of the doors, told her to wait in that room, and then shut the door behind her.

"Widad stood by the door. I wasn't conscious at the time so I didn't see her. I was out of it because of the tranquillisers Dr Behar had prescribed for me. But she was right there in my room, and Khadija had closed the door behind her. Widad took off her yellow shawl and approached the bed. She placed her hand over her mouth so she wouldn't cry out from horror at what she was seeing. I was in a pitiful state. My hair was unkempt. It had been a long time since I'd last bathed. She had only ever seen me with my hair combed and shiny. Now she was seeing me in my worst state. My facial hair had grown long and I reeked of sickness and sweat and a filthy bed. I had become very skinny, my face had yellowed, and my lips were cracked. To put it bluntly, I looked half dead.

"She knelt beside the bed, crying. She held my hand and started to kiss it, running it along her face, wetting it with her tears. She kept repeating, 'Baby, baby.'

"I was in a very small boat. Dr Behar was steering with two little oars. I had my back to him as I leant over the water, searching for my mother and father. My mother appeared beneath the water, calling out to me. She wanted me to dive in after her. She was smiling with the kind of tenderness I had been looking for on the faces of every woman on earth. I hadn't seen it anywhere except with Khadija. Whenever I tried to get out of Dr Behar's boat in order to dive in after her, she would disappear. One time I saw her approaching from underwater. She wasn't waving at me to follow her but swimming right up to the surface of the water. She took my hand and started to kiss it. She moistened it with the water and her tears. I could hear her calling me 'baby'. She always used to call me that. I wanted to jump out of the boat and sink down to be with her, but she started crying and begging me not to. I started wailing. She reached out her hand and began to stroke my forehead. The strange thing was that my forehead was wetter than my hand. I opened my eyes and found that it was all a dream. I had been dreaming I was in Dr Behar's boat but I was actually in my own bed. There was no ocean. Only the normal atmosphere of my bedroom. And it wasn't my mother who was holding my hand, crying, but Widad, dressed like a servant, kneeling beside the bed, crying in anguish as she repeated the word, *habibi*, baby.

I surrendered to the dream. I believed it was real. I had been looking everywhere for Widad, both in the dream and in life. It didn't matter anymore. The important thing was for me to see and touch her. I didn't examine the reality of what I was seeing too closely. I hoped that what I was seeing was real. But it didn't matter. Let it be a dream. There was no longer any difference for me between dreams and reality. She watched me gazing back at her and she froze for a moment before sitting on the bed, holding me. She began to kiss me, unconcerned by my sweat and my many odours. I held her. I caressed her body, my head pressing against her chest. She was crying as she kissed my hair and said, 'Why do you love me? I mistreated you. I thought you would have forgotten about me when they asked you to. I love you, believe me. You have to get on with your life. You have to live.'

"I didn't stop stroking her. I started to doubt that what I was seeing was a dream. When I opened my eyes it turned into reality, and not the reverse. But I still wasn't convinced. How could Widad be sitting on my bed, holding me and kissing me and crying over me? How could she be so close to me? Had she been reduced to a poor woman, dressed like that? But no, it was her. I could tell by her distinctive smell, which I recognised from our trysts in the box at the Roxy Cinema.

I knew the feel of her skin from when I'd held her hand and wiped away the sweat. The whole time I was trying to understand what I was actually seeing and feeling. Was it reality or a dream world? While I was still in that state she suddenly stopped crying. She seemed to be considering something very carefully and furrowed her brow quite seriously. It was the first time I had ever seen her like that.

"'I'll show them all,' she said out loud. 'I'm yours, Nafeh. I'll show them all that I'm yours, your uncle and his pudgy wife and wrinkly Khojah Bahira, whose bad breath I despise. I'll show them all. We'll stick our tongues out at all of them.'

"'Hold on a minute, baby,' she told me, getting up. I followed every move she made, enchanted. She walked over to the door and unlatched the lock, made sure the door was closed and came back. She stood in front of the bed, her back to me, and began to take off her clothes. The bottom part of her shawl fell down as she took off her yellow robe, and then she took off the shawl even though it looked really good on her. She had nothing on underneath but silk red stockings adorned with lace along her thighs. When she turned her torso to release her hair from the shawl I saw the vague elliptical line between her legs. She turned towards me. I just about died from that sweet lump that swelled in my throat. She was smiling at me despite the tears in her eyes and those running down her cheeks. She was naked. An ivory-white body. Everything about her was gorgeous. Everything about her was extraordinary. One moment I believed I was dreaming, the next I thought it was real. She came and lay down next to me, pulled me close to her, clung to me. She reached out to undress me from below, and then took off her lace stockings.

"'I'm yours,' she whispered in my ear. 'Come, take me.'

"I didn't understand what she meant. She started kissing me. I couldn't understand what was happening. She didn't even wait for me to get involved. I was hypnotised, in a dream state. She let me lie there. Then she got on top of me and took me inside of her.

"She was angelic. I clung to her body. Life surged through me afresh. I could hear myself panting as she gasped for air. She was kissing me and weeping. But she was defiant, gentle with me and extremely stern with all those people we'd decided to stick our tongues out at. Her breathing grew faster until she cried out and then cooled off again, quenched at last. She lay down next to me. I held on to her so she wouldn't turn into a fading dream that would be forgotten in a few days. We remained silent, bound to one another. I felt both awakened and depleted. She stood up, put on her clothes, and left the room. She said something to Khadija and then came back inside. A few minutes later she took the serving tray from Khadija. I was so hungry I ate out of her hand. She began to feed me even as she kept on kissing me. I had been saved from the clutches of death for a second time.

"As she fed me, Widad told me everything. She told me it had been the Khojah who betrayed us to my uncle's wife, that my uncle had pronounced his unjust ruling and thrown me into my prison until his daughter Jalila came of age. She asked me to come back to life if I truly loved her, to come back as powerful and handsome as I had been before. I promised her I would. She promised me she'd do whatever she could so we could be together all the time and said we could meet at Khadija's house. Then she put the shawl back on in preparation for going back outside. But she kissed me for a few minutes before she finally left. I heard Khadija take her downstairs. Then the outer door slammed shut."

The old man grew quiet. He leant his head against the head-board and closed his eyes. After he had finished his lunch, I helped him into bed. I started to monitor him. Sometimes he would squeeze his eyelids shut. I convinced myself that he was remembering what had gone on between him and Widad when they were in bed together. I let him reminisce about that state of passion and told myself I'd wait there for him, even if he fell asleep. I drew closer to him. I wanted to watch his skin twitch as he remembered the event. His breathing was laboured and feverish; beads of sweat bloomed on his temples. I could tell how relaxed he was, how much he was enjoying himself.

I moved to the window to observe what was going on outside. It was sunset. The day had ended quickly. I noticed that I could no longer hear the sound of rain. How had it escaped my notice until just then that it had stopped pouring? First I opened the window, then the shutters. Rain was falling softly, the last remaining drops. I took a deep breath. The horizon was clearer now that the low, heavy clouds had dispersed. All that was left were some high clouds which were likely to dissipate in the air at any moment. It seemed we would get some sun tomorrow. I closed the shutters and the window. Was it possible that the rain might stop and the sun might come out in the morning before the story was finished? I was anxious and distressed. I hurried over to switch on the light. I saw Shaykh Nafeh's expression clearly. He was smiling now. I crouched beside the bed and studied the soft creases in his face. He must have been a handsome young man when Widad first decided to give herself to him. He had retained those good looks until that very moment, despite his advanced age. He opened his eyes and saw me there. He was happy. It seemed as if he had been having a pleasant dream that he was afraid might slip away from him. He closed his eyes again and gently nodded his head. I noticed his convulsing hands slowly going slack.

"Hey, Shaykh Nafeh… Are you awake?" I asked him in a near whisper so I wouldn't disturb his pleasant mental state. He reached his hand out towards me and I held it close. It was warm, wrinkled and soft.

"Thank you, my dear boy, for listening to me," he said. "You've allowed me to relive those moments. I'm so grateful that my last days brought you to me."

"I'm so happy that you're happy, but I'm sorry to inform you that the rain has stopped. Tomorrow the sun is going to shine. The end of the story must be upon us. I'm nervous about that."

"Don't worry. You've heard most of it now anyway. I'll try to wrap it up quickly. I wouldn't have any regrets at all if I were to die tomorrow."

"But what about the end of the story? I want to know everything. And what about Ismail?"

"I'll try, but you have to understand something. My whole life I've been trying to recall what happened that day between Widad and me but I always failed. I needed to tell someone like you just so that I could remember. You have no idea how relieved I am right now."

I told him I was afraid for him to go to sleep.

"I know, Shaykh Nafeh, I know. Again, I'm delighted about your happiness, but what happened after she gave herself to you?"

As he drifted between dreaming and wakefulness, he said, "We started meeting at Khadija's house every week, then every three days, then just about every day."

"But what about your uncle Ibrahim Pasha?"

"He was happy for me. But when he saw the splotch of blood on Jalila's underwear, they decided to marry us."

"You didn't run away?"

"Widad recommended that I go ahead and marry Jalila. She said there was no point in my missing out on the inheritance. At first I refused, but she insisted. She said I came from a good family and she was just a dancer, other things like that. Even though she knelt before me and cried, she told me it would make her happy for me to own my father's house and workshop. She believed my uncle was capable of the worst, either forcing me to marry his daughter Jalila or else killing me out of humiliation. She was worried about me and convinced me that she'd wait for me."

He began to speak more calmly, his words halting, as if he were drifting away from me. He spoke with his eyes closed. At first I shook him gently, then more and more forcefully.

On the verge of tears, I asked him, "What do you mean she would wait for you?"

"I had to travel to Paris with my wife in order to go to law school…"

"Why would you agree to that?" I asked aggressively.

"That was my mistake," he replied as though in pain. "I didn't have to get married and go like that, because…"

240

He started to cry.

"Because what? Tell me, Shaykh Nafeh, I beg of you."

He began to disappear into his own kingdom. His hands were hardly trembling at all anymore. What was happening to him? I began shaking him again. With one hand I wiped away his tears and with the other hand I wiped away my own.

"Because… I…" he said, his words spaced further and further apart. "I wouldn't… ever… see her… again… I lost her… for… ever…"

"Why? What happened?"

"Now… let me go… please…" he said, as if tremendous pleasure were washing over his entire body, as if he were back in the arms of his beloved, as if he were reaching orgasm. "I don't want to lose this pleasure. I'm reliving those moments… I spent in her arms."

"Just tell me what happened to Widad," I said hurriedly, sensing that he was about to depart. "Please, I'll kiss your hand."

"Because… she… ran away… from… Khojah Bahira."

Then he exhaled one last time and lost consciousness.

I held his hand and stroked it, tried to rouse him once again but his hand was limp and heavy. The hairs on my neck stood on end. I held his wrist and searched for a pulse. Time passed while I searched, but there was nothing. I drew away from the bed in horror. I muttered, "Shaykh Nafeh… Shaykh Nafeh!" I placed my ear against his chest, where his heart should have been. I didn't hear a sound. Shaykh Nafeh was dead. I cradled him, then started to shake his body as I called out in a hushed voice, "Shaykh Nafeh… Shaykh Nafeh…"

I was overwhelmed by lethal panic, afraid I was going to die. I sat down on the ground, placed my head in my hands.

Could death come so easily? Just a few minutes before he had been talking and shuddering from his illness. He wanted to relive those moments of pleasure so he could die inside them. What a horrible thing. Had I helped him to die? My body quaked as I started to weep. He had only wanted to rediscover that forgotten pleasure so he could die in peace. I had been so captivated by his story that I was almost willing to die if I didn't get to hear the ending. Then there was Ismail. He'd threatened to kill me but he hadn't followed through on his threat because of the old man. Yet now the old man was dead, no doubt he would try. I told myself not to be afraid. I had a rifle. I could defend myself. But I was a man afraid of his own imagination. I'd rather die than kill another human being.

I heard the sound of Ismail's footsteps tiptoeing upstairs. He was bringing dinner. I stood up and moved closer to the door. I wiped the tears from my eyes and placed my ear against the wooden door. I heard his footsteps getting closer. Then he placed the dinner tray on the ground and picked up the lunch tray. I heard him curse me as he walked away, his footsteps receding. I heard him go downstairs. Then silence again. I inhaled deeply, sat with my back against the door and spread my legs on the floor. I had to think. How and when was I going to get out of there? The best time would be at dawn, which meant I would have to spend the entire night with the old man's corpse, and it also meant that Ismail couldn't find out what had happened. If he knew his master was dead he would come straight in and kill me. He knew I wasn't going to use the rifle because I was a coward. He told me as much when I caught him standing on the wooden ladder spying on us from outside the window. But why did the old man have to die? Why now? I had started to care about him and everything connected to the world he'd told me about. I loved Widad as much as he did. I began to love dance and the Khojahs and the *kamancheh* Suad used to play. I loved the handkerchiefs he had used to wipe away the sweat from Widad's hand. I thought about taking them with me to Aleppo. I couldn't live without the traces of Widad, especially the smell of sweat on her hands and the photograph of her standing just above the hat of the French High Commissioner Monsieur de Martel.

But what about the story? Would I lose it now that Shaykh Nafeh had died without finishing it? I couldn't ask Ismail to finish it even though he was the only one who possibly could. He despised me because I had heard the story. Either I would have to give in to him or figure it out for myself. But could I do that? Could I understand why Widad would run away from the Khojah? Or figure out who Ismail actually was and what had happened to Widad and Jalila, his wife? And what about all the other questions that didn't even occur to me as I sat there on the floor, leaning up against the wall?

I looked up at the photographs hanging on the wall, arranged to cover every last inch of the wooden surface. I could use them to deduce the end of the story; that's what I told myself anyway. I'd spend the whole night studying them, until dawn if I had to. Then there was the trunk. It contained piles of folded documents. I'd take them with me to Aleppo. Ismail didn't need them. He hated everything that had to do with the story and its characters. I might find something in there that could unlock all these riddles.

I stood up. I had spotted an old suitcase in the cupboard when the old man had asked me to take out the trunk. I pulled out the suitcase, then the trunk and placed them both on the couch. I brought over the photograph of Widad at the train station and opened the suitcase to put the picture frame and contents of the trunk inside. I discovered that it was filled with documents.

CHAPTER SIX

The Rest of the Story, as Far as
I Could Piece it Together; How I Got Away
from Ismail; and, Finally, The End

I SPENT THE ENTIRE NIGHT with Shaykh Nafeh's corpse. I laid him out in such a way that made it look as if he were sleeping, and then I sat on the floor, rifle by my side, facing the door and the window as I searched through all the papers and photographs and the armoire for any traces that might shed some light on what had happened. I used to say that I have an analytical mind, which is to say that just by glancing over a string of numbers from the Agricultural Bank, I could figure out how well the season had gone, which harvest was better than others… and many other things that are of no interest whatsoever to the reader right now. I'm also good at gathering data, classifying it, and deriving the appropriate interest rates for the Bank in the coming rainy season. Once—and please excuse this additional detour into professional matters—based on the forecasted figures, I expected the following year to be a lean one. I predicted that the volume of rainfall would be low, so I advised my Bank against offering loans as they would only have led to a headache when it was time to collect the monthly repayments from the peasants, who were sure to lose much in that season. As a result, they rewarded me at the Bank by promoting me to Vice-President of the Agricultural Planning division.

With that same desire to analyse data and make sense of it, I sat there working in the departed Shaykh Nafeh's room. In the briefcase were two travel documents for the married couple Nafeh al-Aghyurli and Jalila al-Aghyurli produced by the French authorities in Aleppo and dated 24th April, 1937, which is to say they had already been married by that point and were travelling together from Beirut to Marseille by steamship on 13th May, 1937. Both documents indicated that they were married, mentioning the name of the wife or husband. The journey by steamship from Beirut to Marseille lasted seven days. The French customs stamp was also unmistakable: 20th May, 1937. Nafeh matriculated at the University of Paris and began studying law. He neither visited Syria nor sent his wife back there throughout his time at the university. They spent their holidays travelling around France instead. There were a number of photographs of them in front of the Eiffel Tower and in the French countryside. But the reader must not surmise that this meant the two of them were doing well. There were also a number of letters in the briefcase from Uncle Ibrahim Pasha encouraging them to reconcile, and on every one of those there was a note scrawled by Hamideh Khanum (who was for all intents and purposes illiterate) offering her daughter advice on how to make peace with her husband and be patient with him. I couldn't find a single negative word about Nafeh, probably because his uncle and his wife knew all too well that he would eventually read all the letters. One thing that grabbed my attention in the later letters was the uncle's wife

246

obliquely asking whether or not Jalila was pregnant, although it seemed the answer was always no, because the last time the matter of pregnancy was mentioned her mother had advised her to go see a specialist in Paris.

The final letter was the real bombshell. It was in practically illiterate Hamideh Khanum's handwriting. She wrote to tell the two of them about the tragedy that had befallen her, had befallen them. Uncle Ibrahim had passed away suddenly. They woke up one morning to discover that his soul had surrendered to the Creator, as she put it, and she asked them to come back home to Aleppo immediately, even if that meant Nafeh would have to abandon his studies. What good would studying law do for him anyway now that he was going to inherit the workshop? A few tears had dropped onto some of those words, smudging them, and it wasn't clear to me whose they were—those of the widow Hamideh Khanum or Jalila? An autopsy report by the French coroner who had inspected the corpse was laughable, and made me smile. Under cause of death the doctor indicated that the deceased had died in his sleep: by suffocation. He suspected that my uncle's obese wife had rolled over in her sleep onto his neck and had crushed him. The man had a hernia on his left flank, which was taken as proof that this man had been lifting his overweight wife without the assistance of any servants.

The young couple left France in May 1940, just one month before the Nazi occupation of Paris, which means that they departed the country while Europe was burning during the Second World War, and as the inferno raced towards France with lightning speed. Nafeh dropped out of law school before even sitting his third-year exams. As soon as he got home, he took over the soap workshop and oversaw the division of the inheritance, leaving him with a controlling share in the workshop, the remainder being left to his wife and his uncle's wife. At the same time, it seemed he was also searching for Widad, having learnt, as he told me before he died, about the story of her flight from Khojah Bahira's house. But where had she gone? Nobody knew. In the chest I found a few tickets from the Roxy Cinema dated 1940 and 1941. Apparently he got into the habit of going to the cinema, hoping to run into Widad there, or maybe it was simply so he could remember her—I'm inclined to believe the latter because he would always reserve a seat in the same section where they used to sit together on their dates.

The wheel of death kept on turning. There was a death certificate stamped with the hospital insignia attesting that Jalila Ibrahim al-Aghyurli died during childbirth in November 1945. The document confirmed the death of the foetus as well. According to the report, the cause of death was morbid obesity, which had resulted in elevated blood pressure, leading to cranial haemorrhaging. So Nafeh was already a widower at the age of thirty. I didn't find any pictures hanging on the walls from after that date. I didn't find the division of an inheritance following the death of his wife; apparently he had been in no rush to produce one, and Hamideh Khanum passed away the following June. Ownership of the soap workshop devolved in its entirety, all 2,400 shares, to Nafeh al-Aghyurli.

Nafeh lived alone. There was no trace of the servant Khadijeh. Perhaps she had died as well. He never remarried. He travelled the world instead. His old passports contained an incredible number of entry stamps from many different countries, including India, China and Mexico. The real surprise came in 1950. In the briefcase I found a letter written on brown paper in a woman's trembling hand, which I share with you here and now. I should say that I have taken some liberties in revising the structure. I brought it back to Aleppo with me because it is particularly significant:

My most highly respected Dear Mr Nafeh al-Aghyurli,

Greetings and good wishes from a faithful heart to an esteemed gentleman, etc...

My dear sir. You may wonder what has happened to me and where I now call home. I beg you to forgive me for all I have done, but your affection being ever in my heart, my desire for you to live your life drove me to depart Khojah Bahira's house without leaving an address. Were it not for my profound affection for you I would have come back. That is the reason why I have remained silent all this time. Before you left with your virtuous wife Jalila Khanum, I felt I was carrying your child in my womb. I never had any intention of mucking things up in your life. First I left you, and then one day I ran away from the Khojah's house to the village of Maydan Ekbas, which is the village where I was born and where I lived until my mother's death. It was there that I lied to Shaykh Abd al-Sabbour, the imam of the village mosque, telling him I was married and that the French had imprisoned my husband in the Arwad Prison. The people of the village welcomed me with open arms, and I lived there under the guardianship of Bayonet Abduh until the baby was born. God granted me a son and Shaykh Abd al-Sabbour named him Ismail. I was pleased with such a beautiful name. You must know by now that Ismail is your son as much as he is mine. He was born on New Year's Day, 1938. I then became acquainted with an Egyptian family travelling from Istanbul whose journey had been interrupted in Maydan Ekbas. I invited them to stay with me. Once their problems were resolved they invited me to accompany them to Egypt. I thought long and hard about it. They told me I could become a dancer in Cairo and earn a lot of money. I agreed to go with them. Cairo is such a massive city, with a wide river running through it. They helped take care of my son Ismail whenever I went to dance at weddings to earn a living. But God—blessings and praises be upon Him—punished me, and I became ill. I'm not going to tell you the name of the illness, but I would cough a lot and grow fatigued very easily and I could no longer continue to dance. After a few weeks I started coughing up blood. I feel as though I am going to die soon, my dearly beloved. That's why I sat down to write you this letter. I'm going to write down your exact address and ask this Egyptian family, my only friends in the world, to send my son Ismail to Aleppo along with this letter and the address. If he makes it to you safely, this means that I am dead and may God bless me and may you have mercy on my soul by reciting the Fatiha for me, if only once. I loved you with all my heart and did this only so that you could live an honourable life.

P.S. I repeat that Ismail is your flesh and blood. I swear before Almighty God that he is your son. I pray that his arrival doesn't cause you any trouble with your relatives and that you will take care of him, that you will be able to pretend that he is your servant. He's a smart and sensitive boy. He always asks about his father. He's constantly quarrelling with me and is embarrassed that I'm a dancer.

Cairo, February 1950
Sincerely yours, always,
Widad

The letter calmed me down. The story was complete. There were no more grey areas. I sat in my place, examining Widad's handwriting. Her hand had trembled as she wrote. I tried to imagine the anguish that tormented her during her last few days. No doubt she had suffered a slow and painful death. I was struck with deep sadness for her. Through the story I had come to have great affection for her, through all the things that Shaykh Nafeh had held on to. His love for her was transmitted into my heart.

The idea of writing the story down first came to me as I sat there on the floor. But when I thought about how to actually go about doing it, I realised I had never written a story or even an essay longer than a single page. I hated myself for not being a good writer. I decided that as soon as I got back to Aleppo I would call up a writer and ask him to write it down exactly the way I described it at the beginning of this book. But first things first: I would have to figure out how to get out of there. Ismail was ready to kill me if he sensed that the story was going to make it back to the city, where he was most probably thinking about moving after his father Shaykh Nafeh died. He even threatened to follow me there, to hunt me down if I managed to sneak away. He clearly resented his mother for having been a dancer. He hated the fact that he was a bastard child, and had to pretend he was his father's servant. He had forced his father to move out of the city and into the countryside in order to keep him away from other people, fearful that his secret would be revealed. Life is hard, Ismail. It led me out there to hear your story and to solve its riddles despite the death of the storyteller. But is it worthwhile to try and write it down, to use real names to describe everything and everyone? For example, out of respect for Ismail's secret and my own fear of him, I could change the names of all the characters in the story. I could even change the names of the neighbourhoods and the streets, the village where Badia and Widad once lived. The story could still live on after its characters were gone. The one detail I insisted on retaining was Cairo, where Widad and her son wound up going. As for the rest, dear reader, I decided to dispense with their names. I changed what was manufactured at the workshop Shaykh Nafeh inherited, made it soap despite the fact that it produced something one hundred per cent opposed to soap. I chose soap because one of my childhood friends' fathers used to own a soap workshop, where we spent good times learning how soap was made, wishing we could take part in the process of sliding rings around the individual bars. While sitting among Nafeh's documents and photographs with his body on the bed right there in front of me, I decided what I had to do, and that is what I actually did, as you now know, dear reader. After all, people's privacy and their secrets should be respected.

The chirping of wild birds outside jolted me out of my reverie. I looked out the window and noticed, somewhat embarrassedly, that dawn was breaking. I had to get out of there right away, or else I was sure to wind up a dead man. I wanted to live, so I could carry out my mission of writing down this story and publishing it for others to read. I stood up, gathered together the papers and photographs and scarves I had strewn all over the place, having decided to take them with me, and stuffed all of them inside the old leather briefcase. Everything else I put back in the armoire. I borrowed a jacket from the old man to shield me from the cold, took out a few bed sheets and firmly tied one to another to help me escape safely out the window and down to the garden below. I stood beside the bed and recited the Fatiha over the old man's soul, kissing him and letting my tears flow. I said goodbye to him and threw one final glance around the room. Then I stealthily opened the window and the shutters and tossed down the rope made out of sheets. With the rifle slung over my shoulder and the briefcase hanging from my waist, I climbed down.

My feet safely touched ground in the garden. The sky was clear. The rain had finally let up around midnight. Everything was damp. I heard not a sound as I moved forward. Clutching the rifle, I left the garden, cautiously looking around before finally allowing my feet to run like the wind. I didn't look back. I broke into a sprint and kept on going until I ran out of energy, at which point I stopped and turned around. The house had completely disappeared. I found it strange that it could vanish so quickly. I began walking at a normal pace, and three hours later I came across a shepherd tending a flock of sheep. I came nearer and asked him to show me how to find the main road. After he had pointed out the way I gave him the rifle in exchange for his help. Half an hour later I was able to flag down a passing car. By two p.m. I was knocking on my own front door because I had forgotten my keys back at Shaykh Nafeh's estate. The moment my wife Nadia laid eyes on me, she fainted. Everyone thought I must have got lost in the wilderness and had long since been eaten by wild animals.

NIHAD SIREES – ALEPPO, 1998

PUSHKIN PRESS

Pushkin Press was founded in 1997, and publishes novels, essays, memoirs, children's books—everything from timeless classics to the urgent and contemporary.

Our books represent exciting, high-quality writing from around the world: we publish some of the twentieth century's most widely acclaimed, brilliant authors such as Stefan Zweig, Marcel Aymé, Teffi, Antal Szerb, Gaito Gazdanov and Yasushi Inoue, as well as compelling and award-winning contemporary writers, including Andrés Neuman, Edith Pearlman, Eka Kurniawan, Ayelet Gundar-Goshen and Chigozie Obioma.

Pushkin Press publishes the world's best stories, to be read and read again. To discover more, visit www.pushkinpress.com.

═══

THE SPECTRE OF ALEXANDER WOLF
GAITO GAZDANOV

'A mesmerising work of literature' Antony Beevor

SUMMER BEFORE THE DARK
VOLKER WEIDERMANN

'For such a slim book to convey with such poignancy the extinction of a generation of "Great Europeans" is a triumph' *Sunday Telegraph*

MESSAGES FROM A LOST WORLD
STEFAN ZWEIG

'At a time of monetary crisis and political disorder... Zweig's celebration of the brotherhood of peoples reminds us that there is another way' *The Nation*

THE EVENINGS
GERARD REVE

'Not only a masterpiece but a cornerstone manqué of modern European literature' Tim Parks, *Guardian*

BINOCULAR VISION
EDITH PEARLMAN

'A genius of the short story' Mark Lawson, *Guardian*

IN THE BEGINNING WAS THE SEA
TOMÁS GONZÁLEZ

'Smoothly intriguing narrative, with its touches of sinister,
Patricia Highsmith-like menace' *Irish Times*

BEWARE OF PITY
STEFAN ZWEIG

'Zweig's fictional masterpiece' *Guardian*

THE ENCOUNTER
PETRU POPESCU

'A book that suggests new ways of looking at the world
and our place within it' *Sunday Telegraph*

WAKE UP, SIR!
JONATHAN AMES

'The novel is extremely funny but it is also sad and
poignant, and almost incredibly clever' *Guardian*

THE WORLD OF YESTERDAY
STEFAN ZWEIG

'*The World of Yesterday* is one of the greatest memoirs of the twentieth
century, as perfect in its evocation of the world Zweig loved, as it is
in its portrayal of how that world was destroyed' David Hare

WAKING LIONS
AYELET GUNDAR-GOSHEN

'A literary thriller that is used as a vehicle to explore big
moral issues. I loved everything about it' *Daily Mail*

FOR A LITTLE WHILE
RICK BASS

'Bass is, hands down, a master of the short form, creating in a few pages
a natural world of mythic proportions' *New York Times Book Review*